Get Up, Eleanor

John 14:12 Publications

www.jeffreymcclainjones.com

Cover art from Shutterstock.com.

Get Up, Eleanor

a novel

Jeffrey McClain Jones

For my mother, whose wisdom has blessed my life and the lives of countless others. I love you.

CHAPTER ONE

"What did you say your name was?"

"Paul. Paul Wasser."

"Paul. Thanks for calling me. And for … what you did for my mom."

"Sure. Uh … I'll talk to you when you get out here. Again, I'm so sorry."

"Thank you."

Eleanor Petersen disconnected the cell phone call. Apparently her mother had kept Eleanor's cell number on the refrigerator, and that's how the handyman was able to contact her. Had she been preparing for something like this?

Connie Petersen had fallen on the ice. She hit her head. She couldn't pick herself up. Lying there. For who knows how long.

Just lying there. In the cold.

The medical examiner would know how long. There would be a medical examiner, wouldn't there? Would they tell her how long? Did she really need to know?

"Eleanor? Eleanor!"

"What?" She snapped back to the present—back to school, to her office, seated at her desk. The heat from the radiator behind her chair hovered over her shoulders.

Jackie stood in the doorway. "Has something happened? You're scaring me."

"Yes." Eleanor nodded. Something had happened.

"What is it?" Jackie closed the door and stepped next to the padded maroon armchair in front of the desk. "Is it your mother?"

"Yes. Mom." Take a breath. "She fell. On the ice. She just lay there all night. Maybe …"

"My God. Is she ... ?"

More nodding. "Gone. She hit her head. Her heart stopped. There ... on the ice."

Jackie stepped around the desk and grasped Eleanor's shoulder. "Oh, honey. Oh, Eleanor. Oh, my God."

Eleanor lurched toward her water bottle near the edge of her desk. Her hand shook when she lifted the tall metal bottle toward her. Her right hand trembling, not the left. Not the usual tremors. This was different. This was more.

After a shaky glug, Eleanor clunked the bottle back onto the desk. She swiped the back of her hand across her chin. "Mom was eighty-seven. She insisted on living in that farmhouse all by herself." Deep breath. "I was always afraid something would happen." She looked at Jackie. "But not this. Not like this. Lying out there on the ice for who knows how long."

"Oh, my Lord." Jackie pressed her palm to her mouth, panting and shaking her head.

Leaning until her forehead rested against the front of Jackie's blazer, Eleanor closed her eyes, loosening a knot in her chest. Sobbing. Eleanor allowed the tears. The touch from Jackie had broken that barrier against sorrow. Crossed the distance to the pain.

She had been far from her mother. Far from that woman who lay on the ice with no one to help her.

Where was the dog? He must have known, even if he wasn't out there with her. He would have been barking inside the house. But who would have heard him? No one. There was no one there to hear his alarm. No one to find her. Until too late.

Her weeping hatched a memory of when she was in college. That same heartbroken bawling was all she could do when Gary had left her, when she had lost what she thought was her true love. Lasting love. It didn't last.

These tears threatened to last and last.

8

"That's okay. That's okay. Don't you worry." Jackie stroked the back of Eleanor's head. "Just lean in. Just let it out."

CHAPTER TWO

The LCD display showed the flight to ORD, Chicago, was on time. She tugged her carry-on case onto the carpet and aimed for an open chair at the end of a row in the waiting area. A couple across from that seat bowed in unison over smartphones. Two children silently stared at small tablets, feet pulled up onto their seats.

Eleanor resisted the urge to pull out her phone. She would stay present, outside her phone. Numb but present. This present was just the airport. The gray carpet under her feet was real but impersonal.

Snorting softly, she recalled the mess she had made of Jackie's wool blazer. She would owe her for the dry cleaning.

Then she did pull out her phone. Had Brian replied to her email? She needed him to confirm arrangements for midterm exams before spring break.

There it was. He had everything under control. He'd sent out announcements to the survey course students. Not to worry. Exams would go ahead as scheduled. The seminar students would meet once with Rosemary, her graduate assistant. Their papers would be due as assigned. All under control.

Now she was free to fly to Chicago and drive from there to …

How long had her parents lived in that farmhouse in southern Wisconsin? They moved right after Dad's retirement. How long had her mother lived there alone?

Her phone buzzed. She checked the time before answering. The plane would begin boarding in ten minutes.

"Hello?"

"Dr. Petersen. This is Paul Wasser again."

"Mr. Wasser. Paul. Please, call me Eleanor."

"Okay. Sure. Sorry to bother you. But I wanted to let you

know that I have your mother's dog. Monet." He huffed once. "I have him with me. I'll take care of him for now. In case you were wondering."

She hadn't been. But now she was. "Oh. Okay. You're taking care of the dog. That's good to know."

"Yeah. He's with me and my dog, Dodger. They're good together. He's good."

"He's good?" Good dog. Faithful dog.

"Yeah. I just wanted to let you know. I mean, since he doesn't belong to me, I wanted to be clear that I was just *watching* him."

"You didn't steal him."

He laughed and then aborted that instantly. "Well. Yeah, that's kinda what it sounded like I was worried about." He sighed. "I guess you never know what to say at times like this." He waited as if hoping for instructions. "I was helping Connie with things around her place, ya know. I was ... as I said, I was the one that found her."

Connecting each of his little pieces of confession wasn't important. He was just offering condolences and apologies.

Why apologies?

"You found her?" Eleanor knew that. It wasn't really a question. More an invitation to say more. "That must have been terrible."

"Yes. Yes, it was." His next breath tripped and stuttered. "I don't know how much to say. How much do you wanna know? I mean, we can talk. We can talk when you get here."

"What was she doing? Why was she out there?"

"She had a large canvas with her. She was under that canvas when I found her. It sorta covered her."

A stretched canvas as shelter? That was fitting, or maybe pitiful. Eleanor squelched a sob, holding the phone away from her mouth.

"She kept some of the larger raw canvases out in the barn.

She must have gone out there to get that one and then slipped on the ice on the way back. It was a spot where the old snow kept the meltwater from draining, and it just kept freezing over. I cleared it off and put down salt. But ..."

Was he defending himself? "You cleared snow and ice for her all the time."

"Yeah. That sidewalk was a constant hazard. I don't know how many times I warned her about it."

"She didn't always listen."

He snuffled a laugh. "I guess you would know. I bet you tried to talk her out of living out there by herself."

"I did."

"But she had it her way. She got to live the way she wanted right up to the end. She got the life she wanted."

"And the death?"

"Oh. Well. I don't know. I didn't mean ..."

"No. Of course not. I wasn't really ... Not really arguing. Just thinking aloud. I argue with myself sometimes."

"Yeah. I do that too. I've been chewing myself out for not gettin' to her place sooner. I was supposed to check on the ice at her place. But I was stuck dealing with a flooded basement in town."

He *was* defending his actions. Anyone would.

"I'm sure it's as you say. She knew the risks. None of us could really protect her from every contingency."

"Yeah. I guess you can hear me trying to convince myself that it's not my fault. Not sure I'm ever gonna be able to do that, though."

Was it his fault? In some way? But she wasn't going to blame this handyman for her mother's death. Blame offered no relief. Tears, on the other hand ...

"Well, I should go. I need to board the plane here in a bit."

"Is someone picking you up? Is it Milwaukee or Chicago?"

"I'm flying into O'Hare. I've rented a car."

"Oh. Okay. I'll talk to you when you get here. You're gonna stay at the farm?"

"I had planned on it."

"Careful of the ice." A paralyzed silence followed. Then his voice softened. "I'll get over there to put down some more salt." Another pause. "But be careful, anyway."

Was he afraid she would suffer the same fate as her mother? That would be too much for him to bear, apparently. "Thanks. I'll be careful."

Paul Wasser was the one who had found her mother. But was he the last person she'd spoken to before that?

When had *Eleanor* spoken to her mother last? There was the usual Sunday night phone call. But they had both been distracted. Their exchanged words were the opposite of memorable, the opposite of significant, until now. Now everything had taken on significance. The last visit. The last time Eleanor heard her mother's voice.

She stopped staring at the blank screen on her phone and slipped it back into her jacket pocket. She gazed down at the toes of her black loafers. The carpet beneath them was still there. She was still here. Back from thoughts of the house in Wisconsin and that conversation with Paul Wasser. And now she was stacking sandbags against more of those tears.

After Eleanor boarded the plane, she sat staring out the window, blinking at the itchy blur, hunkering into the tight airline seat.

When had she last seen her mother cry?

There was the funeral. Her father's death. Her mother's greatest loss. That's what she had called it. The way she moaned his name. "Darrel. Oh. Darrel. My love." Her voice had disabled everyone's defenses against total breakdown that day. Contagious grief.

What had startled Eleanor at the time was the contrast with

the smiling woman who persistently faced even bad news with a grin. A cold grin. That was how it had often felt to Eleanor. Her mom wouldn't swear or complain. She just grinned. At most she might say, "Oh, bother." That was the worst.

Until she lost the man who had been her partner and best friend for fifty-six years.

"Best man." That's what she used to call him. "He's my best man." A strange twist. But Connie liked to twist a phrase. She was her own person, with her own way of speaking. Her own way of living.

She hadn't grinned when Eleanor confronted her in the kitchen over the butcher block island after Dad's funeral. "This is where I live. And this is where I'll stay."

"You're seventy-seven years old, Mom. You can't live here all alone."

"I'll get a dog. I've always wanted a dog."

"A dog?" Eleanor could still remember the emptied and washed collection of casserole dishes assembled on the butcher block, a geometrical chaos of round and square and rectangular dishes, yet uniformly Pyrex. Perfect for reheating. They had contained various dishes, but uniformly creamy with cheese. Cheese and butter infused into noodles in ethnically diverse combinations from Italian to Swedish to whatever "tuna hot dish" was. The leftovers would last for the rest of the year. Maybe a dog would come in handy for devouring all those carbs and fats.

"Your father never wanted a dog. He was too softhearted. He never would have wanted to leave a puppy at home, ever. I wouldn't ha' been able to get him to go anywhere."

"So, you've been waiting for Dad to die so you could finally get a dog?" Eleanor could joke with her mom most times. But that jab had been too early, and too sharp.

"Lenny! I can't believe you would ..." And then that grin was back. Flat line. A grin as tight as the seal on the freezer.

Maybe after Dad died Eleanor should have tried harder to convince her mom to stop calling her "Lenny." She hadn't tried very hard before that. Her mom had usually called her "Eleanor" when she referred to an article or book review, proud of her daughter's honors and publications, proud when she was named Chair of the History Department.

Eleanor sat back and closed her eyes. How long had Connie lived on that Wisconsin farm by herself? It must have been fifteen years with Dad. Then about ten without him. Ten years by herself. A stubborn woman. With that stubborn grin on her elfin face.

The white noise of the jet engines cocooned her. Eleanor fell asleep beneath her mother's grin.

When she woke, the plane was just crossing the shore of Lake Michigan. A golden sunset embossed the city. Eleanor pressed her forehead against the window, assessing downtown Chicago. No longer that toddling town. No longer the phoenix resurrected from the great fire. A metropolis of businesses of all sorts and sizes. Maybe she should come out here to The Chicago Historical Society again. Surely she could fill in more details on women-owned businesses in the nineteenth-century.

The flight attendant's announcement erased those thoughts. Eleanor shifted to anxiety about the rental car connection and the drive toward the north and west.

"I'm coming home, Mom."

But it had never been *her* home. The farm was her parents' retirement spot. Not Florida. Not Arizona. They were Wisconsinites. They'd migrated from the Milwaukee suburbs to Dove Lake. Mom would paint. Dad would be a gentleman farmer, managing his investments, reading books, and occasionally doing consulting work for cities around the area. Dinners out. Bridge.

Dove Lake had become Eleanor's surrogate home only because her parents lived there.

Was her mother still there?

Was Connie's spirit lingering in the studio on the first floor? In the bedrooms upstairs? In that kitchen, where she had made pies to give to the neighbors? Was her spirit waiting there for her only daughter, her only child?

As the wheels rumbled over the tarmac, Eleanor leaned into the fact that she was alone. No longer just an only child. She was the only survivor of their little family.

Snap out of it, Lenny. You have to get off this plane, pick up your rental car, and drive over the Wisconsin border.

Get it together, Lenny.

Eleanor.

When she climbed into the Prius, she checked her rearview mirrors and gripped the contoured steering wheel. As she wound her way out of the rental lot toward the freeway, she considered the business ahead of her. House, bank, funeral home, dog. The business of cleaning up after a life. Cleaning up all that was left of her mother, her family.

"That attitude will never do." She snorted, imagining what her mother would say.

"Lenny, you're just gonna have to face it. You may as well make the best of it. That's all we can ever do in life, make the most of what we're given. I know it's a bit of a bother. But you don't have to settle everything all at once. And there will be people to help you."

That's what her mother would say.

Eleanor relaxed into her seat, surveying the broad highway ahead of her. "Glad we had this little talk, Mom. It really helped."

16

CHAPTER THREE

Dove Lake, Wisconsin, had been incorporated in the middle of the nineteenth century, during the boom of immigration and settlement, and the first promise of agricultural prosperity in the upper Midwest. The native nations had been forced west and onto reservations, leaving open prairie. Available land. That was the vision, the dream. It was the attraction for northern European people seeking a new life.

One mystery about the town was the absence of a body of water called Dove Lake. Numerous Wisconsin towns had been named for the lake on whose shores they were built. Not this one. None of the lakes around there had ever been called Dove Lake. Not even a Dove Pond in the lot.

The naming conundrum was the only mystery about the town of which Eleanor was aware. At least, so far.

Approaching the farm from the south and east after dark, a hazy glow smudged the western horizon—the lights of the little business district of Dove Lake. She would avoid town tonight.

Slowing on the county highway, she turned, her headlights catching the quaint and crafty wooden sign painted by her mother. "The Dovecote." Her mother was half Scottish, her maiden name Constance Ferguson. But her name for the farm had been more about teasing her new community for its lack of a lake, dove or otherwise. Connie was the kind of woman who needed to name her farm. And Eleanor hadn't contested that name's cheeky cuteness.

Sitting in the driveway with the high beams illuminating the white slats of the barn, the trip and day fuzzed into silence. Eleanor just sat there.

There was the barn. If she tried, she could probably see the

17

sidewalk, the spot where her mother had fallen. Flat on her back? Under a raw canvas stretched over a pine frame.

Such flimsy shelter. No shelter at all.

That strip of cement was a historic site now. In the story of Eleanor's life, that pavement connecting the white clapboard house with the old white barn had taken on eternal significance. Her mother had passed from this life to the next right on that spot.

Had Connie Petersen lain there, conscious that the next place she would awake would be Heaven? Was she still certain of her eternal fate while she lay there on the ice? Was she even aware of what was happening? If she'd covered herself with that canvas, she must have been conscious, at least for a while. Why didn't she move? Why didn't she get up? Maybe covering herself had been an accident too, not a knowing effort to stay warm.

"Get up, Connie." That would be Dad.

"You gotta see this sunrise." He rose early, even in retirement.

Mom slept late most mornings. But she was a connoisseur of fine sunrises. She would thank her best man for stirring her to see the sun hauling itself off the prairie to the east.

Eleanor breathed a cloud into the car's interior. "Get up, Connie."

She wiped the knit back of her glove over both cheeks and shut off the motor of the hybrid rental. She had selected that car thinking it would be more reliable at starting in the subzero. But this was March. The sub-zeros had rolled away to the north by now. An unnecessary precaution.

It was the thaw that had killed her mother. Melting snow filled the sidewalk with water during the day and then froze at night, or when the next cold front trucked in from the north. Ironic. Her mother had survived the Wisconsin December. She had outlasted the Wisconsin January. And she had beaten back

February.

But not March.

To freeze to death in March. To slip and fall because of the thaw. Eleanor swore. But, of course, she wasn't the first to curse the Wisconsin weather.

She forced herself to open the car door and get out. She checked for clean pavement before settling her left foot on the drive. Then she shook her head at herself.

Standing, she opened the back car door and pulled her suitcase off the seat. She resettled her purse onto her shoulder and extended the handle on the carry-on bag. For some reason it reminded her of going to college, that suitcase. Her mother had packed Eleanor's luggage in the 1970s. Bags were so much more awkward back then. Who had a rolling suitcase in those days? Stewardesses, maybe. That's what they were called back then.

Thoughts, scattered like rock salt on an icy driveway, crunched in her mind and kept her from what she really wanted to remember, what she really wanted to understand.

She rolled her case toward the side door. No one used the front door of her parents' house, though she could see that its stairs had been cleared of snow. She checked for the flowerpot Paul had mentioned. Green. By the back door. Next to the white siding. The light at the corner of the barn showed her the next clue for how to enter this house. How to enter her mother's home. Eleanor would be on her own here for the first time.

But when she stood up after retrieving the cold key from beneath the ceramic pot, her eyes swept across the sidewalk to the barn. She allowed herself to see it. To know that cold surface was still there.

But her mother was no longer there.

Of course.

Eleanor drew a long breath, still gripping the key between her bare fingers, her right glove clutched in her left hand. She stepped toward that patch of pavement. The salt ground beneath her leather soles. The ice was gone. Paul had done his work. He had removed the danger.

Eleanor was standing on that sidewalk now. Was it here? Precisely here? This very spot?

The ice had been her mother's last resting place. Connie was gone. And so was the ice. It seemed a sort of desecration.

Eleanor shook her head and sniffed disapproval at her sentimentality and superstition.

Pivoting back toward the house, her right foot slipped roughly. The layer of salt rolled over the concrete. She startled, fear grabbing her throat for a half second. Then her balance returned, and her feet aligned securely under her. She was walking. Upright. Not following her mother's fate.

Eleanor's stiff fingers fumbled with the key. The car console had said it was twenty-seven degrees. How long ago had she seen that temperature reading? Maybe it was colder now.

She clutched the handle of her rolling bag once the inner door angled open. The storm door banged her backside and shoved her onto the inner landing.

When had she been here last? She needed historical markers now. The last time she had heard her mother's voice. The last time she had seen her mother cry. The last time she had visited this old farmhouse.

"Couldn't you at least get a little townhouse in Waukesha or somewhere? I mean, if it has to be Wisconsin, at least get off this old farm and out of this drafty house."

"But this is *my* home. I love this old house."

"Oh, Mother." Eleanor whispered as she stepped up from the landing into the kitchen.

A welcoming heat awaited her. She flipped on the light, set her gloves on the little counter near the door, and pulled off her coat. The kitchen smelled the same—flour, sugar, cinnamon, a hint of cumin and chili. Fresh scents. That was when it occurred to her that someone had been in the house just that day.

Turning toward the refrigerator, she stopped when she saw the list of phone numbers. Hers was third on the list. Paul Wasser's was at the top. He had probably been familiar with that list. Or had he been strictly an outside man all these years? No. Mother would have at least invited him in to have coffee at the kitchen table.

The table was clean, cleared except for the blond wicker placemats contrasting with the maple surface. Now she returned to what she had started. Opening the refrigerator door, she found the expected casseroles. A yellow Post-it Note adhered to the aluminum cover on the top one. In her mind, she still pronounced it the British way, *aluminium*, from her trips to study at Oxford.

How her mind wandered tonight.

She tugged the note off. "Took out perishables. Mom sent casserole. You know. Paul."

She flipped it over. It seemed unfinished. "You know" ... what?

Well, she did know how people around here would treat the grieving. Consolation casseroles. She had seen it early in life, in Milwaukee—the people from the Lutheran church bringing dinner to the family of the deceased. But these were not resurrection casseroles. They were heavy. Weights to keep the fallen down. Where they belonged. Where they were planted in their graves.

"Morbid." She was talking to herself in her mother's kitchen.

"I know you did the same here. I used to catch you late at night, staying up to paint. Drinking your wine and talking to yourself." Or was her mom talking to Dad? Even when he was alive and in bed upstairs, she might have been talking to him.

Her mother had still not cleaned out her father's bedroom

last time Eleanor was here. Her parents had kept separate bedrooms in the farmhouse. In fact, as soon as she left home for graduate school, her dad had moved into Eleanor's bedroom in Greenfield, Wisconsin.

But Mom never wanted to talk about why. "None of your business."

Suddenly, that anonymous casserole seemed magnetically attractive. Eleanor opened the fridge again. What was it? Lasagna, Wisconsin style? She had eaten lasagna in Syracuse, in Chicago, in New York City, and in Palermo. Here, it would be a lasagna casserole, to be more precise.

No. It was tuna fish. Good enough. Probably better. The smell of it, even cold, stirred her hunger. She set the aluminum pan on the island.

Her image, reflected above the kitchen sink, stopped her. She was still wearing her hat. Pulling the soft knit cap free of her short gray and blond hair, she paused to puff her scrunched locks. No one here to see it but herself ... and her mother's ghost.

Her mom had never been one of those shaming mothers, protecting her own sense of beauty by enforcing cosmetic standards on her daughter. Connie's hair often retained the shape of a hatband, long after the straw fedora had come to rest on one of the hooks by the back door, long past when her floppy fisherman's hat lay on the shelf on the landing.

"Mom. What happened to you? Why couldn't you get up?"

CHAPTER FOUR

She had been surprised to discover that it was nearly midnight when she settled into her father's bedroom. Waking now, she was surprised to see 7:54 in glowing red numerals next to the bed. That would be 8:54 Eastern Time. Eleanor snorted and threw back the sheet and two quilts. She never slept under a quilt at home, only at her parents' house. Though they weren't family heirlooms, those quilts—acquired by her mother after moving to Dove Lake—were part of Eleanor's exit from her real life into the liminal space of a visit here.

"Liminal space." She said it aloud, thinking of George, the Sociology professor she had been seeing most recently. He had explained that his relationship with her was liminal space. He meant it in the sense that their connection was transitional, not in the transformational sense that might have implied rising romance or a commitment larger than dinner and a movie. He was recently divorced. She was part of his transition to singleness.

Anyway. "Up, Lenny." In her father's old bedroom, she spoke to herself as *he* had, back when they lived in the Milwaukee suburbs, and she was late getting up for high school.

Her phone vibrated before she could cross the dull, oriental rug to the hallway toward the bathroom. She turned back and stood next to the nightstand looking at the number. Wisconsin. No name. It must be Paul. She should add him to her contacts.

"Hello."

"Hello. Is this Ms. Petersen?"

"Yes. Eleanor Petersen."

"Hello. My name is Matt Bauer. I manage the Childress Funeral Home. Let me first say how sorry I am about your loss." He sounded as sincere as Jackie had, though less emotional.

23

"Thank you." She closed her eyes. "My mother made arrangements?"

"Yes, she did. My apologies for calling so early. Your mother had a definite plan. But I wanted to talk to you before we proceed. You see, she opted for cremation and no burial. I wanted to call you first, just in case."

In case of what? In case she wanted Connie to be buried, instead? In case she wanted to see her mother's body first? *Should* she want to?

Standing there in her flannel nightgown, she didn't know her own mind. Or maybe this was more about her heart.

"Uh. Well. What ... when ... ah." She huffed. "Could I come and see her first?"

"Certainly. That's what I was calling to check." He paused. "You could come by anytime today. Just let me know when."

"I suppose after lunch. Say, one o'clock?"

"That will be fine. I'll be sure to be here. And, Ms. Petersen, just so you're prepared, your mother's body is being refrigerated. She won't be embalmed. You understand?"

What difference did that make?

It did make a difference. Connie's body would be cold. But Eleanor wouldn't have to touch her.

The cold body of her mother.

Maybe she *didn't* want to see her mother that way.

"Okay. I understand." Had she answered all his questions?

"Again, I am so sorry for your loss. I will see you here at 1:00 p.m. We're on Main Street, of course."

"Of course." The call disconnected. She was going to see her mother's body. *Why* was she going to see her mother's body?

Last night she had tugged against the gravity of the place where her mother had lain on the pavement. Where was that gravity now? The pull to see her mother one more time, to say goodbye in person?

But that wasn't right. She wouldn't see her mother there, really. Her mother wasn't at the Childress Funeral Home. She was more likely in this house. Or in Heaven. That was what Connie had believed.

Eleanor's feet were getting cold. She let go of her phone, clattering it back onto the nightstand.

She would have to talk to a preacher soon. Who was doing the funeral? She had never met her mother's pastor. Connie had usually stayed home from church when her daughter visited, out of deference to the widening chasm between their faiths. As if Eleanor still had *any* sort of faith.

The phone buzzed again. Another Wisconsin number. Was *this* one Paul Wasser? Was she waiting for him to call her? About what?

"Hello."

"Eleanor. This is Paul Wasser."

"Yes. Thank you for the casserole. Tell your mother thank you."

"Oh, good. I'm glad you got it." He paused. "How're you doing?"

"I saw where she fell. I mean, I looked at the sidewalk. Thank you for clearing it." Was there a hint of sarcasm in her voice? Her words of thanks probably came from her engraved sense of polite duty. But she really *was* grateful. Grateful for all he had done for her mother.

He didn't respond right away.

Then he spoke slowly. "I know it was like closing the barn door after the horses already escaped. But you might have walked on it. I mean, of course, you could. You're welcome to … to go to the barn, if you want. She kept some of her bigger paintings out there. There's rooms weathered in. It's not just a barn anymore, as you probably know."

His rambling sounded a bit desperate, like a purge. But the

contents of that purge seemed insignificant. Eleanor didn't need a reminder about the build quality of the rooms in the former barn. But she was strangely grateful to him again. Grateful especially for his discomfort. She sensed a heart behind his stumbling words. True sympathy. Shared grief.

"I'll look out there later. Uh. Why did you call?" Was it just to ask how she was doing? How much did she know about this handyman? Her mother had mentioned him dozens of times over the years. But it was always work-related. Who was he? What was he like? Had he been more to her mother than just a handyman? He seemed friendly and companionable.

"I wondered if you wanted me to bring Monet over. Maybe he could keep you company out there."

Maybe he could. And the dog would certainly have been welcome to come back home, if she were a dog person. She had been shocked to discover that her mother was a dog person. The way Connie spoke to the cocker spaniel had been embarrassing. Eleanor wondered at herself sometimes, worried that she was feeling sibling rivalry with that dog. Monet must be pretty old by now.

"Yeah. That would be okay, I guess. I'm really not a dog person. But it certainly is lonely out here."

"You live in a city back east?"

"A town. A townhouse in a college town." How many times had she just said the word "town?"

"Oh. Sure. I guess not everything in New York is New York City."

"That's true. I'm upstate, a couple hours north of the city."

"I see. Well, anyways. I'll bring Monet over whenever you want. And my mom has a pie she wants me to bring."

"Oh. Well. Okay. I have an appointment at the funeral home at one. Otherwise, I'm here."

"Alright, I'll bring him in a little while."

"That's fine. Thank you again."

"No problem. See you later."

When they hung up, she wondered how long "a little while" was. The range of possibilities boosted her through a brief bathroom routine, less routine for its unfamiliar setting. Even the same old rooms were unfamiliar in the absence of her parents. Both parents now.

She was in the pantry closet looking for breakfast food when she got her third call of the day.

"Hello, dear. How are you doing?" It was Jackie.

"I'm okay. This is all hitting me from the blind side." She squeezed the loaf of bread. Soft enough. "But I guess that's to be expected."

"Uh-huh." She could hear reserve in her best friend's response.

"I'm going to see her body this afternoon. She's refrigerated. But ..." Eleanor had meant to go deeper with this observation but lost the momentum.

"Is anyone going with you?"

"Oh, the funeral director will be there. A guy named Matt, I believe."

"But no one else? What about that handyman that found her?"

"What about him?"

"Maybe he can go with you. I wish I could be there. You shouldn't have to do that sort of thing alone."

"I wish you *were* here. But any of the locals would just be another stranger standing next to me."

"I suppose so." Jackie paused long enough for an extended breath. They both used sound-cancelling new phones, so the rasp of a whole breath didn't come clearly over the connection.

"I stood where she fell. I imagined her there. And I called to her. I told her to get up." Eleanor ran her hand through her damp hair. "I guess that's all absurd."

"Sounds real to me. Do you sense her presence around there? Do you think her spirit is still in the house?"

"You know I don't believe in that sort of thing. I'm not likely to sense something that I don't believe in."

"Um-hmm. Well, an experience like this can change a person. Losing your mother is a big thing, Ellie. Let it happen. Let it happen to *you*, and not just to the people around you."

Jackie, short for Jacquetta, was the only one who called her "Ellie." It had been a tease at first, but they had both gotten used to it over the years."

Eleanor heard a bark close to the house. "I think the dog is back."

"The dog ran away?"

"No. The handyman took him home to take care of him."

"Oh. I thought it was one of those things where the animals know the person is dead, so they run away as an act of mourning."

"I've never heard of that."

"I keep tellin' you that we all have these ancient traditions in our DNA. You don't have to come from Africa to know about that kinda thing."

"You come from Trenton."

"You know what I mean."

Paul knocked on the back door. Eleanor could see him through a gap in the white and yellow checked curtains. "The guy is here."

"Is he handsome?"

"I can't see him. No. I mean. That doesn't matter."

"Sorry. Habit. I still have hopes you'll find someone. I guess you're not thinking about that now."

"I'm not thinking about anything very clearly right now." She turned the doorknob to let Paul in from the cold. It was a dull and windy day, certainly as cold as the night before.

28

The dog pushed through the door, barked once, looked at Eleanor and then took off through the kitchen, on a mission.

"Okay. I gotta go."

"Yeah. I heard the dog."

"He's probably looking for Mom."

After a brief pause. "Take care of yourself, Ellie."

"Okay. I will."

She set her phone down. "Sorry about that."

Paul was standing in the entryway, pulling off brown leather gloves. He had apparently set a bag of dog food on the top step, when she wasn't watching. "I brought Monet some food he likes. I couldn't find much for him here. I'm not even sure what Connie fed him."

The sound of the dog's clinking tags intensified and abated, his nails clicking on hardwood and then silent on rugs. Eleanor listened even as she assessed the man on the landing below her. He was fairly tall. Lanky. He had a full head of hair—brown, due for a cut—and large greenish eyes. She noticed the dark circles around them.

She turned toward the sound of the dog. "He's looking for her, isn't he?"

Paul shrugged. "I don't know. He knows ... He saw ... I mean, he was there. I let him out while we waited for the paramedics. He ... well ... he knew she was down."

"But what does a dog understand about death?"

"I really don't know. I've seen those documentaries where a herd of elephants goes back to where one of 'em died and they seem to mourn the one they lost. But I don't know about dogs, or about Monet. He and Connie were really close."

As he spoke, Eleanor studied his mannerisms. He struck her as a bit nervous. But she was nervous too. Maybe it was Jackie's influence, but she did notice that he was handsome, though not as rugged as she had expected. His face was almost square, only the slightest hint of jowls, strong smile lines, a sort of ball at the end of his nose. His eyes were warm, lively and perceptive. He held a Milwaukee Brewers baseball cap in one hand and ran fingers through his wavy hair.

He was much younger than her. Maybe twenty years younger, certainly no more than forty-five. She gave herself half an eyeroll when she admitted that she had been checking out the handyman.

She stopped staring and spoke up. "Yes. Monet was her most constant companion. The son she never had."

Paul smiled. "I thought I was the son she never had." He braked his chuckling as if he had just heard himself. His eyes fell toward the floor for a second. He attempted a recovery. "Connie and I used to joke about that."

"She was a bit of a flirt."

He laughed harder. "Yeah. I guess I knew that. But it was all in fun. Her and me. She was like the fun mom I never had." Now Paul was rolling his eyes at himself. "Don't let my mom know I said that."

As if Eleanor was going to see Paul's mother any time soon. "Sure. You can count on me for discretion." She saw the pie on the little counter by the back door. Another thing she hadn't noticed when he entered.

"You don't really look like Connie. More like your dad, I guess."

Her mother had been pretty. Everyone said so. Eleanor had known it from when she was small. But the daughter had taken after the father, unfortunately. Her father wasn't unattractive. But he looked like a man. And so did Eleanor, as far as she was concerned. Maybe as far as Paul was concerned too.

"Did you know my dad?" She gestured for him to step up into the kitchen.

He followed as she backed up. "I met him several times over

the years. My dad was still doing most of the work around here in those days. I was in the Army for a while. Then I lived in Texas, until just before your dad died."

"You served overseas?"

"Germany, mostly. Only a short deployment in Afghanistan."

She nodded. The wars of generations past were part of her disciplinary specialty, American history. She had just caught herself fitting this veteran into a historical epoch, a particular generation of the American experience. That was a way to add distance between them.

"Did I tell you how sorry I am about your mom? I guess I did. I even let out some of my guilt about not getting over here sooner." He lowered his head again. "Sorry about that. Sorry about sharing my guilt. I know it doesn't help you any."

"Actually, I think it did help." She connected with his eyes, his head raised again. "I could tell you were struggling with all this just like me, like you were really feeling it. That's different from my friends. They didn't know Mom."

He nodded toward her phone on the island. "That was one of your friends on the phone just now?"

Eleanor sniffled a little laugh. She was leaning against the counter with her arms crossed over her chest. She dropped her hands and rested one on the stainless-steel edge of a sink. "That was Jackie. My closest friend."

"She lives out there where you do?"

"Carlisle University. We both teach there. She's Chair of the African American Studies department."

"Oh. She's ..."

"African American."

He blushed. "Sorry. I guess you can tell I'm from the sticks out here."

"Don't worry about it. She would think it was funny."

"She's not one of those militant types?"

31

"She can get pretty militant where there's some injustice being perpetrated. But she is also very gracious to white folks like me that 'have to work at getting a clue,' as she would say."

"Yeah. That's me. I have to work pretty hard. Or I would if I even felt like I *should* get a clue." He tossed his right hand in the air. "Sorry, that was pretty awkward."

"No harm done."

He chuckled self-consciously. "Thanks. So, you're going to the funeral home, you said?"

"Yeah. She's at ... Oh, I forget the name."

"Childress. They're the only one in town."

"Yes. That's it."

"Burial arrangements?"

"No. She was determined to be cremated. No burial."

"Oh."

"I'm going to see her body before they do it, before they do the cremation."

"Huh. I guess I never thought about that. It would be good to see her before they do that. I mean, not good, really. But it might be important." He gulped a double lung-full and released his exasperation. "I don't even know what I'm saying."

"It's so hard to know. I'm just getting used to people telling me how sorry they are for my loss. I'm working on faking a sincere reply."

"Faking being sincere?"

"Isn't that the only way?"

"Usually not, I think. But I know what you mean. Must ha' been quite a shock. She was completely healthy, wasn't she?"

"Pretty healthy for eighty-seven."

"Really? Eighty-seven? Wow. I didn't know. She might ha' lived to be a hundred, then." Once again, he looked like he was tired of biting leather, having stuck his foot in his mouth one more time.

But all his verbal clumsiness warmed Eleanor. "Thanks for being here for her. I know you were more than just the guy that shoveled the drive."

He turned his head toward the door and then glanced at the bag of dog food before returning to Eleanor's eyes. His face was red. Was that a blush? Or the strain of resisting tears?

She looked away to spare him embarrassment. Or maybe to spare herself more of that tenderizing her heart muscle was experiencing every time she turned her mind loose or spoke to another person about her mother.

"You want me to come with you, when you go see her at Childress?"

Eleanor realized instantly that she did. She did want him to go with her. Paul was feeling less like a stranger to her now. And Jackie was right, she shouldn't have to do this alone.

CHAPTER FIVE

From the window in her mother's bedroom, Eleanor could see the farm pond. On one side, tall pines sheltered the half-acre pond from western winds, certainly the intelligent design of some long-ago farmer or land developer. In the narrow patch of open water, a pair of mallards dug out vegetation along the near bank. That duck couple, at least, thought that spring would be here soon, despite most of the pond still being under ice.

Her mother's room smelled uniquely like Connie. Not just like the house. This room contained her personal scents. The fruity soaps that she favored blended with her honey-sweet perfumes, and with the earthier fragrances of the dried wildflowers standing in vases on nearly every piece of furniture. The ancient dresser, the sideboard, the bookshelves with dusty, hardbound books, books that had travelled here from the home Eleanor grew up in—it was all coated in history.

The dressing table, the bottom quarter of its mirror obscured by stacks of books and assorted painting supplies, bore little evidence of the beautifications her mother would have performed there when she was young. But Connie had never been young in this house. She was nearly Eleanor's age when she moved here. She had jokingly referred to it as her "retirement home." The ducks and geese that visited her pond she called her "retirement community."

When Eleanor extricated herself from the memory-laden air of her mother's bedroom she heard a pounding and a bark downstairs. Perhaps the dog wanted out. How was that done? She tried to remember. Should she hook him to a leash or just allow him to run? She would check by the back door for a reminder.

Reaching the bottom of the popping and groaning staircase, she could see the dog lying under the dining room table, his head up, alert. The pounding was from outside the back door. Monet barked again. Apparently, there was no bell out there. Or their visitor was disinclined to use it.

As she strode through the kitchen, Eleanor could see a small person from the chin down. A plaid coat from decades past, a gloved hand reaching for another knock. Eleanor padded down the steps on sock feet and pulled the door open. She hadn't locked it after Paul left.

"Hello?" She addressed an elderly woman with a severe hunch to her back.

"Eleanor? I'm Audrey Benson. A friend of your mother's."

"Mrs. Benson. Yes, of course, I recognize you."

"Call me Audrey." She turned and waved toward someone sitting in a dark sedan on the driveway. "My daughter."

"Please come on in." The wind was chasing last year's leaves up the driveway. The temperature was probably above freezing again. Audrey's face was lined and pale, except for her cheekbones and nose—nearly blood-red from the cold.

"She'll come back and get me when I text her." Audrey glanced stiffly over her shoulder and raised a hand halfway to indicate the departing car.

"Oh. That's fine. Come on in and have a seat." Eleanor was reciting lines as if from a Tennessee Williams play. She had no clear idea of where Audrey should sit or what they were going to do. But these automatic replies seemed to be her part, her lines in the script someone else wrote for her.

"Thank you. I suspect you have a lot of things to take care of, so I won't burden you with a long visit."

Audrey was tugging at her second glove and stepping very delicately onto the kitchen floor. She forged ahead toward the kitchen table. She knew her way around, of course. Audrey was probably her mother's best friend. She would have sat in this kitchen innumerable times, certainly more often than Eleanor had.

"Can I pour you some coffee?" There was almost a whole cup still in the carafe. Eleanor turned off the coffee maker, suspecting that remainder was a bit burnt. "Maybe I should make some fresh." That was a weak attempt to upgrade her hospitality, a late recovery effort.

"Oh. No thanks. I had my two cups today already. Good for the circulation but still makes me jittery if I overdo it." She draped her coat on the back of one maple chair and pulled at another with her left hand. "How are you doing, dear? This was such a shock, wasn't it?"

Loading up with a fresh breath, Eleanor nodded before deciding how much to open her soul to this stranger, a woman who had been no stranger to her mother. "I hardly know even what to think."

"I know. I know. I just keep trying not to think about Connie laying out there on the frozen pavement." Audrey dropped her head as her voice clutched with emotion. She rocked slightly side-to-side, sitting now with both hands spread on the polished tabletop in front of her.

Eleanor slipped into the chair across the table, her back to the window. She grabbed a lavender box of tissues from the counter and pushed it toward her guest. It bumped against the wicker placemat.

"I've been obsessing about that same thing. I don't know if I'm just deluding myself with the thought that it would have been so much easier if Mom had died in her bed, or in a hospital with some disease we saw coming. Is that right? Would it have been easier to accept?"

Alternating between shaking her head and nodding, Audrey busied herself with wiping her nose and cheeks, lifting her thin wire-rimmed glasses away from the strokes of the folded tissues. She seemed to have two or three Kleenexes involved in the operation. "I don't know. You could be right. Either way, you could be right. Just fooling ourselves maybe. But it's such a shock. Such a shock."

Eleanor glanced at the carved cuckoo clock on the wall to her right. It was past eleven thirty now. Where had her morning gone?

"I'm going to Childress at one o'clock to see her body before the cremation." She didn't complete the invitation, in case it was inappropriate to offer it.

Years of studying death rituals in various cultures in the Americas, mostly from previous centuries, only reinforced Eleanor's sense of absent traditions, missing guidelines for what she was supposed to do next, and with whom.

"You want me to come with you?"

"Paul Wasser is going to meet me there, so I won't be alone. But I was thinking you might want to come as well. We're not going to have a viewing otherwise."

"Just Connie under a sheet in a cold room?"

Internally, Eleanor winced at this description. Up to this point, the room at the funeral home had been a transparency, a blank with no character of its own. It was just her mother there.

Cold? Probably.

Inviting? Certainly not.

"Maybe you don't want to remember her that way."

"No. I'd go if you needed me to support you. But I'm not from people that go in for wakes and viewings so much. I know she's gone. She's not layin' under a sheet at the funeral home. She's looking down on us with an artist's appreciation for the scene." She glanced toward the ceiling, though Eleanor knew her guest was thinking much higher. Audrey, at least, was picturing Connie in Heaven right now.

Eleanor liked the idea of it. But Heaven was no more specific to her than her anemic imagination of the viewing room at the funeral home.

A prolonged silence from Eleanor seemed to prompt some concern from Audrey. The old woman leaned her torso to one side and lifted her head sideways to survey Eleanor across the table. "Do you want me to pray with you?" She looked like she had more questions. But she let her lips fall still after a few small twitches.

"No. Thank you. I appreciate it. I'm grateful for my mother's faith. I ..." How much to say? "I'm glad for your confidence that she's in a better place now. That feels good. She would be glad for us to think of her that way." Maybe she was digging a hole out of which she knew no likely exit, but Eleanor didn't want to fold her hands and bow her head after all these years. And she couldn't be sure that Audrey wasn't here to try and bring her back into the fold.

Nodding and lowering her eyes to the table again, Audrey seemed satisfied. "Okay. You just keep me in mind if you need someone to talk to. Your mother and I shared everything, two old widows finding comfort in each other's company." She seemed to hunker down a little more. "I just find it so ironic that she's the one that's gone, her being the one with so much energy." Again, her voice tightened before locking shut. After Audrey inhaled a calming breath, she reached for her coat and rummaged until she pulled a smartphone from one pocket.

"Does your daughter live nearby?"

"Yes. We're right on the edge of town over here. The last place before you see the Dove Lake sign." She indicated the direction with three fingers between punching the screen with her index finger. "She had to go back to keep an eye on a lunch she's cooking."

Eleanor contrasted Audrey's pokey texting style with the

students she often watched dancing their thumbs over the surface of their phones, as if the glass were molten and they dared not touch it for more than a nanosecond at a time.

She waited for Audrey to finish before speaking again. "I expect there are lots of things to do around here. One is deciding what to do with Mother's things. Please feel free to take whatever mementos you can think of, maybe some of her paintings."

Pausing her efforts to reinsert her phone into her coat pocket, Audrey made the swiftest movement Eleanor has seen so far. "Her paintings? You don't want to give those away too lightly. Those are worth quite a lot of money these days."

"Oh." Eleanor stopped there, wondering if Audrey was exaggerating, the way a loyal friend might. Simultaneously, she conceded that she had lost track of her mother's artistic success.

"She nearly sold out the show at that place by Lake Geneva. And her showing in Madison was written up in the paper up there." Having straightened her posture with sudden effort, Audrey strained to keep her head up and her watery gray eyes focused on Eleanor. "Maybe you didn't know about all that." Her eyebrows were stretched high. "No, you should think carefully about what to do with her paintings. There are a lot of 'em and they're all worth thousands of dollars, I'm quite certain."

Feeling caught in the act of neglecting her mother, her deceased mother who was this woman's dearest friend, Eleanor tried to redirect. "That doesn't mean that Mother wouldn't want you to have your pick from the paintings, at least one painting."

Audrey relaxed her neck and shrugged with one shoulder. "You're probably right. But you should still take some time to study that before you make any decisions."

Letting her eyes wander around the kitchen and toward the dining room, Eleanor found Monet sitting by the doorway, as if he were listening in on their conversation. But she looked past him, trying to recall seeing any of her mother's paintings around

39

the house. "Where would her paintings be? Out in the barn?"

"Well, some are in galleries around the area, as far away as Springfield, Illinois and Minneapolis. But I'm sure you'll find quite a few in the barn. Maybe some downstairs. Have you been in her studio?" The sound of a car crunching up the drive started Audrey pulling her gloves out of her coat pocket.

The studio was the former master bedroom on the first floor. With a bathroom attached and large windows on two sides, it had been a perfect painter's studio, overlooking the farm pond and with plenty of room for easels to remain standing.

"I just couldn't go in there yet. I managed to stand in her bedroom for a little while this morning. I'll get to the studio."

Audrey stood slowly and reached for Eleanor's near hand. She patted it gently. "I understand completely. I had such a struggle talking myself into coming over here. It's just not the same with Connie gone." Abruptly ceasing her comments and her offered consolation, Audrey turned toward the back door.

Eleanor attributed the lack of ceremony in her departure to Audrey's intense emotions and her close friendship with Connie. Her mother was casual and comfortable with everyone. She wouldn't begrudge a silent, tearful retreat today.

Walking slowly toward the door, the process of winding her scarf around her neck decreased Audrey's pace even further.

A woman perhaps a bit younger than Eleanor was at the back door. She brushed a lock of red hair off her forehead as she held the storm door open. "So sorry for your loss." That was perhaps in lieu of introductions. Eleanor just nodded her acceptance of that standard condolence.

"Remember what I said about calling me to talk. Feel free. And don't let anyone carry away any paintings until you know what they're worth." With that, Audrey grasped the offered forearm of her daughter, eased down the two steps, and squeezed out the door to toddle toward the car.

Audrey's parting words were a little less circumspect than her earlier comments about the paintings. She seemed to be implying that Eleanor didn't know what she was doing when it came to the disposition of Connie's paintings. And it was true. Eleanor accepted the fact of her ignorance as a sort of afterthought. Almost all this experience seemed to be coming clear to her only in "oh, yeah" moments.

Looking again at the cuckoo clock, she rode the momentum of Audrey's cautions. She paced past the dog and through the house, toward her mother's studio. "Come on, Monet. You can show me around." The cocker spaniel followed dutifully, looking up at Eleanor every time she paused to glance at him. He apparently had questions. She wished she could answer them, even if some of her own remained unaddressed.

CHAPTER SIX

Childress Funeral Home was in a low, dark structure that could easily belong to any town Eleanor had visited in North America. She had visited hundreds by this point in her life. But the proprietor in that generic building, Matt Bauer, was clearly practiced at a personal touch and at applying that touch to total strangers.

"It's such a difficult time. You just let me know if something makes you uncomfortable. Honesty is the best policy in these situations." He was probably in his late thirties, balding, pale with yellowish-brown hair combed over his shiny head. His eyes seemed to seek an entry point and then retreat subtly, not really looking away but averting to a different part of her face, away from her eyes to her mouth or to her cheeks or to her fly-away hair.

Eleanor knew she was trying too hard, assessing him too closely, bearing down on each of her auditions for a recognizable role to play, something to define the way she should act toward these people she didn't know. Even though she had accompanied her mother through many of the funeral arrangements for her father, Connie had been entirely in charge back then. Eleanor had just been her assistant, an acolyte to the woman who knew what to do, or at least who knew how to act like she did.

Had it been this same funeral home? Maybe the name had changed. But Eleanor found no inspiration to begin a historical investigation.

Paul Wasser arrived just after Eleanor. He remained a step behind her as the three of them slipped apologetically into the small viewing room off the main corridor. The room was empty, almost as anonymous as Eleanor had imagined. It did have a cross on one wall. That hadn't been part of her imagination. Facing her there, that cross was funeral decoration, appropriate to the occasion, not religious or spiritual in any way. Few people in this rural community would be offended by a cross in this empty room, with its indoor-outdoor carpet and pale paneling halfway up three walls.

Matt excused himself as Paul and Eleanor stood waiting in the middle of the room. She noticed three chairs against the wall behind her, next to the door through which they had entered. Maybe she would need to collapse into one of those chairs when she saw her mother. Certainly, that was their purpose. No one would want to sit and meditate in this room, to contemplate the body of their deceased relative. Or would they?

The door through which Matt had exited swung both ways, swinging inward now as he butted it open and pulled a sort of hospital gurney in after him. For a moment, it reminded Eleanor of the time her mother had endured gallbladder surgery. Was her mother Matt Bauer's patient now? A failed patient, certainly.

"Do you want me to stay? Do you want a moment alone?" Paul seemed to be having second thoughts, or maybe one of those afterthoughts Eleanor had been fumbling from her pockets as she shuffled through this odyssey.

"No. This is fine. You don't have to go anywhere." She almost said, "This isn't a big deal, don't worry about it." Or something to that effect. She might say it even if it weren't true. But she didn't.

Paul just nodded and stood with his Brewers cap clutched in two hands. He hadn't dressed up at all, and neither had Eleanor. She felt accomplished for having showered and put on clean clothes that morning. Now she remembered she would need to press her black dress, having foregone the option of a garment bag.

What a profane thought.

Under a white sheet lay the form of her mother. The form of

her mother's body. Beneath that sheet, she also seemed to be covered with several layers of blankets. Eleanor banished cynical thoughts about efforts to keep her mother warm in the refrigerator.

Matt pulled back the sheet to reveal his patient's head and neck. He discretely folded it there and then excused himself with whispered words and stealthy steps. He may have said, "I will leave you alone with her."

Eleanor wasn't alone. Paul was there, though he stood as still as one of those chairs by the wall. She certainly didn't feel like she was with her mother. This strange-looking woman was a poor facsimile of her mother, a stiff, gray likeness of Connie. The work of some amateur sculptor, perhaps.

Eleanor stepped next to the bed. Maybe she would recognize the woman from closer.

No. This dead person was *not* her mother. Even when she had seen her mother asleep, napping in the middle of the day, Connie had been mobile and vital. Her color had been warm and her features ... alive. Her mother was a living person. This was not her mother.

Yet, of course, she knew this was Constance Petersen, wife of Darrel Petersen, mother of Eleanor Petersen. The facts were undeniable. The facts, however, were cold. They were like the book history with which Eleanor had been educated, not like the living history discovered by traveling the country to see sites and to interview people. Even if this cold person under this sheet was her mother, Eleanor wouldn't mourn *her*. Instead, she would mourn the loss of the quirky woman with the messy mop of hair and a pencil-thin paint brush forgotten behind one ear. Where was *that* woman?

"I'm keeping busy, Lenny. No need to worry about me." Where was *that* version of her mother?

The woman in her memory was probably too young. Connie

had been preserved as a seventy-seven-year-old in her daughter's mind, perhaps. Had Connie grown feebler since then? There were hints at Christmas.

"Should I have known, Mother?" Eleanor stood right over the body now. She glanced over her shoulder, checking for a reaction from Paul. Had she spoken aloud?

I should have insisted. I should have taken better care of you. The pressure in her head forced her eyes shut.

Everything shut down.

Sorrow. Just sorrow.

She sensed Paul touching her on the back.

But she didn't venture to touch her mother's body.

When she stood outside the front door of the funeral home, Eleanor could recall slices of conversation inside, some of it significant. But it all remained contained in that low building, with its 1950s architecture and its odd mix of florescent and incandescent lighting. Outside, in the half sunlight, she was looking at Paul.

"I hope I remember all the things I agreed to in there." She didn't mean to confess that to him. She was just ejecting worries, as if clearing the way for a flow of true and meaningful words.

"I can help you remember, in case you're really serious." Paul seemed to understand her thoughts both spoken and unspoken. He looked toward Main Street and a pair of pickup trucks passing each other in opposite directions. "How's Monet taking it?"

The question sounded funny. Eleanor blew a small laugh through her nose. Monet, after all, was a painter who had been dead longer than her mother. But she didn't say that.

"I feel like I'm neglecting him. What do you think about taking him? I mean permanently."

"Oh. Well. Hmmm. I'll have to think about that. I got the feeling that Monet was waiting to go home the whole time. I don't know how long that might go on." He looked away for a moment and then back. "I probably have room. And Dodger won't mind. You really don't want him?"

Here was one of those partially obscured truths. It would have been obvious to her in a rational state. Did she want to keep the dog? Of course not. She didn't want a dog. She wasn't going to take a dog back to New York with her.

She felt her shoulders sag, deflated by a weary realization that she was neglecting more than the dog. She was staying at a safe distance from everything, thinking only about things that other people insisted she face by asking her questions. Right now, she welcomed thinking about her mother's pet, as shelter from harder thoughts.

Paul seemed to be waiting for something, but maybe he wasn't sure what.

Eleanor slipped one hand into the pocket of her dark blue car coat. "I really can't take him long-term. I think I was just accepting him back at the house as a way for him to mourn, and as a temporary arrangement until we find him a home. I can't take him back to New York."

She rubbed past a realization now that she had insanely assumed that the dog would just stay at the house when she went back home. But, what about the house? Was she going to just leave it without arranging for its future as well? What about her mother's things, especially the paintings?

"I'm just getting my mind around all the things I have to take care of. Could you help me with the dog? Find him a home?"

He nodded. "I'll take him for now and see if we can keep him."

"We? I never bothered to find out if you're married."

"When I say 'we,' I mean me and Dodger. I'm not married." He looked toward the street again, as if he were embarrassed. But maybe Eleanor was just projecting her own embarrassment on him.

"So, you want to come over now? To get Matisse?"

"Monet, you mean."

"Yes." She chuckled. "Him and any other impressionists you might find at my mother's place."

"I can never remember which ones were impressionists and which were post-impressionist."

Was he showing off his sophistication with that comment? It might have been one of those undergraduate pretenses at knowledge. But Eleanor slapped those thoughts aside. "I'm sure I can't help you there. And it turns out that I don't even know as much about my own mother's paintings as I should."

"She has a lot of 'em over there. Though maybe she's sold a bunch. I know people around here consider her a kind of art celebrity. Or *considered* her that." He breathed a sigh almost big enough to make a significant contribution to the billowing wind flapping at Eleanor's bangs.

"See you at the house? Or do you want to come by later?" She didn't remember him answering that question yet.

"I'll follow you over there now."

"I should probably follow *you*. I still get turned around, even on Main Street." She was embellishing a little, but only a little. She persistently mistook east for west around here.

It wasn't until they both had pulled into the driveway by the farmhouse that Eleanor noticed an unusual shape to the old snow by the sidewalk where Connie fell. The piles next to the sidewalk had been chopped off, like strip mining the top off a mountain. And a fresh pile of slushy snow lined the end of the drive, by the barn. Clearly, Paul had tried to minimize the chances that snowmelt would get trapped on that sidewalk again. That was thoughtful, if too late. Apparently, he was protecting Eleanor against killer ice.

With Paul climbing out of his truck just next to her rental, on the double-wide part of the driveway, this thought felt like a wicked accusation. Against Paul? Against ice. She rejected all accusations by turning her thoughts to the dog. Monet was barking from inside.

"I don't remember him barking a lot. He was pretty quiet when I was in the house with him."

"He's probably just greeting us. That's how I think of it. He'll quiet down once he sees us."

Inside the house, Monet did quiet his barking. But he maintained a hearty panting, while looking constant questions at the two humans entering the house.

"He probably needs to go out. I'll take him." Paul reached for a leash by the back door.

"Did mother walk him when he needed out? I don't remember."

"Only sometimes. There's a chain hooked to the railing out there that she would put him on if she was in the middle of something, and if the snow wasn't piled up too high by the house."

That sounded familiar. She must have seen that arrangement when she visited. Eleanor just stood staring, as Paul hooked the leash on Monet's collar.

While Paul and Monet patrolled the perimeter of the property, a task she observed out of her father's bedroom window for a moment, Eleanor contemplated what she was doing. She had wandered, sleepwalker-like, up the stairs. She seemed to be seeking an overlook from which to assess what she had done thus far.

She had just returned from seeing her mother's body. That had happened. That was real. That had proved to her that her mother was really dead. Was that the purpose?

Now she was in the process of giving away her mother's old dog. This further testified to the surety of her mother's death.

It was definite. It was final.

48

CHAPTER SEVEN

While Paul was still backing down the driveway, with Monet in the truck cab, Eleanor's phone buzzed on the kitchen table. She picked it up and took one breath before answering.

"Hello, Jackie." She turned and walked toward the living room. When she ambled past the stacks of books and papers, something sticking through the mail slot in the front door caught her attention. The U.S. mail was delivered to a box by the county road. That mail slot was a vestige of an earlier time or perhaps entirely misplaced.

"Hello, dear. Tell me all about it. How are you doing?"

"What day is it?"

"Ah. That bad, is it?"

"Seriously. I have no idea what day it is."

"Thursday."

"Seemed like a weekend to me, for whatever reason." She was pulling the yellow note through the mail slot. A fraction of a legal page.

"Sure. That's entirely understandable. Are you getting support from your mother's friends out there?"

"I am. And here is a note from her pastor. He must have come by while I was out." She unlocked the bolt and opened the front door. That note reminded her that not everyone would think of the front door as strictly ornamental. And there she found three casseroles stacked on the wooden porch, next to the door, casseroles in aluminum pans. Disposable pans. Convenient. "More casseroles here on the front porch. First time I checked there."

"So, this is really rural, white America. This is the authentic experience."

"Well, it is mostly white. No denying that. But I think my mother attracted some artists and free thinkers, among her many admirers. Apparently, her paintings were gathering something of a following in recent years. More than I knew."

"I'll Google her." Jackie paused. "Constance, right?"

"Yes. Constance. That was how she signed her paintings. That was how she was known in the art world. It does sound more artistic, as well as more puritanical."

"Oh. Here's her Wikipedia page. A decent-length biography."

"Wait. My mother has a Wikipedia page?" Eleanor's voice hit an unfamiliar peak.

"Right here in front of me. You brought a laptop, didn't you?"

"I haven't even unpacked it. Which reminds me—I have to unpack my black dress to press it." She lugged the last of the casserole dishes inside to the broad bookshelf by the front door. She wouldn't have been surprised if her mother had placed a bookshelf *over* the front door, given how little she had used it.

"What does the pastor say in the note? Oh, here's a review of a show in Milwaukee last year. 'A Living and Breathing Portrayal of Rural America.' That's the title. 'Living and Breathing.'" Jackie fell silent, as if muted by the irony of repeating that phrase.

"The pastor says to call him for funeral arrangements and anything else I need. And he scrawled a bit at the end. 'Casseroles are not from me.' I guess he didn't want to falsely receive credit."

"Very holy of him." Jackie didn't sound critical, more distracted. Probably still reading about the artistic career of Constance Petersen.

"Does the Wikipedia article note her death?"

"Uh. Back. Back. No. Not yet deceased according to this. I could update that."

"Sure. I guess you may as well." Several faculty members that

Eleanor knew were active contributors to Wikipedia, Jackie included.

"So, you're going to get some consolation from this pastor?"

"I don't know about consolation. We have to make arrangements. Mother designated him as the officiant for her funeral, I expect. I guess we'll schedule it for Monday."

"You want me to fly out there for that?"

"Oh. No. That would be way too much trouble. No. Just keep calling me and waking me up. Like alerting me to what day it is." She left the casseroles on that bookshelf, warning herself not to forget them entirely. But something was drawing her back to the studio now.

Much of her adult life, Eleanor had been the celebrity in the family. She had been salutatorian of her high school class. She had been in The National Honor Society. She was written up in the Milwaukee paper when she was selected for her first summer program at Oxford University. Her first guest lectures evoked congratulations from her parents, as did her first book and her full professorship.

In contrast, her mother's painting had been nothing more than a hobby. That was a common attitude for women in the 1970s. Only the bold and radical asserted themselves as serious artists. Her mother was too mild for that. And perhaps her talent had yet to be fully formed, along with her identity as an artist.

Eleanor listened to Jackie reading parts of a review from the *Chicago Tribune*, as she looked at the paintings in the studio. Her mother's style resembled Andrew Wyeth's in its realism and her use of color. But her subjects were generally more expressive and welcoming, at least as Eleanor saw them. And she saw them now through new eyes. Even comparing some aspect of her mother's work to a respected artist such as Wyeth would have seemed silly twenty years ago. But maybe Eleanor had already been neglecting her mother's art back then. Maybe Connie had established herself already.

"What's the earliest review you find?"

"Gallery review? Let me look at Google. There are thousands of mentions. Some are another person entirely. But the majority are the artist Constance Petersen. I see one here from 2011. Madison, Wisconsin. Go Badgers."

"Is that all you know about Wisconsin?"

"Ha. That and the history of populist progressivism that has frustratingly evaporated in recent national political alignments."

"Okay. Sorry I brought it up."

"I can keep digging. But you should probably be doing this, right?"

"I'm thinking that I have more immediate obligations. I have her paintings themselves. Apparently, dozens of her paintings. And they seem to be worth a lot to the art-buying public."

"Ah. I guess that will complicate things. You will also have to consider the inflating value of her work, now that she's no longer ... painting."

"No longer painting. Yes." Eleanor stood in front of an unfinished acrylic of a large, old barn. Boards slipped askew, it had nevertheless been splashed with red and white paint, a late attempt at reviving it. Then one more collapse and another. Perhaps it was an economic collapse. But her mother was fairly nonpolitical in most areas of her life, probably her art too. At least, that was what Eleanor understood. Maybe she would need to reevaluate all such assumptions.

"Well, dear. I need to get to a meeting. You sound like you're doing okay. But it sounds like you have lots of work to do on many levels."

"Yes. It's true. Good thing spring break is coming."

"Call me when you need to talk."

"I will. Thanks, Jackie."

"You're welcome, Ellie."

Turning now to another painting, finished perhaps, of a crow sitting atop a wooden fence post, with curls of barbed wire dangling from it, a deep longing percolated. The art was beautiful. Compelling. But Eleanor really missed the one who created that picture of solitude and rustic beauty.

CHAPTER EIGHT

Her last truly significant conversation with her mother had been over Christmas. They spoke over the phone at least once a week. But those low-energy calls generally fell short of momentous, often short of intimate.

In December, during her visit just before the new year, she had found her mother stretched out in the living room. That time Connie was awake, not napping. She was, in fact, reading Eleanor's most recent book, her gray brows knitted closely in scrutiny of some concept or story. Eleanor tried to imagine which part Connie was reading with such intensity.

Connie turned the page and lowered the book. "Ah. You caught me catching up on my academic reading."

"Well, that book is supposed to be more accessible to the nonacademic public."

"Sounds like what your publisher said about it."

"Something like that."

Connie sat up straighter. "It *is* fascinating to see how women over the years kept fighting, even when all the economic cards were stacked against them."

Eleanor tried to recall if she had used that card metaphor in the book but couldn't recall. Her mom had been a bridge player back in the 1980s or so. But she didn't know if Connie had played since then.

Seeing her reading that volume had sparked some curiosity about her mother's education. "You think you still benefit from your Lake Forrest education?"

"I expect so. If I had stayed home and cooked and cleaned after high school, or just gone to work in a dime store, I doubt I'd be able to comprehend something like this." She lifted the 500-

page hardbound book in reference. Letting its weight settle the volume between her side and the arm of the couch, she had grinned at her daughter.

Connie was curvier than she used to be, but still what Eleanor would call slim. Certainly, her arms and legs had thinned over the years. Right then, her mother's feet were propped on the old mahogany coffee table Connie had inherited from *her* mother. Her mother never would have let Connie prop her feet on it like that. Apparently, Connie saw Eleanor noting the placement of her feet. She lifted a pink terrycloth slipper at her and waved it back and forth.

"Have you put any more thought into arrangements for your future?" It was the tough conversation that Eleanor just kept pushing, hoping each passing year added new weight to her concern about her mother's isolation.

Monet had lifted his head, where he lay on the floor beneath Connie, as if he too was interested in revisiting this sorest topic between them.

"I actually did put some thought into it recently. I was talking to Alva Kroeker about her arrangement. She has a girl that comes out to do some housework and wash her hair and go pick up her groceries and meds. I'm hearing from others too, that there are lots of ways to prolong living independently these days. I'll keep an eye on that. I think I might like some help cleaning this house sometime soon."

Eleanor had allowed herself an evaluative survey of the house that day, from a cleaning perspective. But that was only a pause. A small bubble of hope was rising.

"I'm glad to hear you're thinking about that. Let me know if you need me to help pay for any of it."

"Are you making big bucks from these books, dear?" Connie tapped the book under her arm.

"Uh. No. Not really. But I don't have kids to put through

college, and I don't need to save up to pass anything on when I die. So, I can help when you need it."

"That's sweet of you. Thanks for offering. But I'm doing pretty well."

At the time, Eleanor had assumed—if it were true—that this was entirely due to her father's financial planning skills and some good investments her parents had made over the years. It had not occurred to her that her mother was making a substantial income from her art.

After she left a message on the pastor's voice mail, just before sunset on that Thursday, Eleanor decided to go out to the barn to see what was stored out there. A sort of treasure-hunting intrigue accompanied her out the back door and over the dry pavement. It looked as if Paul had paused to clear away some of the salt so it didn't constitute another sort of slip hazard.

Eleanor clutched her black cardigan close against the wind. She should have grabbed one of her mother's jackets, instead of plowing into the cold in just a sweater. This thought diverted her back to that small bag of personal items Matt Bauer had handed her at the funeral home. Apparently, her mother had been wearing only a cashmere cardigan when she ventured out to the barn that day, earlier this week—this very long week. That pink sweater was folded still in the white plastic bag lying on the kitchen floor, where Eleanor had dropped it. White plastic, as if it was from a generic grocery store. That cashmere sweater must have been from Macy's or Nordstrom's.

She grunted frustration at these wandering thoughts. She pulled at the storm door on the barn and found that the inside door was locked. She twisted harder at the handle, in a fit of even more frustration, and the door squeaked open. She fiddled with the inside knob as she pushed into the still interior. The door *had* been locked but not pulled all the way shut. Eleanor turned the button on the knob inside, unlocking it. Then she changed her mind and locked it again.

Now she battled the squirmy thought that her mother had been the one who had pulled that door shut behind her but hadn't checked that it latched. Had Connie been distracted? Was she weak or disoriented?

Of course, on a regular day—one when Connie didn't fall and freeze to death on the sidewalk—failing to latch that door would have been an insignificant oversight. In this wilderness of grief, however, the unlatched door was an ominous landmark. Eleanor shook her head in argument against making a big issue of it and left the door open a few inches, the storm door blocking enough of the wind and cold. She wriggled against locking herself into this unfamiliar barn.

She had come out here with her mother several times over the years. She had even fetched something once on her own— maybe a tool or one of those raw canvases—as a favor for her mother. But Eleanor had never explored all the rooms and spaces in this big box of a building.

It had started out as a working barn, as far as she knew, for straw and hay storage, with some animal stalls, perhaps. Before her parents bought it, this farmhouse and barn had already been separated from the crop land, the land sold off to a large interest. Only a bit more than an acre remained, including the pond. And the barn had been converted to a workspace for an automotive hobbyist. It still smelled slightly of motor oil and gasoline. But the dominant smell now was linseed oil. The most pungent element of her mother's art.

The ceiling was open in the central corridor. The walls of that corridor, down which she now walked, were hung with old sketches—pencil and charcoal drawings from decades past. Her mother had explained to her that she still found inspiration from her early attempts, as if their primitiveness was a catalyst.

Eleanor stopped and studied a sketch of a young girl and a

cat. Much of it was rough, implying that Connie's subjects had scampered away before their images could be fully captured on paper. But she knew that her mother worked mostly from photographs, not from live models. Even the barns and fences, which wouldn't fidget and fuss, posed for her via photographic images, many of which Eleanor had seen stacked around the studio.

Two doors stood opposite each other near the end of that corridor. One stood halfway open. From it came that linseed odor, the smell of oil paintings. She opened the other door and noted much less of that familiar odor. She pushed in. When she turned on the light, she could see rough pine racks on which were stacked dozens of paintings along the opposite wall. To her right were stacks of more canvases, many tied in bundles. The lack of odor was not from a lack of paintings, just a lack of linseed oil. Her mother had switched frequently back and forth between acrylic and oil painting. Now that Eleanor thought of it, Connie must have only been using acrylics in the house recently. There was very little of the oily scent in there, even with the windows shut for winter.

The pine racks along the wall had numbers printed on them in black ink. The numbers were years. Some years had only a few paintings in them. Others ten or more. She pulled one painting from the set marked 2014. What she found stunned her—a woman in a sort of peasant blouse and skirt. A deep green shawl stretched behind her shoulders, where she held its golden tassels in each hand. The subject looked away from the viewer. The woman's face was young, but not girlish, with long eyelashes and a sweep of dark hair. A golden and ochre background set off her brown eyes and milky skin. It was stunning. Beautifully done. The image invited the viewer into the life of that woman, that nameless woman.

Eleanor flipped the 30" x 24" canvas over and found a name. "Yvonne #6." It was tallied in her mother's neat hand, blue pencil on the back of the wood frame.

"Yvonne." Not just a photo. A person. "I wonder who Yvonne is, or was." She checked the date again. 2014 wasn't long ago.

She spent nearly an hour pulling out canvases to see her mother's work. What she couldn't determine was why *these* paintings were here and not in a gallery somewhere. Were they lacking in quality, in her mother's estimation? Or were they too precious to sell?

In all, she found six paintings of Yvonne in that storage room. Most in a similar costume, all staged to enhance her large Southern European eyes and prominent cheekbones. Somehow, of all the paintings Eleanor found in those rooms, the ones of Yvonne evoked the most intense melancholy. And they awoke a drive to investigate. To investigate Yvonne's identity and Connie's art.

CHAPTER NINE

When Pastor Virgil Meers called her back on her cell phone, Eleanor was eating cold lasagna casserole off a lunch plate and sifting through files in her mother's upstairs office. The lasagna had been warm when she started.

"Ms. Petersen. Or, I suppose, it's Dr. Petersen."

"You can call me Eleanor." She leaned back and stared into a dark corner of the stuffy office.

"All right. You can call me Virgil, then. That's what your mother called me. She didn't go in for titles. She treated people like people, not titles." He hung for a second. "That's one of the things I appreciated about her."

"How well did you know her?"

"Well, she was part of the church for all the twenty-some years that I've been here. I suppose I got to know her as well as I did any of the older women in the church."

"Did she flirt with you?" She was remembering what Paul had said about their teasing back and forth.

"Ha. She did have a great sense of humor. But I don't think I ever felt like she was flirting. Certainly, never anything inappropriate. Nothing serious."

He had said more than she expected. But he wouldn't know how sober her concern might be.

"No, not serious, of course." She rotated her shoulders against stiffening pain. "But I had wondered if her flirting was really as innocent as it seemed, especially after my father passed. I often wondered if she was lonely." What was she saying? Once she had started down this way, she couldn't find an offramp.

"I can understand your concern. A mother living alone. I didn't know your father as well. But I thought of them as a warm and loving couple. She certainly missed him."

"Yes. She certainly did miss him. I tried to ask my mother about their relationship at various points, especially after he passed. There were some things I didn't understand."

"Hmm. Well, we've gotten off to a brisk start."

"Yes." She shook her head at herself. "I suppose lots of things are getting stirred up over here, alone with my mother's memories. I'm missing my father too, now." She rested her forehead on one hand. "And there's the whole confessional element."

"With me? I'm not a Catholic priest."

"Lutheran, of course."

"Lutheran Church—Missouri Synod."

"Not the evangelical kind?" She possessed only sketchy notions about the different sorts of Lutheran groups. She had grown up in a Lutheran church in Milwaukee but had bailed out in high school, as soon as her parents allowed her the option. Since then, church had become primarily a cultural phenomenon, occasionally relevant to her historical research and little more than that.

"Our church is probably more what you would consider mainstream evangelical than the Lutherans who have that title in their name. In a town like Dove Lake, we might not look so different from your average Bible church in many ways. Certainly, our faith is very compatible with the broader evangelical community."

"Are you recruiting me?"

"No. But I do want you to know where I'm coming from, as you and I prepare for the funeral service. Your mother wanted a service fitting to her church home."

"And she told you that I might resist that?"

"No. Not really. I think she said you were agnostic but not antagonistic."

"Did she really say that?"

"I might have dressed that up a bit. I've been working on my sermon all day. Once I hit a preaching rhythm it's hard to get out of it."

"Okay." She wondered for the first time how she would feel at the funeral that her mother had arranged. "I do want to have the service the way Mother would have intended. I guess we can go over the plan, and I'll speak up if something seems offensive to me."

"We are accustomed to funeral services including friends and family from a variety of faiths and perspectives. So, we are practiced at avoiding offense."

"I might just test you on that." Why was she feeling so free with this stranger? Maybe because he was clergy. Was it a perverse urge to provoke him? Catholic or not, something about talking to this pastor made Eleanor want to confess things.

After a small laugh at her comment, he stuck to business. "When should we meet to discuss the plan?"

"I'm available anytime tomorrow."

They set up a meeting at his office for the following morning at ten o'clock. And that ended her first conversation with Virgil Meers. An odd exchange, probably only from her side.

She thought about him the rest of the evening—an ongoing conversation. His tone lingered in her head, like the smell of woodsmoke on her clothes. Someone's fireplace was, in fact, tinting the air as the night deepened. That hint of smoke tempted Eleanor to follow suit, but she suspected that her mother hadn't kept up the chimney maintenance. That was the sort of thing to which her dad would have attended. Was Paul now the one caring for all aspects of this property? She might need him to continue doing that.

This raised another question. Was Paul contracted to remove ice whenever it appeared? Was he obligated to check on her mother every day? He wasn't her caregiver.

Hunkered over her mother's desk, Eleanor shoved aside that line of questioning.

She was searching for papers. No lawyer had contacted her yet. Was there someone for her to consult? Who managed her mother's money? Did Connie pay her own bills?

A desk lamp gooardnecked over the clutter on the big old desk, Eleanor pulled at drawers and searched the room for obvious file storage. She hadn't noticed any such storage elsewhere in the house, or in the barn. This office was as cluttered as a recycle bin. Certainly, anything important would be here somewhere.

Though much of her document research was electronic these days, Eleanor had entered academia before the proliferation of digital archives and internet connections. And she still relished the warmth of old documents and the smell of ancient manuscripts. Ruffling through piles of bills revived a little of that nostalgic attraction. The tactile appeal of paper enhanced the obsessive focus, which erased time from consideration. But she did glance at the clock just before midnight.

"Well. How long have I been at this?" She slid a file full of medical bills back into the three-drawer cabinet next to the desk, a file named for the supplemental insurance provider. Then she noticed a file labeled "Cards Received." She pulled the manila folder out of the back of the top drawer. She suspected that her father had imposed the alphabetical system on these reams of important and not-so-important documents.

But the first card in that folder was to her *mother*.

And it was from Eleanor.

"Mom. I am so thankful for a mother who inspires me, and so many others, to keep pursuing our dreams. Love you. Eleanor."

A Mother's Day card from two years ago.

Eleanor sucked a hasty breath to make up for the thin supply she had been sipping when she read that card. This could get sad. Very sad. She skipped the next few cards in the file. They were mostly in order. What was the oldest card in there?

Toward the back of the folder she found one entitled, "To My Wife." A traditional card from an old-style company. Inside, the printed script said, "Have a blessed and beautiful birthday." Then her father's tight handwriting ran to the bottom of the page and onto the back of the internal flap.

Dearest Constance,

I still think of your name as perfectly appropriate. You have been my constant friend and faithful companion for all these years. And you have not only tolerated my quirks and foibles, but you have showed me grace and mercy year in and year out. So many others would have left years ago when they found out about my "preference." But you have stayed, and you have never even hinted that you regretted that decision.

I believe there is a special reward awaiting you in Heaven, for loving me in spite of my limitations, and loving me so faithfully and so constantly.

I love you now and forever,

Darrel

The date was 2009. Her mother's birthday had been a month before his last heart attack. The one from which he didn't recover.

"Dearest Constance." Eleanor could understand his praise for Connie's loyalty. Though she had often wondered if there was a level of regret, some hidden dissatisfaction behind her mother's pressed and creased grin.

She pictured her father writing this. He was a bit unsteady toward the end, his hands trembling the way hers did now, only worse. Still, he managed a neat script. Years of practice, no doubt.

But what was he saying about his "preference?" Not his

preferences. It was singular. "Preference."

What an odd phrase. Her father had been particular about many things—food, literature, music. He had taught Eleanor to appreciate classical music, to the extent that she still did.

"Preference." Which preference?

He couldn't be referring to ...

Eleanor sat up abruptly.

What was he saying?

Flipping the card over, she reread it, even starting from the cover and "To My Wife." This time, she flipped the card to the back cover. There she found her mother's handwriting in blue ballpoint ink.

My Dearest Darrel,

You have gone from me now, before I could adequately thank you for this sentiment. With others around us at dinner on my birthday, I knew I couldn't fully react. And then I let it slip. What a regrettable procrastination.

Can I still respond? Is it really too late?

I never regretted my decision to stay with you. How could I? You were always my very best and sweetest friend.

Oh, how I miss you ...

There the words stopped at the bottom of the back cover. Eleanor flipped the card around, opened it, closed it. She pawed at the pile of cards in the folder now open on the desk.

"How I miss you..."

It was a complete thought. But not a completed communication.

"Mom." She whispered into the cool darkness beyond the cone of light from the desk lamp.

"What was happening? What did you do?"

But she knew the answer. She had long suspected *something*. But not this.

Now, in the absence of both her parents, the rest of her small

family, she had to face this numbing family secret.
   Alone.

CHAPTER TEN

At eight o'clock the next morning, Eleanor tapped on Jackie's contact icon in her recent calls. It would be nine o'clock in New York. Friday. Jackie had no exams to administer on Friday. But she was probably in her office.

Eleanor was seated in her mother's office. It used to be her father's. This leather desk chair had been his desk chair until a decade ago.

Jackie answered after two rings. "Hello, my friend. How are you doing?" Jackie's rich alto familiarity nearly extracted the tears Eleanor had been stopping up inside.

She sighed heavily. "I found something last night. I found a card from my dad to my mom. It was from just before he died."

"Oh, dear. I think I need to come out there. This is a lot for you to bear on your own, Ellie."

Jackie didn't even know what Eleanor had found in that card. But she knew her so well, she could read volumes in her voice.

"My dad thanked her for staying with him in spite of his 'preference.' When others would have left him long ago."

"Oh. Really? His preference?"

"Yes."

"In quotes? That's how you said it. As if it were in quotes."

"Yes."

"Oh. Does it mean what we're both thinking?" She didn't wait for Eleanor to answer. "But you thought there was something. You mentioned to me that they had separate bedrooms."

"That could have just been because my mother snored."

"But you said they weren't intimate."

"I didn't know that for sure. But I did think of my mother as

67

cold." Eleanor tried to moderate her accelerating breath. "I remember once when I was a teenager and my dad patted my mom on the backside. I thought it was cute. But she gave him this homicidal stare. It was a sort of 'how dare you?' look. You know?"

"You thought it was her that wasn't interested."

Eleanor leaned back and rotated the chair slowly away from the desk. She regarded the pale day outside. From here, she could see the barn past a bare tree.

Jackie's voice was gentle. "Does 'preference' necessarily mean gay, for their generation?"

Eleanor waited. "What else could it mean?"

"I guess it could mean other things, except that you already had evidence, and good old intuition, that their marriage was ... nontraditional."

She clicked her tongue. "Yes. I always knew that much. I just had no idea *how* nontraditional."

"This is a startling discovery, of course." Jackie's voice was contemplative. "But does it really change anything?"

"No. Not really." A heaviness was slowing Eleanor now. "You know I'm not freaking out over some homophobic nightmare. But ..." She dropped her head and felt the resistance of tight neck muscles. She was wearing her mother's pink terrycloth bathrobe. It still smelled wonderfully like Connie.

Jackie was silent.

"This intensifies my sense that I really didn't know my parents. This is a big thing to not know about them."

"But you did know, on some level."

"No. I judged my mother for being cold. How could I do that if I knew my father was a homosexual?"

"You don't think he was ever unfaithful to *her*, do you?"

"I didn't before. Not really. I had wondered if there might be some dark history that led them to the separate bedrooms."

"When the snoring explanation wore thin?"

Eleanor paused to appreciate her best friend. "I'm so glad I called you."

"Me too. Are you sure I shouldn't fly out there after I grade papers?"

"No. I know you have that trip to see Thomas's family." She watched a robin land on a branch in that tree. "And I'm not gonna be able to work through all this right away. I can't even begin to address all the logistics on this one trip. I'll have to get back here in the summer to really close things down."

"Okay. It sounds like you're prepared to pace yourself, not fix everything."

"Yes. There's so much I can't fix. Now I have a new shock to recover from." She turned back and leaned an elbow on the desk, propping her head, with her fingers entwined in her hair.

"A little at a time. You don't even have to *understand* everything now. Just get through the funeral and the basics."

"That's right. Of course. Thanks, Jackie."

"You're welcome. You knew *I* wouldn't go ballistic over this particular revelation. But best not to call certain folks you know around here."

"You think Henry would offer me condolences at my tainted heritage?"

"Only in private. He knows better than to say something like that publicly ... now."

Eleanor pictured the conservative philosophy professor with whom she had served on an academic committee. Henry Chalmers was several years older than her and a several dozen degrees more anti-gay than any of her friends.

"Okay. I'm not getting caught up in even a mental debate with Henry over this."

"Right. Focus on you, and what you have to do to put your mother to rest."

"Thanks again."

"Love you, my friend."

"Love you, too."

Closing the call, she stood immediately, defying the weights that were trying to anchor her in that chair, threatening to confine her there for the rest of the day. She had a funeral to plan and a pastor to meet.

"Oh, God. I hope he's not a right-wing nut."

She laughed at the unintended phrase "wing nut." That allowed her head to rotate away from abstract cultural debates toward the very real need for coffee, food and a shower.

The Lutheran church was also on Main Street, just two blocks from the funeral home. In the parking lot, Eleanor tugged at her medium blue skirt to straighten it and lengthen it just a little. She shook her head at the power of old habits. Could she identify an actual exchange with her mother over how short her skirt was, a terse debate on the way into the Lutheran church they had attended in Milwaukee? Eleanor was a teenager in the sixties and seventies. Some version of that conversation had certainly happened in those days. She had struggled back then with two forces opposed to her wearing short skirts. The one was her parents' religion. The other was her fat knees. In the end, the knees were decisive. Then the debate turned to wearing jeans to church.

Was that why she wore a skirt today? Was she changing her position on jeans in church, or slacks perhaps? Or had she overcome her shame at those chubby knees?

"Try not to trip up the walk to the front door, Eleanor. That's enough for now." She didn't say that aloud, she was almost certain.

"Hello, Eleanor? I'm Virgil."

She met him at his office door.

He was wearing jeans.

They were relatively new jeans. And he wore a button-up shirt and a respectable gray sweater vest. Low business casual. The sort of thing a professor at her university would wear. Had Virgil dressed to suit her? But he probably hadn't given her that much thought.

"Hello. Thanks for meeting with me."

She was practicing that skill which separated a layer of her internal dialogue from the social interactions required of civil society. It was a bifurcation honed during innumerable meetings with students sporting haircuts, tattoos or piercings at which she longed to stare, that she longed to study and to comment upon. None of which she ever did. Eleanor could talk to a girl with blue hair and double nose piercings in exactly the same tone she would use with a girl with an expensive haircut and designer clothes ... and the same as a pastor in jeans ... in a church.

He gestured to a chair in front of his desk. "Of course. It's more than my job to serve at her funeral. With Connie, it's my privilege. One last service I can offer her. She was such a blessing to this congregation. She was one of the people that made my job most enjoyable." His tone seemed strenuously upbeat, as if he was putting in a good effort. His eyes cut toward her and then away a few times, as if assessing the effectiveness of that effort.

She seated herself as he did the same. "You were pretty close to her then?" Had they covered this on the phone? Maybe. But she didn't strain to recall. Instead, she absorbed the visual impression of Virgil Meers, beyond his casual attire.

He was perhaps not as old as Eleanor, but probably close. He wore black wire-rimmed glasses. His dark, wavy hair was just short enough to keep it from looking frizzy or curly. Gray at his temples ran down into his sideburns, which might have last been styled in about 1989. A slight sag to his chin showed possible weight loss recently. His hands looked younger than his face, certainly younger than the raw hands of a farmer his age. His sympathetic eyes were dark blue with gray rims, his eyelashes adding an elegance or beauty to his face, the sort of eyes that would have looked good on a daughter or mother. If he had a daughter. Was he married? He wore no wedding ring.

"I knew your mother fairly well, as I said. And I knew quite a lot *about* her. Other folks in the church liked to tell me about her. She was interesting and entertaining, but she was also inspiring to lots of folks." As his voice rose and fell, it seemed to do the latter more than the former. Was Virgil Meers running out of fuel for his simulated effervescence? Or was he missing Connie Petersen more and more, as he was forced to talk about her?

"It's good to hear of church people saying positive things about each other." As soon as she said that, Eleanor rebuked herself. She intended to keep her anti-church prejudices to herself. She shifted in her seat and glanced away.

"Oh. Yes. I'm sure we've all heard about church gossip that's destructive. But that's one of the things I'm proud of around here. I think there is very little negative gossip. About your mother, I would hear things like, 'Did you see the article in the Madison paper about Connie?' Things like that."

"I'm only now appreciating how proud other people were of my mother." Eleanor sat looking at him across his broad, oak desk. She was willing to take the role of the student on this side of the desk. Virgil the professor.

But he stood and rolled his chair around to the end of his desk so they could face each other with no large obstacle between them. "Can I get you some coffee or tea? I have a pot that's warm, but I can crank it up to a full boil in a minute or two."

"Oh. No. Thank you."

The shades seemed to come down over Virgil's face at this point. It couldn't be her refusal of the coffee or tea. Maybe he had just run to the end of his practiced social buoyancy. Was he better with parishioners than with a stranger, and an agnostic one at that?

He pushed his glasses up the bridge of his nose a bit. "I guess I have to warn you that I'm feeling pretty emotional about Connie's death. I know I'm supposed to be consoling *you*. But I'm still needing some consolation myself. It was so sudden. Totally out of the blue. She seemed like she would live forever sometimes." His eyes fell repeatedly toward a low bookshelf beside Eleanor. But he elevated them back to her eyes again and again.

"Sympathy is important in your job, of course. But I sense that you sincerely loved my mother, and that's a wonderful discovery." Eleanor was still doing that bifurcated interaction, her mind speculating over the pastor's marital status, while offering a sincere spoken response to his emotional confession.

Her response seemed to silence him.

In that pause, she noted that she had spoken very freely with him just now, much as she had on the phone. And now *he* was confessing to her. In the depth of his silence, she sensed that he had much to confess. Not crimes or misdemeanors, perhaps, but some pain of his own that predated the death of Connie Petersen.

"Well." He said it with enough force to break free from that moment of contemplation. "We have some things to discuss."

And, from that point, Eleanor followed Virgil's lead. He led her through the arrangements her mother had requested. And he led her through the options available within those plans. Though he didn't offer Eleanor the option of opposing her mother's wishes, he did frequently pause for her to respond to Connie's preparation. Eleanor offered no resistance. His generous affection for her mother inspired an expectation that Virgil would apply Connie's wishes just as she had prescribed.

"I hope that doesn't offend you, or others who might not believe the way Connie did," he said once.

Eleanor attempted to shift the focus from her own lack of faith. "She probably had some artist friends who weren't Lutheran."

"Certainly. Or ones who weren't Christian in any way."

Eleanor nodded again and again, a mute assent. Virgil wasn't what she had feared. He seemed like a man who would make an educated effort not to offend, and one who would endure a lot before suffering offense himself.

"You've been very gracious. Feel free to do this the way my mother wanted. I trust you." Only the briefest tug slowed that last phrase. She was accepting this pastor's judgment after only this short acquaintance.

Then Eleanor remembered the revelation she had found in that birthday card from her father. Her curiosity about Virgil's reaction compelled her. Was that mischievous curiosity?

"I discovered something last night, in my mother's papers, that shocked me."

Virgil had braced one hand on the arm of his chair, as if to stand up. But he relaxed back into the leather desk chair as soon as she started her doorknob confession.

"What's that?"

"Apparently, my mother discovered some time ago that my father had homosexual preferences."

"Oh. You found that in her papers?"

"Uh. Well, it was a birthday card, with a sweet note of appreciation from my father. Just a month before he died."

"Oh. I see." He nodded subtly. "He was grateful for her acceptance of him?"

"He was very grateful that she stayed with him in spite of his 'preference.' That's approximately how he expressed it."

"And ... that was a shock to you?"

He's good. This pastor. A veteran counselor, clearly. And probably a good poker player.

74

"I knew something was ... different. I think I always worried about what was misaligned in their marriage, what interfered with their intimacy." She tipped her head toward him slightly. "I seem to feel compelled to confess to you, despite your lack of a confessional."

He grinned primly. "We don't have the requisite furniture. But we do accept confessions of all sorts, including intense concerns about our parents, even deceased parents."

"Are you married?" She could almost hear the cracking and shattering of that glass wall between what she was thinking and their polite conversation.

He propped both elbows on the arms of his chair, fitting them into visible dimples in the padded leather. "Why do you ask?"

"Oh. I suppose that's out of bounds. I'm sorry."

"No. It's really not out of bounds. The people in my congregation know that I'm no longer married. My wife passed away fifteen years ago." He hesitated. "She died of a brain aneurism. It happened very suddenly." He seemed to roll into a bog here that stopped him completely. His head tipped and his hands slacked beneath his chin.

Eleanor could see no way of towing him out of the mire into which she had just dragged him. "I'm ... I'm sorry. I ..."

"Oh. No." He sat up straighter. "I'm not really mourning my wife right now. Actually, I was just realizing one reason I'm having so much trouble with Connie's departure. It was so sudden. Just like Joanne's death. Very sudden. Shocking." He focused more sharply on Eleanor's eyes. "I guess your mother's death triggered those added feelings for me." He pursed a sort of grin at her, his upper lip puffing, where a mustache would have been.

Her mind was wandering again, noticing that he hadn't shaved that morning, and maybe the morning before. His stubble was uniform in length and not so heavy as to darken his face significantly. Sections of his whiskers were gray or white.

He seemed to be waiting patiently during her contemplation of his face.

Eleanor felt herself blush. She was tripping toward some misplaced thoughts about Pastor Meers. What was happening to her brain?

"Well." He broke the silence much more gently this time—wearily, really. "I think we have enough to go forward from here. I'll stay in touch with you and contact Matt at the funeral home." He stood this time, uninterrupted. "Don't hesitate to call me. All phone confessions are confidential. And calls are not monitored or recorded."

"Good." She grinned at his little joke as she stood up. "I feel like a freshman these days. I don't know what to do next, and I feel like I'm completely unqualified for any of it."

"You're fine. You're doing fine."

Eleanor seldom hugged anyone. She and Jackie exchanged a lot of strokes and back-pats, shoulder rubs and arm squeezes. But, right now, she was fighting a crazy compulsion to embrace Virgil Meers.

He rocked forward and then stepped around her as he gestured toward the door. "I'll walk you out."

For the first time since she arrived at the church, Eleanor heard voices from somewhere in the building. She and the pastor weren't alone. But what did that matter? She wasn't worried about being alone with him. No temptation. Not really.

CHAPTER ELEVEN

She took calls from Paul, from Jackie and from a lawyer, of whom she had still not found solid evidence in Connie's papers. But Eleanor only spoke to each of these out of a tangled distraction, unable to disengage fully from digging through her mother's history.

"Tell me about the pastor." Jackie called late in the afternoon. "How was he?"

"What do you mean, 'how was he?' He was fine." After that retort, she realized that Jackie wasn't asking if the pastor was holding up under the strain. She was probably thinking about the cultural and religious gap between her friend and a rural pastor.

"Did you tell him about your father?"

Of course, Jackie meant her father's homosexuality. But Eleanor toyed with ignoring that implication and forcing her friend to say it explicitly.

"My father. Yes. I did tell him about finding that card. I told him everything."

"Everything?"

"Okay. He's this gentle and attractive single man about my age. Yes, I found him interesting, more than just as the man doing my mother's funeral. And yes, I did spill my guts to him."

Jackie remained quiet for a second. "Oh, well. It's good that you can trust him." Her tone was gentle, like she was trying not to scare off some wildlife from her back yard.

"I keep confessing to him. And I don't even believe in any of that. You can see just how unhinged I am."

"Unhinged, maybe. But it's a stressful time. You shouldn't judge yourself too harshly. It's a unique sort of trauma."

Eleanor didn't regret letting Jackie into her vulnerability with the Lutheran pastor. The real rub here was that freshman feeling. Eleanor was behaving like a confused girl. And the business of her mother's death was strictly for grownups. She was supposed to be a grownup.

"I think it's really just me being upset and alone. This pastor is a widower with obvious emotional wounds. I guess I found him very approachable." She allowed a long sigh.

"Okay. That's good. That's what you need, right?"

"Sure."

On the phone with Paul, Eleanor had begun negotiating ongoing care for the house when she returned to New York. That propelled her into her mother's computer, to find out more about Connie's banking arrangements. Eleanor would meet with the lawyer regarding the will tomorrow morning, but that probably wouldn't get her all the specifics about the financial footing of her mother and this house.

Fortunately for Eleanor, her mother had not password-protected her computer. She was uniquely grateful for the lax security. But she would have been surprised if it had been otherwise.

She looked for links to bank accounts or maybe budgeting software. But Connie wouldn't have done her own books.

Eleanor opened the email client and waited for new messages to load. There were twenty thousand messages in the inbox. When was the last time Eleanor had helped her mother to clean up her computer? It had been years. The computer was still running Windows 7.

How far back did those emails go? She scrolled and scrolled and scrolled. She stopped when she got to 2009, the year her father died. There were emails from her father to her mother. The influence of that last birthday card from her father drove Eleanor now.

A link in an email from him. *"Financial planning for your*

later years." Another email with a link, this one a reply from him. Connie had sent him an article about Cocker Spaniels.

"What do you think?" Was the subject line of another message from her father to her mother.

The link: *My Husband is a Homosexual ...*

"Oh, Daddy." Eleanor clicked on the hyperlink, but the browser couldn't find the ten-year-old article.

"What do you think?" What were you asking, Dad?

"And what did *you* say, Mom?" Eleanor looked for the Sent Items folder. Only six thousand emails in there. "Brother."

She scrolled toward the bottom of the Sent Items folder, to the date when her father sent that article link.

"Oh, this is not us. We don't have anything to worry about." That was her mother's reply. Her upbeat, tight-lipped reply.

Were you in denial, Mother? Did you really have something to worry about? How could you just ignore it?

But she didn't really know if her mother had ignored the pain. Maybe she had confided in someone, maybe even in Virgil Meers. Eleanor sat up straight, feeling the ache of hours of poor posture. It was dark again. She hadn't eaten. Disgusted with herself, she stood up and strode out of the office. For an instant, she slowed to avoid tripping over Monet. Then she remembered that Paul had taken the old dog to his place. She missed the dog for the first time. She kind of missed Paul too.

Hmm. Your mother died. You're alone in this big farmhouse in rural Wisconsin. You are more than a little confused. You haven't eaten anything since that bit of tuna casserole at one o'clock, or thereabouts.

At the top of the stairs, she reached back to turn on the upper hallway light. The desk lamp had lit the way thus far but would be little help going down the creaky stairs. Creaky stairs. Creepy stairs. Creepy house.

She thought she felt a warm puff of air on her face, like a

breath. A draft? A *warm* draft?

Even in houses reputed to be haunted, Eleanor had always felt safe inside her skepticism, cloaked in the protection of her rational mind. That mind seemed to be malfunctioning today.

A breath? A ghost? A warm ghost?

She snorted an impatient sigh through her nose. The harsh sound of that breath reminded her that she was feeling congested, her nose dry and scratchy. The house was dusty. She would call tomorrow to get a cleaning service in here. It was overdue.

She turned on the kitchen light to find her mother *not* there in her nightgown. Not poking around and stepping over the dog. And Eleanor recalled that email reply.

"This is not us."

Maybe you were right. But what was? What were you two? And why didn't I know? Why don't I still know?

She considered the merits of four casseroles stacked on the top shelf of the fridge, before closing the door and turning to the apple pie on the counter. She should probably refrigerate that, too. But first she would eat some. Not all of it. No, don't go there.

Why had she asked Virgil whether he was married? Maybe she was wondering how he felt about heterosexual love, and also about the other kind. Maybe she was just interested in him, as a person. A man. She had liked him instantly. She trusted him, without assuming that he was perfect. Perhaps she had graduated from that kind of childish assumption. Perhaps she wasn't really ensnared in freshman follies.

She had been a sophomore the first time she really fell in love. So maybe she wasn't safe yet.

With the fork clenched between her lips, Eleanor hastily wrapped the aluminum foil back over the top of the apple pie, forbidding herself to eat more. Pulling against the vacuum of the fridge door, she left it standing open, adding its cold, white light to the warm incandescence of her mother's old bulbs. Connie probably had a lifetime supply of those old bulbs down in the basement.

The basement. What would she find down there?

Eleanor laughed at her own ominous note to that thought. The cuckoo clock said it was past eleven thirty. Time for bed. Weariness was bringing out her crazies. Her odd thoughts were like items tumbling out of a stuffed closet.

Now she rummaged back to that one old item that had fallen into her thoughts just a moment ago.

Gary Wilmington. Her first love. Sophomore year. And junior year. And never forgotten. Obviously.

As she undressed upstairs, she caught a glimpse of herself reflected in the window. She was standing naked in her parents' house remembering Gary Wilmington now. Eleanor snatched her flannel nightgown from atop her suitcase. More than modesty, she sought shelter. Her mother had died and left her vulnerable. Her mother had left her.

"How could you do that to me?" She said it. She didn't scream it. She didn't yell it. She didn't even whine it. But there it was. Blame. You did this to me. You left too early. Too suddenly.

But Eleanor had left first. She had left her parents as soon as she could. There was the internship at the university library in Boston after freshman year. The travel study program—with Gary and others—after sophomore year. She had left her parents before they left her.

She, however, had retained the option to come home to them. They couldn't return to her. Not now. Not ever.

Eleanor slept fitfully that night. Perhaps the result of too much apple pie. Perhaps it was Gary Wilmington's fault.

Or her mother's.

CHAPTER TWELVE

On that Saturday morning it seemed obvious that Irwin Bechler had opened his law office only to meet with Eleanor.

"Sorry about my casual attire." Mr. Bechler was probably well into his seventies, or maybe just a very tired and stressed sixty-something.

"I appreciate you seeing me on a Saturday."

"Well, I assumed you would leave soon after the service on Monday, so I wanted to catch you while you're still in town, or in the area, I should say." He was wearing a light blue V-neck sweater over a white polo shirt. They offset his ruddy complexion and enhanced his light blue eyes. If the weather were warmer, Eleanor would suspect he was on his way to the golf course. The sun was shining, but the temperature would spend little time above freezing that day.

"Yes. I won't be staying long." A thought stepped forward out of the shadows. "Let me ask you something. Should I be thinking about liability regarding my mother's death? I've just assumed it was an accident and that no one was to blame, in the sense of legal liability."

"You have reason to believe someone was liable?"

"It's just that it was an accident involving ice, when she had a contract with a handyman to clear ice and snow." She shrugged. "I'm just checking that I'm not being naïve by ignoring any thought about whether the handyman should be held accountable for the ice."

"That's Paul Wasser these days, isn't it?"

"Yes. He was so nice that I just forgave him immediately. I was still mad at my mother for insisting on living by herself. Blame seemed to rest mostly with her. I just didn't want to bypass any legal implications of the way she died. In case there might be any." The more words she required in order to explain this tangent, the more she regretted starting it.

"Well. I could check with the sheriff's office about that. But I had been assuming that it was a simple accident that didn't implicate anyone."

She shook her head sharply. "I don't think it's worth any trouble. I just wondered if *you* had any concerns about it."

"I didn't before now. But I will call Ed over at the sheriff's and see what he thinks." He scowled at her. "Connie had a contract with the Wassers? Do you have a copy of that contract?"

"No. My mother's gifts didn't include careful business documentation. I doubt I'll find anything in writing."

"But you're feeling like your mother was ill-served by the handyman service?"

"No. I was just wondering if you had thought about that. I was just going to let it go unless you advised otherwise."

Mr. Bechler twisted his mouth for a second. "No. No one around here has said anything against Paul, like that. I think folks are just seeing it as an accident that could have happened to anyone, especially an elderly person. I know *I've* been more careful since your mother slipped and fell."

Eleanor lifted a small grin at him. "Okay. I just didn't want to be naïve, just trusting Paul Wasser because I thought he was a nice guy." It occurred to her now that this might be exactly how everyone in town was thinking about it.

"I'm not primarily a liability and litigation lawyer, though you have to do a little of this and a little of that in a small town. I wasn't thinking about liability."

"It's okay. Let's just forget about it. I'm certain that's what my mother would want. I doubt she lay there on the ice cursing Paul Wasser. She was probably just worrying about who would take care of her dog, if she was conscious at all."

"Do you know whether she *was* conscious as she lay there?" Eleanor could hear a lawyer's investigation gearing up. That query would go to the question of the suffering of the victim.

"The funeral home guy ... uh, Matt, at the funeral home offered to show me the medical examiner's report. I didn't take him up on that. But he did say it was clearly a case of a severe head trauma. Her heart stopped eventually, in the freezing cold. But it was the knock on the head that started it all. So, maybe that means she was unconscious the whole time." For the first time, Eleanor wondered if Paul had cleaned up the blood. No blood stain on the sidewalk. Didn't Connie bleed?

"Uh." Mr. Bechler nodded. Perhaps he was thinking of calling the medical examiner now.

"But, no. Let's forget that. I don't want anyone to get in trouble. I know Paul is feeling guilty. I expect that's punishment enough, if he deserves any blame at all." A rewind and a do-over would be so good just now.

"Okay. Okay. Yes. I think you're right about that. Okay, let's get to the reading of the will."

He unfolded a several-page, legal-sized document and began to read the template *Last Will and Testament*, which began with very little of her mother's personality. The specifics of the disposition of Connie's property, however, were more interesting, and more like her.

"To my agent, Virginia Whitworth, I entrust all of the paintings that are in galleries at the time of my passing, except for any of the paintings done at the cabin in Minocqua. Those should go to my daughter, Eleanor. Regarding the paintings in my house or in storage, the ones of Yvonne Marketti must not be sold or publicly displayed without express approval of the subject. They should be offered to Yvonne, for her to do with as she pleases."

That explained a little about those beautiful paintings of Yvonne. But other questions spawned out of those sentences.

The next surprise came with the dollar amounts. "To the Milwaukee Children's Project, I donate one million dollars. To the Northern Wisconsin Gallery of Art, I donate three hundred thousand dollars." In all, there were eight large donations totaling almost two and a half million dollars, including the Lutheran church and something called "The Dove's Nest."

"Wait. She has that much money? And without selling the farm or all her paintings?" Eleanor suddenly worried that she needed to sell off her mother's things in order to fund these donations.

"She has it. And a bit more. Your father was a smart investor. And your mother's art was growing in popularity every year. I know of one painting she sold for twenty thousand dollars down near Chicago."

Eleanor nodded, and then changed her pace from pensive to permissive. "Go ahead."

"To my daughter, Eleanor, I entrust the rest of my worldly possessions, including any funds remaining in the investment accounts at Hampton and Claussen, after taxes owed."

Mr. Bechler paused to explain. "Given the size of her estate, there won't be any estate tax. That clause was first put in there when the exemption was much lower, and her donations smaller. The remaining amount will be well within the current exemption."

Eleanor took a deep breath. She had worried that her mother's disheveled business style would mean paying off assorted debts. But Connie wasn't in debt. She wasn't struggling. She had left a significant bequest. What a relief.

The only burden left on Eleanor was what she had expected, the obligation to sort and dispose of her parents' possessions. But she drifted away from these thoughts when Mr. Bechler cleared his throat with obvious intent.

"Yes. Go ahead." She could tell that she had missed some

details, but she would reread the document when she returned to the farm.

"If my dog, Monet, is still alive after I go, then I entrust him to Paul Wasser, who shared my love of Cocker Spaniels and whom Monet always trusted."

Connie didn't even consider the possibility that Eleanor would want the dog. Her mother knew her well enough to anticipate what had already passed between Eleanor and Paul, regarding Monet.

Finishing with more template language, Mr. Bechler finally looked up at her. "So. There you have it. I have account names and numbers, and passwords to financial institutions. He tapped a legal-sized manila envelope on his desk. Here is a copy of her safe deposit box key, as well. And you can call my office any time, if you need help figuring out what to do with any of this." He seemed ready to head off to whatever he had planned for that late Saturday morning.

"Thank you again for your time. And thank you for your service to my mother. She was clearly well served by the people she knew here."

Mr. Bechler stood and reached across his desk. "We all respected your mother, and she was very much loved around here. She brought her own flavor to town but only ever made the people around her feel better about their own uniqueness." An unexpected epitaph. But recognizable, nonetheless.

Eleanor just smiled, gathered the stack of envelopes and stepped toward the door. She had to turn back to get her coat, but then headed quickly out toward her rental car, anxious to release Mr. Bechler to the rest of his day.

At the door he stopped her. "If you want me to pursue any questions of liability in your mother's death, let me know. But we'll just leave it be for now, right?"

"Yes. Certainly. I'm satisfied the way things are. And I think mother would be, too."

He nodded, grinned and turned toward his Cadillac Escalade, after reaching back to check that the front door of his office had locked behind them.

Driving toward the farm, Eleanor was trying to outrun a mob of worries spawned by how little she had understood about her mother. But a person walking in a bizarre fashion on the sidewalk derailed those thoughts. She slowed to watch more closely.

It was a woman. Each step she took looked like a kick, as if she were wading into a room full of balloons and kicking them aside. She wore a knit hat with animal ears sticking up. Dark hair blew around her face, tangled with the long ties dangling from the hat. Eleanor gaped briefly before returning her eyes to the road.

Where she lived, in a large town near the Hudson River, Eleanor was used to seeing homeless or hapless people stepping strangely along the sidewalk. She didn't know of any halfway houses or mental hospitals around Dove Lake, but she suspected her mother would have known about them.

Instead of motoring back to the house as fast as possible, Eleanor impulsively allowed her desire to explore American towns to provide a respite from her grief. She slowed further and pulled over next to the diner, near the north end of Main Street. She would see if they had good coffee and perhaps a muffin.

She was feeling penitent for her neglect of her mother's life here in Dove Lake. Maybe she should start taking a closer look at the town that had embraced Connie so warmly.

The wind was aggressively cold, against the best efforts of the March sunshine. Eleanor hit the lock button on her key remote and squinted to see inside the diner. "Roger's" was scripted in red and white across the big windows. Maybe it wasn't a coffee shop worthy of a university town, but she hoped to sample some local flavor, if not a good latte.

A bell rang above the door, though the woman behind the counter had already looked up to watch Eleanor entering the diner.

"Hello. Go ahead and take a seat wherever. You're late for the breakfast rush and early for the lunch rush." The woman chuckled as if appreciating the cleverness of her own observation.

The humor might have been that there wasn't ever much of a rush at this eating spot, though Eleanor could imagine it being popular on Saturday mornings, perhaps more so a few decades ago. She sat down in a booth by the windows.

"You just visiting?" The mid-thirties woman with a hearty Wisconsin accent paraded around the counter and over to Eleanor's table. "You look familiar."

Though her mother had been thinner than her, Eleanor knew that she had inherited Connie's likeness in a sharp beak and big, green eyes. People had often recognized the family resemblance, even though she carried those features on a rounder head atop a stouter body.

"I'm Eleanor Petersen. I'm here to put my mother's things in order." She wondered if Marcy, the waitress identified by her name badge, would have heard of Connie's death.

"Eleanor Petersen? Who's your mother?"

"Constance Petersen. Connie."

"Constance. Sounds like a pilgrim name. But Connie sounds familiar. She's older?"

"She was older than me." Eleanor grinned.

"Uh. Yeah. Of course. I was just trying to place the name."

Laughing to let the waitress off the hook, Eleanor changed the subject. "Do you have muffins, and such a thing as a latte?"

"You're from the city, I guess. Madison?"

"New York. North of New York City."

"Oh. Wow. Yeah. I guess you had to come back here for your

mother. Oh, wait. Your mother *died*?" Eleanor hadn't said it explicitly. Now the implication had landed. "I heard about an older woman that fell on the ice." Marcy quickly powered down her mouth.

"That was my mother, Connie Petersen." Eleanor was still forcing a grin.

"Oh. I'm so sorry. Oh, you poor thing." She seemed to restrain herself from taking Eleanor's hand.

Eleanor appreciated the restraint. "Just coffee with cream and sugar, if not a latte."

"Oh. No. We do have a latte machine. I even know how to work it. Lucky you. What flavor? We have vanilla, caramel and hazelnut."

"Vanilla, please."

"And you said a muffin?"

"Yes. Not an English muffin though?"

"Uh. No, blueberry muffin or something like that?"

Eleanor nodded. "Or bran."

"Let me check what we have. We get some from the bakery every morning. But they don't always make it this far into a Saturday. I'll go look."

"Okay. Thanks."

Eleanor suspected that Marcy left in search of refuge from their awkward interaction, as well as in search of baked goods. It was minorly interesting that the waitress had heard the story of a woman fallen on the ice but hadn't recognized her mother's name. Eleanor was pondering that when she glanced out the window. For just a second, she thought she saw someone peeking at her around the corner by the front door. But there was no one there now. She looked toward the counter. Marcy was maneuvering around the latte machine. Eleanor looked back outside.

There it was again. Or there *she* was again. Someone with

long hair, probably a woman, had ducked out of sight. Eleanor sat perfectly still for a few seconds. But she knew how to play this game. She extracted her cell phone from her purse and checked for messages. She had heard a buzz or two while she was meeting with Mr. Bechler. Remembering those messages added some authenticity to her ploy. As the messaging app loaded, she shifted her eyes toward the window without raising her head.

From that angle she couldn't see her clearly, but someone was definitely watching through the window. Eleanor recalled the odd woman kicking invisible balloons down the sidewalk. This little cat-and-mouse game was eccentric enough to implicate that stranger. Eleanor looked toward Marcy now.

"We only have one scone left. It's raisin. You want that?"

"Oh, yes. That would be fine."

Marcy glanced outside. Eleanor resisted the temptation to follow. She interrupted Marcy's turn back toward the counter, however. "Excuse me. Marcy. Did you see someone outside, a woman who might be watching me?"

"Oh. Do you know her?"

"Well, no I don't. But I noticed someone sort of spying on me. I wondered if *you* knew her."

"Uh. I don't know her personally. I've seen her around plenty. People sometimes buy her coffee. I think she lives in a sort of group home near here. She's ... uh ... I guess you'd say she's disabled."

"Do you know her name?" Eleanor was thinking about inviting the woman in and offering her coffee. It was just the sort of thing her mother would do.

"I'll ask in the kitchen. Roger will probably know." She headed back toward the kitchen, diverting just briefly to renew the coffee of a pair of middle-aged men sitting in the back of the pale blue and gray restaurant, almost half of it still glowing in the late-morning sun.

Eleanor didn't want to wait for Marcy. She was afraid the strange woman would escape before the waitress returned. Standing, as if she were heading to the restroom, Eleanor abruptly turned toward the door. She could at least call after her if the woman ran away.

Instead, Eleanor nearly crashed into the woman in the entryway. "Oh. Pardon me. I didn't realize you were coming in." Actually, the odd woman might not have been coming in, only lurking between the inside and outside doors.

But the woman didn't run away. She stood still and stared at Eleanor, instead. "I think I know you. Do you think so?"

It was a strange question, except that Eleanor was having a similar experience. "I do. I think I do recognize you from somewhere." The fact that she had rarely ventured far in this town, during visits with her mother and father, stood against this impression.

"You look like Connie."

Eleanor wobbled. Her knees nearly gave out. The shock that ran up her spine twisted her and shook her with a small seizure. "Oh ... You knew my ..."

Then she knew where she had seen her. "Yvonne?"

"Um-hmm. You have her eyes."

"Uh. Do ... Do you want to come in and have coffee with me?" Eleanor's voice cracked. She gestured spastically toward the booth, the inner door pressing against her.

Yvonne nodded. "Roger says it's okay. If someone invites me. You're inviting me. Aren't you?"

"I am."

"Okay then."

Eleanor held the door for Yvonne to safely traverse the threshold, as if she were Roger's gatekeeper. Roger, the owner, presumably.

91

Yvonne sat down and looked away from Eleanor. "I saw you sitting here, didn't I?" She didn't pull off her hat or coat, resting bare, red hands on the table.

"Yes. I think you did."

"Uh, huh. You look like her. I saw you. And I knew you weren't her. But I thought you might be like her."

"I'm her daughter. Eleanor."

"She has a daughter. Or you are her daughter."

"She had a daughter. Me." Something occurred to her. "You know that ..." Eleanor suddenly wondered what it might mean for this woman to hear it. How well did Yvonne know Connie? "Did you know that ... were you aware that ... she died? Connie died."

Yvonne stared, though not exactly at Eleanor. "Died? Oh." Her face began to twist in stages. Gradually more and more intensely. Horror expanding her eyes and dropping her jaw.

"Oh. No. No. No. No." She started to gasp. Her volume escalated. "Oh. No. Oh. No."

Standing abruptly. "Connie." She almost sprinted to the door.

"Yvonne!" Eleanor bumped the table and dodged Marcy, who was carrying her scone and latte. A flash of the waitress staring open-mouthed passed her peripheral vision.

"Yvonne."

Outside, Eleanor couldn't see her. She had vanished like a specter. But, of course, that was impossible. Eleanor stepped to that corner where Yvonne had been hiding before. She twisted her neck and found a walkway as wide as two people. At the far end of that walkway Yvonne was disappearing from view. Eleanor took one step in that direction and then decided against it. She turned back to the front door of the diner, pausing to catch her balance by leaning on the aluminum door handle.

When she stepped through the inner door, a man was

standing at the counter looking expectantly at her. Perhaps he thought that he needed to apologize for something. He wore a white cotton cap atop his large, round head, his white apron stretched tightly over his belly.

"Do you know her?" The middle-aged man leaned into the question. "Yvonne? Do you know her?" He elevated his black caterpillar eyebrows over his round dark eyes.

Starting with a deep breath, Eleanor tried a first draft of an explanation. "My mother knew her. She painted some beautiful paintings of her. I found them a couple of days ago. I recognized her from the paintings. But I've never met her before." Her voice was quaking. Her hands were shaking visibly.

"Who's your mother?" The trailing tone at the end of that question implied that the man might know the answer.

"Connie Petersen."

He started nodding, wiped his hands on a dingy cotton cloth and walked around the end of the counter. "I'm Roger Holtz-man." His voice barely rose above a whisper. Then he seemed to recover. "This is my place. I knew your mother." He twisted to his left. "She donated that painting over there." He aimed a stout arm at a large canvas depicting a main street scene that might have existed in the past life of Dove Lake.

"Oh. Very nice." Eleanor stepped away from the light coming through the doors and front windows so she could see the paint-ing without so much glare on her contact lenses. "Oh. I recognize her style. Wonderful."

She tried to corral her breathing. This was a lot.

"Connie was a wonderful woman. I am so sorry she's gone." Roger's eyes seemed watery. Teary?

Marcy had set down the scone plate and coffee mug and ap-peared not to know what to do next.

Eleanor shook Roger's hand. "Sorry I upset Yvonne like that. Apparently, she didn't know my mother had died. It was thoughtless of me."

"Oh, don't worry about that." Marcy's offer of a free pass was certainly sincere, but Eleanor didn't need it.

She just nodded and returned to her seat in the booth. Her knees still vibrated. She tried not to look like she was collapsing into the seat. Maybe she needed some calories to catch up with what she had just spent in pursuit of Yvonne.

"I can imagine your mother painting Yvonne. She's a striking woman. Used to be more beautiful when she was younger. I wonder how long ago that was." Roger was staring out the front window.

"I'm not sure when she started, but one of the paintings was marked 2014, as I recall."

"Oh. Not so long ago." He quirked a grin. "I saw the two of 'em in here having coffee. Probably quite a few times, over th' years."

Marcy shrugged, perhaps regretful that she couldn't help her boss with his recollection.

Eleanor just nodded and eyed her morning snack. She was suddenly very hungry.

"Well, so glad to meet you. And my condolences on your loss." Roger made half a bow and retreated toward the kitchen.

Eleanor looked at her scone. She thought of Yvonne's over-wrought escape. Something of that panicked retreat pulled at her, like the wake of a large ship. Part of her had gone with Yvonne, out that door, down that alley. Maybe it was the part of Eleanor that was ready to stop hiding the pain, ready to run shouting the news of her mother's death.

CHAPTER THIRTEEN

In her mother's kitchen, at noon on Saturday, Eleanor gazed wearily at the stack of envelopes from the lawyer's office. She paused to regret not visiting the bank and the safe deposit box. But she was already at the end of her emotional energy for the day. It would have to wait for next week.

More urgent was her desire to find Yvonne and apologize, or maybe console her. But even that urge remained confined to the impotent realm of good intentions and not something Eleanor would do right now. She picked up the papers and carried them through the kitchen into the dark central hallway next to the dining room.

Looking over the heavy railing, up the staircase, a bulging weight slowed her intended climb. The total mass of her loss had expanded in the days since receiving Paul Wasser's phone call.

The oppressive resistance she faced up those stairs now recalled the days after her father's death. His death had also been sudden.

They were out to dinner with friends when he and Connie had left early. Indigestion ended that night out on the town. Not until they had reached the house did the intense chest pains begin.

Eleanor had long understood that her father's heart fluttered tenuously inside him, and she had been grateful that he had survived so far into his life without any severe infarctions. That status quo had graduated to an expectation for her. Not of immortality, of course, but of continuity. An expectation of a future.

Climbing those stairs, when Eleanor first came home to comfort her mother and mourn her father, had seemed impossible. She usually slept on a fold-away bed in the room that was now her mother's office. After her father died, she had considered staying on the couch in the living room, instead. Something up those steps threatened to engulf her and smother her.

That something was absence.

No longer would her father be up there, in his room buttoning one of his Oxford shirts and sliding his feet into his leather slippers. No longer would he be gazing through reading glasses at his papers or studying the computer monitor pensively. No longer could she expect her father to be there for her. Not now or in the future.

This time, the loss seemed even greater. Even greater than the sadness of losing her beloved father and enduring the sorrow of her mother's death. Now, Eleanor was truly alone. After her father's death, she had maintained a connection to him through her mother. Now there was no one.

And now, Eleanor had discovered things about her parents, in the aftermath of Connie's death, that stretched her loss back into the past. More than a future without her mother, she was facing the evidence of a lost past, as well.

Clearly, she hadn't done all she could to know her parents, especially her mother.

She strenuously stifled a fit of tears and forced her foot onto the first step. One step might be enough to puncture the membrane of dread that swelled out of the most intimate rooms of the house. Her parents' separate bedrooms.

What had Eleanor missed by not realizing her father's sexual preference? What had she neglected to see in her mother's sacrifice of a normal marriage, Connie's costly choice of faithfulness to the man she married?

Eleanor's decades of illuminating the stories of empowered women, women who shattered centuries-old walls of prejudice and restriction, might impugn her mother's choice. Didn't every woman deserve a fulfilled life? Didn't her mother deserve to be freed from the expectations that she would submit her desires to the will of her husband? In this case, she was submitting to his lack of desire for her.

Ah. Those abstract questions that swirled around seminar tables in the wood-paneled academic buildings at Carlisle University, and hundreds of universities around the world, couldn't touch her parents' lives. Connie wasn't a sexual identity. She was a person. And she was a much more complex person than Eleanor had realized. But was her mother a hero for staying with her uninterested husband?

Was a lifelong friendship good enough? What had she called him? *"My best and sweetest friend."*

He was a sweet man. A gentle man. And never the stifling *gentleman* of his and previous generations. Darrel Petersen was a good man. And he was a good friend to her mother. What was wrong with keeping that friendship together under the guise of a marriage? Is any marriage really more than that?

But what would Eleanor know? She had stayed unmarried all these years.

As she settled the pile of papers in the center of her mother's desk, she now had another question to ask, another question that wasn't just an historical examination.

"Did I stay single because of you two?"

During college, she had fallen in love. She had begun to build the hope of a life conjoined with Gary Wilmington. No one questioned the assumptions behind those hopes. Though her best girlfriends were serious students, determined to make their own way in the world still dominated by men, she heard little opposition to her drive to become a wife.

She and Gary had met in Eleanor's first political science class her sophomore year. He was a political science major. He harbored political ambitions in those days. Youthful ambitions. She had stared wide-eyed at his confidence about impacting the world. Only later would she question that inherited confidence manifest in a typical well-to-do white male. At the time, it was entirely admirable to Eleanor.

Eleanor. She was still struggling to rid herself of the nickname her father had given her. *Lenny.* A childish name. A boyish name.

Now, at nearly sixty-five years old, Eleanor stood wondering about that, too. Why had her father called her by a boy's name? Just in fun? Or was he passing on his own gender confusion to her? Passing it unconsciously perhaps.

She had told her friends in college that it was because her father had always wanted a son. But that was just what one said about such things back then. Eleanor could recall no signs of her father mourning the absence of a son to carry on his name, or a son with whom to do manly things. He had been a bookish man with only moderate interest in spectator sports. No hunting, fishing, ball playing for him. No. Eleanor had been fully gender-qualified to share her father's fascinations in the 1960s.

They debated politics. He worked as a civil engineer in the towns and suburbs around Milwaukee. He knew politics on a street level. "What do you think about the evidence that realtors are only selling houses in our neighborhood to white people, Lenny?"

Such questions, at age eleven or twelve, had included her in her father's world. He invited her into his need to challenge inequities and injustices. There might have been little that her father actually did in his job to right those wrongs. But, in his heart and mind, these were crucial questions that responsible citizens should answer.

Lenny.

Sitting now in her mother's chair, her black loafers kicked off beside the desk, Eleanor still identified with that nickname. Some part of her was "Lenny." Jackie was still the only one who called her "Ellie," the most obvious nickname for Eleanor. The name Ellie had been too frilly and fragile for her, when she was a girl. As much as she wanted to be slender and graceful like her mother, Eleanor refused to fake it by adopting a nickname that would have fit her mother better than her.

She had been a thinker, a scholar and a debater. Little physical grace, few feminine frills, no artistic inclinations. Lenny. She rebelled against that name only in college. And maybe then it was more about being a teenager than about ambitions to recover her femininity. Had she ever thought of it as something she needed to recover?

She had been feminine enough for Gary Wilmington. At least at first.

Sitting with her back to the desk, Eleanor stared out at the partly sunny day. A giant shadow sailed slowly over the driveway and toward the county highway. The urge to climb into bed and pull the covers over her head nearly ended her day. But her weariness made following even that impulse unlikely now. She was more likely to stay right where she was.

Her phone rang.

"Hello, Eleanor, this is Virgil Meers."

"Oh. Hello." Again, she engaged him externally, without releasing her internal turmoil.

"We just had a question about flowers in the church. Are you allergic?"

"Allergic? To flowers?"

"It's a precaution our funeral committee has put in place. It doesn't do for the family to be suffering allergy symptoms on top of everything else. Other folks have a choice about attending and about where to sit. But you'll be in the front row, of course."

"Oh. I guess that all makes sense. No. I don't have a significant allergy to flowers."

"Good. Good for you and for the folks who donated these

wonderful arrangements. Now, is it okay with you if we use some of the arrangements in the church service tomorrow morning?"

"Uh. Sure. Why not?"

"Well, you know, some folks might be sensitive about things like that."

"Uh-huh."

"One more thing. Will you be speaking at the funeral? Your mother left that up to you, remember?"

"Hmm. Can I get back to you on that? I hadn't put much thought into it yet."

"Of course. No problem. Will I see you at church tomorrow?"

"Is this part of your Saturday call-out-the-parishioners push?" She offered this as a tease but wondered about the nature of his last question. Was he inviting her? Inviting her as the bereaved family member of a deceased parishioner? As something else?

"I do sometimes try to drum up attendance with Saturday calls. But that often has to do with identifying people who need the church van or someone to pick them up. There are quite a few elderly folks in the congregation."

"More elderly than you and me?"

He laughed. "Yes, indeed. More elderly than you and I. I suppose we're about the same age."

"I was guessing that. I'm sixty-four."

"A liberated woman unafraid of telling a relative stranger her real age. I'm assuming that was your real age."

"I wouldn't lie to a pastor."

"That's good. Good policy." He hummed for a second. "Does that mean that you were honest with me about any offense you might have taken from your mother's rather evangelical funeral service?"

She nodded for a few beats before attempting an answer. "I think offense is generally a matter of degrees. And tolerance is something I've advocated all my life. I'm willing to endure a little bit of discomfort for the sake of my mother and her friends."

"Yes. I understand. I can fully relate. You know, I have to say things from the pulpit once in a while that aren't exactly what I believe. But one has to choose one's battles, or what's worth offending for."

"Ah. Yes. That sounds like the task of a university professor. We have to avoid claims to capital-T truth when behind the lectern, even if we still believe in some of those."

"Interesting. I'd love to talk to you about that someday. Though, I suppose you won't be staying around long after the funeral." Had he already fished this in front of her during their meeting?

"Midterm exams are finishing up today. Spring break begins, or has already begun, for most students. So I don't have to get back immediately. But I'll try to return before the end of the week." She grunted. "That reminds me, I need to change my return flight."

"Returning later?"

"I've discovered so many things I didn't expect. I think I need to take a little more time to work on some of the logistics. Arrangements for the house are probably more complex than I anticipated."

"Of course. Well, feel free to ask for help. I know people around town, and I can get you connected to resources."

"That's part of being a pastor?"

"Leading the sheep to pastures and fresh water. Those are very practical needs."

"Yes. They are." She smiled at the picture of Virgil leading her to some grass for grazing. She realized she was hungry. The clock on the wall said 12:28.

"Alright. I'll let you go, and I'll get back to my telemarketing calls for boosting church attendance."

She breathed a brief laugh. "Okay. Thanks for checking in about those items. I *may* attend church tomorrow, in honor of Mother."

"Good. Good to hear it. Well, blessings on the rest of your day."

"Thanks."

He sounded pretty happy about the prospect of her attendance. Had she offered that impulsive possibility to impress him? To keep him interested? He did seem interested. Though the nature of his interest was entirely unquantifiable.

Raising herself out of the swivel chair, she wondered what things Virgil felt compelled to say from the pulpit with which he didn't entirely agree. That would be a fascinating conversation. Was her fascination based on a hope that she might find him less religious and more like her?

She snorted at herself and stepped back down the stairs, toward the kitchen and perhaps a different casserole this time. Was there one with some green vegetables in it?

CHAPTER FOURTEEN

Eleanor stood in the doorway of her mother's office. It was Sunday morning. She looked at her laptop propped open in the middle of the desk. She hadn't been able to figure out wireless access to her mother's Internet connection but had pulled the network plug out of her mother's desktop and connected it to her laptop. That had worked for catching up on personal and work email, late into Saturday night.

Now, in the morning, she was contemplating whether she could follow through on her half-promise to attend church. The obstacles to doing that were immense and aggressive, a phalanx of titans arrayed against her. And, of course, they existed only inside her head.

"Ha. Phalanx of titans? Classical historical references, Eleanor. Time to update your metaphors. Less violent ones, perhaps." That was what Jackie would advocate, as would others in Eleanor's own department.

This recalled emails from colleagues, condolences from coworkers. George had almost waxed warm and sentimental for a sentence or two. But he did skillfully maintain his emotional distance. "Your friend, George." Constrained, but authentic.

She leaned in the door and caught sight of the square clock on the wall. She had fifteen minutes to get to the Lutheran church. She was dressed. A major victory. Slacks and loafers. She was hoping the old ways hadn't survived with Virgil's aging congregation. The only nice dress she had was her black one. And she wasn't about to be that woman in mourning, wearing her black dress everywhere she went. Her slacks were black. Actually, the cardigan she had on was also black. It had been included for the funeral but would have to do double duty. Her mother's good sweaters would mostly be too tight in the shoulders. And Connie's baggy old sweaters might be recognized by her friends at church. That would be creepy.

Of course, there was the skirt she packed, perhaps with a blouse from her mother. But Virgil had already seen her in that skirt.

What did that matter?

Stalling. Still stalling.

She harrumphed at herself and turned toward the stairs. Her leather soles on the hard wood, and then on the tamped-down carpet, counted her determination to break her isolation. With only phone calls since she left the diner yesterday, she needed to breathe outside air and see actual human beings.

Even if it was in church.

As she drove into town, she tried to remember the last time she had been in a church, other than weddings or funerals. Perhaps it had been before her father died. There was one Easter when her parents almost insisted that she accompany them. It was a difficult Sunday for them to miss church, of course. She usually avoided visiting on religious holidays for that reason. Eleanor had been running away from church since high school.

Really? Was that it? Was she running away? That would imply intentionality. It would imply a relationship, a breakup.

Had she made the coffee too strong that morning? Her hand tremors seemed worse. Of course, nerves intensified the vibration. "Face it. You're nervous. Are you afraid they'll convert you? Or are you nervous about seeing ..." Not ready to say that aloud yet, not even to herself.

The small parking lot that wrapped around the compact, white church building, with its familiar steeple, was more than half full. Less than half empty, perhaps. Eleanor took the closest parking space to the driveway, her best escape route. The more in-demand spaces would be the ones nearest the door, if the congregation skewed toward senior citizens. Most old-line Protestant churches did. Eleanor knew that. She knew more demographic data about churches than what motivated the faithful. She was, however, savvy enough to arrive there for the main worship service and not for Sunday School. That smaller setting would be too personal, she knew.

She skipped up the concrete steps to the front entry, as organ music pushed out through the door. Pulling the door open, she slowed to allow her eyes to adjust. The foyer was dim, the only windows high and narrow, and the sun standing now on the other side of the building. Cold again outside, at least the day was sunny.

A short man wearing a light gray suit smiled at her from next to the sanctuary door. The volume of the organ music might have ruffled his hair if he had more to ruffle. Eleanor returned his smile and accepted the bulletin with a small thanks. She was drifting, rolling along, like a patient on a gurney. It was like when she had been carted around the hospital from one testing lab to another last year, with the blood clot in her lung.

She was having a little trouble breathing now, her head swimming slightly. But she managed to land in a pew second from the back. Virgil Meers entered from a side door onto the stage just then. Was that what they call it in a church? A stage? Or was there some religious term for it? She hadn't paid close attention to things like that when she was a girl.

Now she was paying attention to Virgil and feeling her breathing regulate. The organ music had stopped. Perhaps that helped, less of the feeling of a horror movie. She forced herself not to laugh at that thought. If anyone recognized her, she didn't want to be seen laughing in church on the day before her mother's funeral.

Her mother might be laughing. Connie could laugh on the day before, the day of, and the day after her own funeral. It might be a low chuckle with that flat smile of hers, her eyes getting up and going for a walk to some far-off place, perhaps a place that only existed in her imagination.

Eleanor scanned the sanctuary, shifting her eyes more than her neck. She wondered where her mother would have sat. She must have owned a regular spot. When Eleanor—Lenny—had accompanied Mom and Dad to church in Milwaukee they used to joke about putting a brass plaque at the end of their pew. The three Petersens sat there always in the same order. Lenny on the end, so she could exercise her restless legs with a trip to the restroom, whether she needed it or not.

Now she realized that she was needing a restroom. Would there be a commercial break when she could make an artful exit? She was suffering from ill-timed coffee before coming to church. And then there were the nerves which seemed to penetrate all the way to her bladder. "The tiniest bladder in the world," her mother used to tell her. Eleanor tugged her focus off her need of a restroom to what Virgil was saying.

Only now did she address what her automatic sensors had registered. He had noticed her, glancing her way more than once. While standing during the congregational singing, he executed a brief glimpse in her direction that he must have practiced for decades. The pastor surely dared not survey the congregation boldly. He dared not cast his authoritative gaze upon a single member more than others. At least not in this sort of church. He surely wouldn't be pointing from the pulpit, stabbing at the sinners with the wrath of God. No, those images were from a different stream of American Christianity. And from a personality different from the thoughtful and humble pastor she had met.

The service seemed categorically familiar. That is, she didn't recognize the particular songs. She didn't anticipate the next item in the order of service. She didn't understand some of the announcements. But everything she heard seemed fitting. She expected the funeral would be the same.

Should she say something at her mother's funeral? Worrying away at that stone in the pocket of her mind erased the remainder of that Sunday service from her awareness. Hopefully, Virgil wouldn't ask what she thought about anything said in that service. Maybe she wouldn't get a chance to speak to him about it.

Wrapping up the service with a reminder of the funeral the next day, Virgil woke her from her mental tossing and turning. Dozens of eyes turned in her direction, though Virgil did refrain from pointing her out. And she wasn't asked to stand and introduce herself during the announcements, as she had done at Jackie's church many years ago.

Maybe that was the last time she had been in church. But that experience in an African American congregation in New York resembled this one only in a very pixilated way.

Then more organ music marked the end of the gathering. Eleanor slipped on her coat and stood to leave. But an old gentleman with a sweep of white hair across his dark pink head interrupted her escape.

"Miss Petersen, is it?"

"It is. Eleanor."

"Eleanor. I'm so sorry to see Connie go. It was too soon. She was the liveliest of us all. Such a shame." He was shaking her hand, his hand even colder than hers. In his eyes she saw expectation. Did he think she would recognize him?

"I'm Earl Johnson. My wife and I used to go out to dinner and to plays with your mother. She was game for driving all over the area to find good theater."

"Oh. I believe you. Yes, she took me to a quaint little opera house north of here, just last year."

"That must ha' been Stoughton. We went there with her a couple o' times."

Eleanor noticed a queue forming behind Mr. Johnson. In fact, after he excused himself, with sincere condolences, eight more people stopped to talk with her. As they did so, she also thought she noticed a few giving up on waiting to speak with her. She would probably see those well-wishers the next day.

One woman, with dyed brunette hair, and several large age spots on her sagging face, clasped Eleanor's hand for a full minute before letting go and reaching for her phone. "I wanted you to see these." She held a smartphone in knotted hands, tapping away at the screen. Then she turned it to show Eleanor. Zooming in with a thumb and forefinger, she accidentally advanced to the next photo. Photos of paintings.

"We have five of your mother's paintings in our house. But I suppose that's boasting about our riches." She cocked her head sideways just slightly, probably including the hunched man standing tightly at her elbow. The last of the congregation was filing past, some smiling knowingly, as if they too had been offered a look at Mrs. Songer's art collection. Or maybe they also had paintings signed, "Constance Petersen."

"At first, we were just supporting her, encouraging a local artist, you know. But then folks started catching on. And I think your mother's work improved over the years. This last one." She stopped scrolling at a picture of a cat squeezing out through a screen door to a rough wooden porch onto which the viewer was about to step. "I think this one is marvelous. It reminds me of my father's farm, back too many years for me to admit."

Mrs. Songer paused and looked up at Eleanor. "She was a treasure, your mother. She was a true gift to this town and to all of Wisconsin, if you ask me." At which point she choked up and had to resort to waving a hand to excuse herself. That hunched man took hold of her arm and sauntered away with her, out into the foyer, following the last of the departing congregants.

That left Eleanor sighing away tears and staggering toward

the front door. She found Virgil waiting there in his clerical vestments. Remembering then her need for a restroom, she forced herself to ignore that need yet again. Turning to run away from Virgil would certainly send the wrong message.

"Eleanor. How are you holding up?"

Right now, her answer to that sympathetic inquiry stood at the end of that queue of Connie's friends and fans. Once again, Eleanor felt as if she were cartwheeling from a new discovery of something about her mother.

"I just talked to several people who loved and respected Mother so much. I really don't know what to say. I am completely overwhelmed."

Virgil pursed his lips and lifted an arm as if to take hold of hers in support and comfort. But he stopped himself. They weren't alone. A man and woman were discussing something along the side of the foyer, beneath one of the windows—something about a repair. Would Virgil have acted on his apparent impulse if he and Eleanor had been alone? Was that allowed?

Most of all, she wondered if she *wanted* him to touch her, to console her. Appropriate? How would she know? How much did she even care?

Perhaps the pressure of tears was adding to her need to relieve herself. "I'm sorry. I need to use the restroom." She gestured toward where she thought that might be located.

He pointed in the same direction. "Just down that hall." Virgil smiled his permission and perhaps an apology.

By the time she finished in the women's restroom, the church building was quiet. No voices, no music. Nothing left to recall the gathering that had filled it only twenty minutes before. When she reached the front door, however, she found Virgil waiting outside, dressed now in a suit and tie.

"No clerical collar?" She hadn't calculated that question, neither to shame him nor even to satisfy a curiosity. The change of costume had simply shaken loose an instant response.

"Usually not, unless I'm going visiting, to the hospital or such. I was raised in a different tradition and tend to use the vestments and collar as little as I'm allowed."

"And you are allowed?"

"No one is strictly keeping track, as far as I can tell. I think I won a large measure of latitude from my congregation when my wife died. They seemed to save me some extra grace for little things after that."

Eleanor was walking toward her car with Virgil close beside her. "I can see that you have a very sympathetic church."

"We have done a lot of life together, losses and victories along the way. I feel welcomed and accepted by them and hope I communicate the same."

Standing now next to her rental car, Eleanor continued to follow her impulses in conversation with Virgil. "I think that sort of acceptance would have kept me interested in church if I had seen it when I was young."

"You left the church when you were young?"

"Yes. I stopped following Mom and Dad to church. I guess leaving was mostly me declaring myself grownup and independent. But I did have some gripes about the way religious people acted in the sixties and seventies."

"Ah. Yes. That was a challenging time for traditional church people. A lot of young people turned away in those days."

Now that her need for a restroom was satisfied, she felt mostly tired. Eleanor worried it was a symptom of depression.

Virgil seemed to intuit her mood. "I'll let you go. You could use some rest, of course. And will you be thinking about what to say tomorrow?"

She nodded. He was only slightly taller than her and eye-contact with Virgil was easy. "I will. I'll work on it today. I'm sure I'll have something." Her electronic key in her hands, she studied the unfamiliar device for a second. "The only question is whether I'll be able to deliver the eulogy."

He grinned sympathetically. "We have a solution for that. If you write it out, I can step in for you, in case you find you can't speak."

"You've done this before."

"Too many times."

She allowed her whole face to relax into a smile, before hitting the remote unlock button and waving her keys in farewell.

"Goodbye." He stepped back a foot. "I'll see you before eleven tomorrow."

"Yes. Before eleven."

CHAPTER FIFTEEN

With nearly forty years of experience delivering prepared re-marks in the form of class lectures, Eleanor was determined to serve her mother with those skills. She suspected Connie might have intended her eulogy as an opportunity to show off her ac-complished daughter. Being a mother comes with bragging rights. Connie had exercised those rights at every opportunity.

The trick now, beside the fact that this was *not* an academic lecture, would be to say enough to be heartfelt without her own words breaking her down to tears in front of a gathering of strangers.

None of the nephews and nieces that still survived had been close with her mother, as far as Eleanor knew. And even if they did attend, they wouldn't be familiar to Eleanor these days. So, the funeral would definitely be a gathering of strangers, strangers to Eleanor. But the attendees would not have been strangers to her mother. Which was part of the challenge.

Eleanor spent nearly two hours Sunday afternoon drafting, editing and refining her remarks after another helping of the la-sagna casserole. She dumped what remained of that culinary consolation, suspecting it had reached the end of its healthy shelf life. Tapping her fork on the edge of her plate as she reread the final section, Eleanor considered rewriting it entirely. She might not be able to say these things aloud.

Then her phone rang.

"I hope you don't mind. I bribed Paul Wasser to give me your cell phone number. I guess your mom disconnected her land line."

"No. I don't mind. Is this …?" Eleanor could picture the old woman she had met that first full day at the farm. How long ago was that?

"Audrey Benson. Sorry, I'm not the best at introductions. Get right into it most of the time." She cleared her throat. "I called to invite you to dinner tonight, if you want. I'll have a couple of your mother's old friends over here, and we wanted to offer you an evening with some company. You're all alone over there at the farm, aren't you?"

Pausing to recover from the emotional knock to the head dealt by writing the eulogy, Eleanor tried to recreate the question. "You want me to come for supper, tonight? To your house?"

"I live on the edge of town, next to my daughter's place. Just a few friends. Very casual evening. No expectations. In case you don't wanna be alone tonight."

"That would be wonderful. Thank you. It's so good of you to think of me." Eleanor's throat squeezed shut and tears stung her eyes.

"Good. Can you get here by six?"

"Um-hmm. Yes. I can." Fortunately, that was enough words. As loudly as Audrey projected over the phone, Eleanor suspected she was hearing impaired, so perhaps she had missed the gravel clogging Eleanor's voice.

Rereading and editing some more, she finally printed her mother's eulogy. She didn't pick it up off the printer, however, interrupted by another round of intense silent tears at the very idea of a eulogy for her mother.

Sitting in the armchair in the corner of the office, the one that smelled the most of Cocker Spaniel, she ripped tissues out of a box in quick succession.

"If I can't cry now. When can I?"

As if calling to answer that question, Jackie's name appeared on Eleanor's phone as it buzzed on the corner of the desk. Eleanor rose from that chair and grabbed the phone, sliding her thumb to answer. She needed her other hand for swiping at the dog hairs she imagined covering her backside.

"Hello, my dear. I'm getting requests. Including from one of your graduate students. Folks want to know whether it's okay to call you and offer sympathy and support."

"Graduate students? Is that Rosemary?"

"Yes. And she implied that one or two others would like to hear your voice and to offer their heart-felts."

"Well. They can call. Let them know that I might be with people and not able to answer. But even seeing that they called will be comforting. Of course, Grace and David and Amanda can call. Have you been gatekeeping?"

"I have. But I don't want to leave you isolated."

"I'm going to dinner at the house of one of Mother's old friends."

"Old as in elderly."

"Senior, as in citizen, not as in about to graduate."

"You must be having a bit of culture shock, hanging with the older generation. See what you've been missing by staying away from church all these years?"

"I've met some sweet old folks here. They all have glowing stories about Mom. Oh, and there was the woman in the mysterious portraits."

"Oh. Tell me about that."

Eleanor described the portraits she had found in the barn, and she started walking that direction as she spoke. She was following a current pushing her toward her mother's art, especially the paintings of Yvonne.

"So, when you saw her on the street you had no idea this was the same woman?"

"No idea. Even when she came in to sit down with me, I still hadn't figured it out." Eleanor pulled the back door open and stepped into the billowing cold.

"And she was just overcome with grief at the news that your

mother had died?"

"Yes. She sure was. I should have been more circumspect." Eleanor arrived at the side door of the barn and began fiddling with the doorknob. She wrote herself a mental note to find the key before she finally followed through on locking this door. Then she heard a call coming through on top of Jackie's. "Hey, you mind if I take this call from the handyman?"

"Handyman. Hmm. I think I'll bypass the obvious humor in that term. Isn't there a more politically correct version of that?"

"Can I take it? I'm not sure why he would be calling."

"Of course. Call me later when you get back from the sewing circle, or whatever."

"Okay."

"Paul."

"Eleanor. Did I catch you at a bad time?"

"Just a call from a friend back home. What can I do for you?"

"Actually, I was thinking maybe you wouldn't want to be alone this evening. I'd like to take you out to dinner, if you're available."

"Well, that's very considerate. I appreciate it. But Audrey Benson got to me first. She has some friends coming over and invited me to her house. I don't suppose you would want to join us."

"What, like as your date?"

"Ha. Not exactly what I was thinking."

"Sorry. It was the sorta joking I did with your mother. I guess I forgot myself for a minute."

"No problem. I get the humor. I wish I could have seen you two together. I bet Mom was entertaining as the flirty old woman."

"I always got a kick out of her. Never a dull moment."

"I envy you the time you spent with her."

"Well, it wasn't so much time maybe, just stopping in for

coffee after plowing the drive or trimming trees or something. Mowing the lawn. Lemonade in the summer, you know."

"No alcohol involved?"

"No. No booze. Strictly sober."

That triggered a thought that Eleanor could take a bottle of wine with her to dinner that night. Or ... maybe a regifted casserole. "So, sorry about dinner tonight. I'll be around a few more days. Maybe another time."

"Okay, I'll call again after tomorrow."

"Right. After tomorrow."

Arriving at Audrey Benson's little ranch house, as the sun settled amidst approaching clouds, reminded Eleanor of being a girl, visiting old aunts in Zion, Illinois, or in Wauwatosa. Dinner with her mother's friends recast her as a girl for the first time in a long time. Even with Connie, in recent years, she had been more like a sister. At least she generally felt like a grownup.

"Hello, hello. Come on in, Eleanor. Here's Denise Cartwright, and Gretchen Moore. These are two of the girls that used to get together with your mother and me for a game of cards or to go out to dinner." Audrey stepped back from the front door tentatively, gesturing toward two women Eleanor didn't recognize.

"Oh, you played bridge with her?"

"Not so much bridge lately."

"We liked Spades. Your mother always shooting for the moon even when she had only a ghost of a chance." Denise shook Eleanor's hand. She was probably a bit younger than Connie.

"I always wanted to play rummy. Used to play it with my husband years back." Gretchen shook her hand, hanging on for a few extra seconds. "You sure have her eyes." Gretchen's own eyes blinked back tears when she let go. She was small but not slender, perhaps older than Connie. She wore her russet hair swept back into a knot on top of her head. Who helped her with that knot? Her stiff neck and arm movements implied that question.

Eleanor remembered that she had left the wine in the car, a bottle pilfered from her mother's basement. But she left it there, not wanting to interrupt the greetings.

Denise was chatting away about Connie's card playing habits. Apparently, Eleanor's mother was no more competitive at spades than she had been at Monopoly. When she was a child, Eleanor and her father had invented Monopolistic Charities, by which they would donate excess wealth to Connie in order to prolong a game, keeping it at a three-person contest as long as possible.

"I don't think she cared at all about the cards," Audrey was saying. She had invited them all toward the dining room.

Her daughter was setting food in the center of a table that would seat six. "I'm not staying, I just helped Mom out with the hot dishes. She's not strong enough to cook big meals these days."

"I'm Eleanor. I don't think I got your name."

"Debbie. Pleased to meet you." She looked like she would say more, but perhaps she recalled then that she had offered condolences already, though not her name.

Seated at the table, Eleanor to Audrey's right, they began to practice an improvised version of passing the food dishes. Gretchen seemed to have weak hands. She spilled first green beans and then some gravy. "Such a klutz. Sorry, girls. Not as handy as I used to be." She shook her head and kept her eyes on the food being offered but not handed to her.

"I think it was Connie that started us calling each other 'girls.' Don't you?" Denise arched her makeup-enhanced eyebrows to a point in the middle of her forehead. She was looking at Audrey.

"Probably. She had a penchant for influencing other people

with her way of looking at the world. I guess that's why her paintings did so well. Lots of folks wanted to see things through her eyes."

Eleanor followed another one of those generous impulses her mother's death had released. "Speaking of mother's paintings. I want all of you to come over sometime and take a look at what she had stored in the barn. I pulled a bunch of them into the house just so I could enjoy them. I have them sitting in chairs like a bunch of guests. Though some are landscapes, of course." She was babbling, concentrating some on not overfilling her plate with the steaming food.

"You brought a bunch of 'em inside? Oh, that sounds fun. I'd like to come over to see that. I'm not sure it's right for us to take any of them, though." Denise was attentively spearing green beans. She glanced at Audrey. They must have talked about this between them.

Eleanor glanced at Audrey as well, lifting her fork to begin eating. "I attended the reading of the will. Mother made provision for some galleries and for me. And there seems to be plenty of her art to go around. I know she would want you each to take at least one."

"I told her to hold off on that. Not too sure she knows what she's saying with that grand offer. Maybe more generous than she knows." Audrey remained hunched over her plate, speaking in a low, resigned tone.

"I've been doing some research about her paintings. And I know how much she donated to charities. She was quite successful. But I see no reason for not sharing a little bit of that with her dearest friends."

Gretchen was sitting with her hands in her lap. Subtle sobs rocked her in her chair. "I'm gonna miss her so much. How can I think of outliving Connie? It's just not right. She was the best of us."

Seeing the old woman's head shuddering, her shoulders shaking, Eleanor forgot her own restraints. She blurted a sob that proved to be only a small introduction to what she had brought to the table.

"Now look what you've done." But that was all Audrey could say.

Gretchen's tears infected her as well. Dropping forks and knives, they formed a weeping quartet. When Audrey began struggling to reach for a tissue box behind her chair, Eleanor stood briskly and grabbed it for her, handing the box to the hostess but snatching two for herself first.

The evening wasn't all tears. They did manage to eat the food while it was still warm. And by the time the meal was finished, Eleanor was lounging in layers of comfort and contentment. The catharsis at the start of the meal had tightened her stomach, but that loosened as they ate, talked and began to laugh together. Like survivors of a disaster, they had bonded through that flood of tears.

After dinner, the four women sat around the living room, sipping coffee and eating almond cookies. "You brought a bunch of her paintings into the house, you say? What made you think of that?" Gretchen leaned to one side in order to look at Eleanor, seated next to her on the couch.

Collecting a few stray crumbs off her black slacks, Eleanor surveyed the other women. "Her art was a revelation of who she was. It's a way for me to be with her now, I guess. Really, I just missed her and felt like I could get some of her in the house with me." She smiled benignly at Gretchen, and then remembered something. "And I met a woman named Yvonne who used to model for Mother."

"Oh. You met Yvonne." Gretchen was nodding, perhaps avoiding eye contact.

"Where did you see her?" Audrey attentively placed her

coffee cup on the small table beside her chair.

Eleanor retold the story of meeting Yvonne.

"Oh, I had no idea Connie painted her. I thought she just befriended Yvonne out of charity, you know." Denise was nodding and staring past Eleanor.

"I remember finding Yvonne over there for one of those modeling sessions." Audrey began with a smile that faded slowly. "Yvonne was all dressed up in this sort of gypsy dancing girl costume. Like Carmen. She seemed like she was playing a part or playing dress up." Audrey signed. "She seemed to be having the time of her life. And Connie was dressed up too, as I recall." Audrey slowed to consider the curtains next to her chair. "I think she was wearing some exotic turban or something. Those two really got along well most of the time, and that was the best I saw of it."

"Mom had difficulty with Yvonne sometimes?"

"Oh. I think there were some problems. But you must remember that Yvonne has trouble relating to people. She hears things in her head. And she never knows whether something you said to her, or even something you did with her, really happened. She's always asking whether you really just said something or not."

Denise and Gretchen were both nodding and looking toward the floor.

"Connie insisted on bringing Yvonne along with us when we went out to eat different times." Gretchen grinned somewhat painfully and raised one eyebrow at Eleanor.

The other two seemed to be remembering something about that. "Um-hmm," they both said.

"Do you know how I can get ahold of Yvonne?" Eleanor finished her coffee and wondered if it would keep her up at night, before clattering the cup into the saucer with her left hand. That hand betrayed her tremors the most. She should have sat with a table on her right.

"She stays at The Dove's Nest house on the other side of town." Denise aimed one eye at Eleanor, as if she knew she was telling her something important that she didn't know. "Your mother had quite a bit to do with the founding of that place. It's a sort of care home for folks that can't really get by on their own. Me and Connie used to volunteer over there. I've been thinking of checking if they need me again. I'll give you the number so you can call to see if Yvonne will meet with you."

Eleanor bypassed trying to recall what her mother had said about her volunteer work. "I would talk to one of her caregivers?"

"Yes. The other Connie, Consuela, is her daytime caregiver most days."

"The *other* Connie." Gretchen echoed it mournfully.

CHAPTER SIXTEEN

Dinner with "the girls" ended in more tears and hugs—the sort of minimal contact hugs that seemed to preserve space for a third person in between. A slim person, perhaps. Even after those Wisconsin hugs, the visit remained warm and vibrant in Eleanor's mind, right through to the following morning.

This was the day she would join the town in saying goodbye to her mother. She scuffed on bare feet into the office to pick her eulogy off the printer. She didn't look at it. Instead, she focused on the paintings propped along the wall of the upper hallway. She flipped on the hall light to see the depictions of barns that she had grouped up there. Her mother's house was cold this morning. It was certainly the earliest Eleanor had awakened on this visit. The homey paintings comforted her against the cold. And she descended the stairs on the way to her morning coffee.

Eleanor set the eulogy on the little lamp table in the central hallway downstairs. There she hit another light switch. Paintings of farmhouses and fencerows lined the dining room, propped on every surface that would hold one, some on the floor leaning against chairs and shelves or the rare exposed wall. Through the small hall to the kitchen more canvases extended Connie's embrace of her daughter. The display ended at the kitchen. In all, she had carried more than thirty paintings in from the barn. She had also unstacked at least twenty in the studio. Those were mostly still life depictions of flowers in vases or wildflowers scattered on various wood surfaces. Some of small animals.

With the coffee beginning to drip, Eleanor shuffled toward the living room. She wanted to see the paintings in there, including those sitting on the couch like guests arrived for tea. But the guests were all the same. One woman. In exotic costumes that

122

highlighted her Mediterranean features and her lustrous eyes.

Would Yvonne be at the funeral? Was she allowed?

Eleanor planned to contact her the next day, after the funeral. Now, she stood in the living room with seven portraits of a playful and joyous woman. Perhaps there was a wildness in her eyes. What looked like the snap of adventure might have been the edge of insanity. Was that what Connie had wanted to capture? Or did she paint Yvonne just for Yvonne?

In her will, she had insisted that Yvonne should choose what happens to these paintings. Until that happened, Eleanor would enjoy them. And she would welcome Denise and Gretchen over for a private showing, to enjoy them at least one time.

The mundane demands of that funeral day eased behind the images in the paintings—farm dogs looking expectantly at the viewer, cats slinking away, ducks on the pond. These all accompanied Eleanor through her preparations. Getting in the car required three trips, including one to retrieve her paper copy of the eulogy. She had emailed it to her phone. But she wanted it on paper in case she had to hand it to Virgil to finish.

Her mother's ashes contained in an urn. A church full of strangers. Paintings lining the walls of a house that had never belonged to Eleanor. Virgil Meers and Paul Wasser. The old girls her mother loved. All of it was like a fencerow around the fringes of Eleanor's mind. She was walking among these people and things. But at a distance. A necessary distance. Alone in the space they allowed her.

Over and again, she lost track of how she had gotten somewhere—not remembering the ride to the church, the walk up to the pulpit or her steps back down to the front pew. There would be no burial. The urn was entrusted to Eleanor the same way her father's urn had been entrusted to Connie a decade ago. Did Eleanor awaken from her trance when a murmur stirred over the mention of there being no burial? Maybe it was her own internal murmuring.

The people who attended, who processed with her to the fellowship hall for a lunch reception, flowed like one giant creature—an organism with multitudinous eyes, dozens of hands and feet. All moving as one. Mourning as one.

The others in that crowd had inhaled in unison when Eleanor read the story of her mother's speech to her before she left for college—the permission, the blessing and the challenge she offered her girl.

"The world isn't so big as to not notice you out in it, Lenny. Expect to make an impact and you will. But you know you will always have a home here, and you can always come back, whether to celebrate or to find some consolation."

She told the gathered mourners that she was here, by her mother's side again, needing some of that consolation. And they cried with her. That vast creature with many heads and many hearts sighed and sniffled and sobbed with her. They too were here for consolation, here for Connie and for recalling the joy she had given them.

The conjoined sorrow and sympathy that reached its crescendo during the eulogy, stretched a hand toward Eleanor, from the fringes of that field on which she had been wandering. After that, they were walking with her as they had walked with her mother.

Eleanor came to understand then that she wasn't alone at the funeral, not as she had feared she would be, as Jackie had feared she would be. Her contacts with Connie's friends, with the handyman, and with the pastor had established a partnership that wouldn't leave Eleanor abandoned. She recalled their faces afterward—sometimes wet with tears—even if she couldn't remember a single word they had said to her.

Before she left the reception, something freed Eleanor to stand and invite everyone to come by the house to see the paintings she had spread throughout. She had intended only to give a reminder to Denise and Gretchen, and perhaps Audrey, but it had escalated into a general invitation. Perhaps it was the intoxication of the thin air, where she had drifted high above the world in which she had once lived as the daughter of Connie and Darrel Petersen, a world she could see now only by looking back from a lofty altitude.

When she finally left the church, she had to return once to retrieve the urn, her mother's ashes forgotten for just one moment, in the wake of missing the living and breathing woman.

Eleanor arrived at the farmhouse to find Paul Wasser already there, his blue pickup parked by the barn. He stood next to it with a gray fedora clutched between his hands, where she had seen that Brewers baseball cap before.

"I thought you might need a little help with the gallery in there." He lifted the hat with one hand toward the house.

Eleanor craved a tight, extended hug, like the one Jackie would give her right now. But she evaluated Paul only briefly for that position and left his candidacy for later consideration. "Thank you. I surprised myself with that invitation. The house is a mess. I hope they'll only see the paintings." She stepped toward the house and stopped herself. "Maybe we could grab a few more." She nodded toward the barn. She was pretty certain she had still left it unlocked.

"Sure." Paul led the way, without any visible hesitation.

"You helped her set this all up?" She gestured toward the big barn.

"That was my dad and Ralph Brubaker. They built the storage areas in there and set up the heating and AC for the paintings to be protected. I just kept it going and helped her move stuff sometimes." He pushed inside, apparently not surprised that the door was unlocked.

"I should keep it locked. I keep forgetting." Her voice

thinned as she realized she was still carrying her mother's urn.

"I'll make sure the key is where you can find it when we go in. And then I'll come out to lock it." So, perhaps, Paul had been thinking about the need to keep it secured, just reserving his advice.

Her impulse to collect more paintings came from realizing how unkempt the house was, wanting to hide as much of that as possible. A dozen more paintings would surely help. When they both bumped and rattled out the storm door into the afternoon grayness, an old sedan was slowing to park next to Paul's pickup. Debbie was driving, and Audrey, Denise and Gretchen were all on board. While Paul and Eleanor propped paintings by the back door and against the fence rail, Debbie busied herself with pulling two walkers out of the trunk.

Denise was holding a huge leather purse, dressed in classic pumps with low heels and a heavy wool coat. All black. Her funeral uniform, perhaps. "Can I help?"

Eleanor began to refuse but then realized that she was still needing to do something with that urn, at least for a moment. "Sure. Would you mind?" She offered Denise a facial apology and held out Connie's ashes.

"Oh." That was all Denise could say. She wrapped an arm around the urn as if she were holding a toddler against her hip.

Those early arrivals helped with moving the paintings already inside as well as placing a dozen more on available surfaces. The panorama of Connie's paintings became the captivating focus for everyone already crowded shoulder-to-shoulder on the first floor.

"Are there more upstairs?" Gretchen was staring at a painting of a black and white cat asleep around a terracotta flowerpot which contained an amaryllis tipped slightly away from the viewer.

"Yes." Eleanor offered her hand. "Do you need some help?"

"I got her." Debbie took Gretchen's arm and waited for her to turn away from her current obsession.

During that afternoon, dozens of others knocked on the back door or walked right in. A few mistook the front door for what it only appeared to be, but Eleanor had also left it unlocked and the artworks clear of it.

Virgil arrived in the company of a young woman with startling blue eyes, pale skin and voluminous dark hair fastened in a knot atop her head. Who was that young woman? Eleanor's mind raced in search of a possible explanation, packets of paranoia left ripped open where she rummaged about. Before she could investigate directly, one of her mother's neighbors interrupted her.

"Are you gonna sell some of these, Miss Petersen?" Mr. Walters, from down the road, was poised before a painting of a rusting tractor surrounded by tall grass, in front of a faded barn.

"You can't afford one of these, Cecil." A woman, that Eleanor presumed was Mrs. Walters, scolded him condescendingly.

Eleanor pushed past that tone. "I haven't decided what to do with all of them. I know I have an obligation to Mother's legacy as an artist. And I'm afraid these won't be affordable for everyone."

"You could buy a new pickup for what you'd pay for one of these." That woman turned away, a sour note lingering behind.

"Well, not a *new* pickup." Mr. Walters seemed confident that he knew something about the value of both pickups and paintings.

Eleanor just nodded.

That was when Virgil approached her. "What an inspiration, Eleanor. What a magnificent celebration of your mother's art." Wonder and appreciation shone from his face.

But Eleanor was still distracted by that attractive, young woman next to him.

"Oh. This is my daughter, Candice. Candice, this is Eleanor."

Candice reached a thin hand toward her. "You probably don't know that I studied painting here in the studio. Your mother was a delightful teacher."

"What?" For a second, it was as if the world had turned over sideways. This young woman wasn't whom Eleanor had feared. And she had brought with her another new image of Connie. "No. I didn't know. Oh, that's wonderful." She stared at Candice for a second. "I would love to talk to you about that."

Candice smiled a teary reply. The hubbub around them insisted on the postponement of their discussion. Eleanor returned Candice's smile and transferred that mute bond to Virgil, a man full of surprises.

A tall woman with golden hair was looking over Virgil and Candice's shoulders. She slowly shook her head and smiled almost deliriously as they excused themselves to make way for newcomers.

"Eleanor, I'm Virginia Whitworth, Connie's agent." She offered her hand. "This is stunning. What a unique way to remember your mother, and so appropriate. She would have loved this." She teared up and just stood there with her lips quivering. An intake of air and a roll of her eyes.

Eleanor knew instantly that she liked Virginia Whitworth. Of course, her mother had liked and trusted her. Eleanor would join Connie there. "We have lots to talk about. Did you get a letter from the lawyer about the will?"

Virginia nodded but didn't speak. Couldn't speak. That too fed Eleanor's heart with trust for the well-dressed agent. They finally released hands and Virginia moved further into the impromptu gallery. Eleanor imagined her mother offering her hand just so, in covenant with this professional woman. For whatever reason, that almost made Eleanor laugh. Instead, she stopped at a grin, until another visitor offered his condolences.

The time in the impromptu gallery was nothing like her ethereal drift through the funeral. But Eleanor did begin to falter, as she met and thanked the patrons. When she stood propped against the wide doorpost between the living room and the dining room, Paul approached, holding two glasses.

"Should I pass the word that the gallery is closing?" He handed her a glass of red wine with his offer.

"Huh? Oh. Oh, yes. Thank you. That would be very kind of you. I think I've spent all I had to spend today." She called on a last store of energy to raise her eyebrows and stretch a tight-lipped smile. It was the offspring of her mother's little grin, perhaps.

When she pried herself off that doorpost, she sipped the wine Paul had handed her. Virgil appeared at that moment, following Candice this time. Would he disapprove of her drinking?

"That looks like a good idea. Just one, though." Virgil was regarding her from a three-quarters angle, with a little smile. It might have been a teasing smile. But Eleanor was distracted by the fact that Virgil had assumed the same angle and the same expression as the old man in a painting behind him, an oil propped on top of the sideboard.

Eleanor laughed. She pointed one finger as she raised her wine glass. "You just did a very accurate impression of that old man over there." The way it came out, with the glass of wine in hand, reinforced a feeling of intoxication, a feeling that recalled faculty parties over the years.

"Oh. I hope I don't look *that* old." Virgil was turned away to evaluate her comparison.

Candice spoke up. "If you did, we would never tell you." She had turned back from checking that portrait. She offered Eleanor a confiding smile, as if they had an understanding.

That understanding probably birthed out of Candice's loyalty to Connie. Like Paul and several others, she seemed to be granting Eleanor grace that belonged to her mother. But maybe that's how grace works. She would have to ask Virgil about that some time.

Shifting the wine, Eleanor accepted Virgil's offered hand. But this was no handshake. He hung on. A clasp of hands. Friendly. No substitute for that missing hug, perhaps, but warm and welcomed, especially from Virgil.

Perhaps she was on her way to inebriation, with thoughts like that. Or maybe Candice and Virgil were conspiring to seduce her into such imaginings. Eleanor read a sly signal from the daughter, a hint of the sort of permission that sprouts from concern about a lonely parent. Eleanor knew that feeling well.

She leaned toward Candice. "Good night. So good to meet you. We really should talk sometime."

Virgil nodded at his daughter with a look that must have been approval.

Eleanor followed Virgil and Candice out to the kitchen. Paul was there reiterating his polite apologies about the gallery closing. Eleanor waved when Virgil looked back at her from near the back door. The wind ruffled the scarf he wore around his coat collar as Candice waited for him.

Then Eleanor turned to reenter the dining room. Her mother's paintings were there, still there after all the people had left. Everyone except Paul. A minute later, he came in from the back door with a pair of keys looped onto one finger. Heading to the key rack, he nodded to Eleanor.

"Thank you for checking on that. I kept forgetting to lock it and I never got around to finding where the key was."

"Folks don't lock up around here all the time. But I think your mother meant to keep that locked. She was forgetting things more and more, I noticed." He paused as if wondering whether this was his to say. But her raised eyebrows invited him to go on. "Connie seemed to get caught up in her own thoughts more toward the end."

"Umm." Eleanor wasn't finding enough of a flame to light that torch. She would have to explore those corridors later. She looked at Paul for a moment and realized that she also had no more energy for the hug she had imagined between them.

"Well. You've been very helpful as always. I'll contact you before I leave, to make sure everything is in place."

"Are we still on for dinner?"

"Oh. Yes. I forgot. Sure. Say, Wednesday? I fly out on Thursday."

"That's fine with me. Is late okay, after seven?"

"Yes. That'll work for me."

"I'll come by and pick you up."

Though that felt like a date, contesting the offer would have escalated the awkwardness too much. "I'll see you then."

"So, you're gonna leave the paintings in here for now?"

"For now." She wasn't making decisions. Not tonight.

CHAPTER SEVENTEEN

In her eulogy, Eleanor had attempted to reproduce a conversation she had with her mother before taking the plane toward college. Revisiting those words stirred the pot and wafted a scent she hadn't inhaled for a while. It was like the spices of a good chili, awakened by lifting the lid and scooping the ladle down and through. Eleanor had occasionally stirred that memory before her mother's death. In doing so, she had credited her mother for the empowering message.

But more often, she had replayed a particular rebuff that she had witnessed from her mother to her father. It was during her first Thanksgiving break, just three months after that farewell speech.

Freshman year established the pattern for school breaks. They had decided she would fly home from Boston to Milwaukee even for the short Thanksgiving holiday. It was just a long weekend back in those days. Perhaps she made that first short trip because she was away from home for the first time. She later wished she hadn't been in her parents' house that weekend, that she hadn't seen her mother deflect her father's affection.

That was how the scene had been captured in her mind, until now. Now that it was too late to take Connie's hand and bring her along to revisit that scene.

Wednesday night, before the holiday and the guests, the big meal as the main event, Eleanor was supposed to be sleeping. The exhaustion of the ride from Amherst to Boston and then the flight to Milwaukee, piled on top of her first ten weeks of college. She had gone to bed early. But the spin of the travel and the excitement of being home tossed her back and forth in bed for what must have been an hour or more.

She didn't remember creeping out of bed as if to catch her parents at some secret holiday activity. It wasn't Christmas Eve in the rambling ranch house in Greenfield, Wisconsin. And she wasn't ten years old, furtively awake. But her parents clearly didn't notice their eighteen-year-old in the shadows at the end of the hallway. She stood paralyzed there, wanting to stay and to retreat at the same time.

"You don't wanna do that, remember?" Her mother had pushed her dad's hands away.

"Maybe tonight I do."

"You've been drinking, so you *think* you do. But really you *can't*."

"I can't because you won't let me?"

"You know why you can't."

And then Dad had appeared to deflate, as if his wife's words had punctured him. He sank back into a couch cushion and stared toward the fire. Eleanor couldn't see the fireplace from there, only the orange glow on her parents' faces. Her mother smug. Her usual straight grin. A thin line. A negative sign.

Her father looked like he might cry. Eleanor had never seen him so sad, so defeated.

That image of her mother and father staring at the fire remained clear, even if she wasn't remembering exactly the words she had overheard. In her memory, it was a startling picture of her mother wounding her father. At eighteen, Eleanor knew that her mother had betrayed her marriage, she had rejected the man she had vowed to have and to hold. And *this* was the woman who had urged her daughter to go out and make a mark on the world, the woman offering love and acceptance always awaiting her at home.

Over forty-six years later, Eleanor lay in the bed that had been her father's, his bed in his separate bedroom. Separated *not* because of the selfish hypocrisy of her mother. Separated by his "preference."

She rolled onto her back and stared at the ceiling. A sharp pressure behind her eyes reminded her of that second glass of wine. Virgil had been right. He wasn't just joking. It had been sage advice. Advice ignored. Headache earned. Judgement.

God was certainly judging Eleanor for unfairly blaming her mother. Eleanor was being judged because she had judged. She would never have a chance to apologize, now that she recognized that she had made her ruling out of ignorance.

Could she now reimagine the meaning of that fireside scene?

There was that sad expression carved into her father's face. Was it defeat? Defeat that had been handed him many years before?

There was her mother's buttoned-down grin. Was that a painful grin? The pain of costly faithfulness?

"Did I even know you? Either of you?" Percolating emotions cut her off. "Do I know you now? Now that it's too late?"

She stared still at the ceiling, as if its mottled pale grayness reflected her leeched complexion amid the fog-gray sheets. A sort of numbness rushed in to protect her from the regret, regret that threatened to drag her into depression. Eleanor couldn't move. She couldn't be expected to get up.

She closed her eyes and fell back to sleep.

"Get up, Lenny."

"Get up, girl."

Her father's voice.

"Get up, Lenny."

"Eleanor, get up!"

She was startled awake. Who was that?

Her phone.

She reached to the bedside table in time to see that it had been a call from Grace, one of the assistant professors in the History department. The two of them weren't friends. But Grace was the ideal employee. And she did have some friend potential. Perhaps their positions in the university organizational chart were all that prevented a real friendship. That and twenty years of age difference. Jackie, on the other hand, was less than ten years younger than Eleanor. It worked between them. It worked because Jackie was the chair of a different department. They were peers.

Grace had tried calling the day before, as well, perhaps not getting her dates right. Would she really have intentionally called on the day of the funeral?

Now Eleanor was awake. The bedside clock said 8:30. It offered no retraction nor amendment to that claim. Until it said 8:31.

Flinging the covers back, she tried to generate momentum, the opposite of the last time she awoke. Had she really been awake? It was hard to tell. Was this depression? Perhaps David would call later today—her psychology professor friend. Maybe he would call with his wife, Amanda. Young and beautiful Amanda. She would surely call.

Amanda had been one of David's students when he first taught in Boston. Why bring that up now?

Eleanor strove for a bustling pace. More momentum.

She hadn't displayed any of the paintings in the bedroom. That would have added an awkward wing to her little gallery. She slowed as she passed images and scenes on the way to the bathroom. She would stack these, maybe all of them. Even the ones of Yvonne would have to be stacked. She couldn't bring Yvonne over here to see those seven portraits all sitting around the living room, like a support group for former gypsy dancers.

"Ha." That was funny. Wouldn't it be good to really laugh again? Someday.

After a shower, Eleanor dried her hair with a towel, one of the benefits of her short haircut. Her phone buzzed again.

Unknown caller. She had met a few unknown callers in the past several days, so she picked it up. She settled the ragged pink towel onto her shoulder.

"Hello, Eleanor. This is Candice. I hope it's okay for me to call today."

"Of course. I guess we left things pretty vague yesterday. I'm glad you took the initiative." Was she addressing this young woman the way she would one of her graduate students? Candice had been her mother's student after all.

"I'm flying back to Portland later today. I was hoping we could get together before I leave. Do you have time for lunch?"

"Yes. I'm just realizing that I have no appointments today, and I haven't yet figured out what I should be doing. Do you want to meet in town? One thing I should do is check Mother's safe deposit box."

"Sure. Have you tried The Caboose?"

"I have not. Where is it exactly?"

Candice gave directions to the small restaurant near the abandoned train station at the north edge of town.

"I'll meet you there at noon." And they ended their call, Eleanor returning to fluffing her hair for a moment.

While still wearing her mother's terrycloth bathrobe, she stooped and sorted, scooped and stacked—roughly organizing the paintings in the upstairs hallway, settling some of them in her mother's bedroom. She had hesitated about displaying paintings in there. But that room was one that most needed the cover of the art display. The door was blocked open by a massive pile of books and magazines.

"Were you a hoarder, Mother?" Eleanor set a stack of six medium-sized canvases against her mother's dresser. There she paused to pull open the slender jewelry drawer at the top.

Oh. That was a mistake.

Her mother owned only a few pieces of expensive jewelry,

136

favoring more artsy pieces that she found at craft shops. Something designed and crafted by a woman living in Namibia attracted Connie more passionately than a box from Zales or Kays. Still, there were a few of those pricey pieces. A diamond bracelet. A long string of perfect pearls. Those were gifts from Eleanor's father. But her mistake was looking at the little pendants of cats, butterflies and flowers, hand-painted by people whom her mother would have loved if she had met them, even if she couldn't pronounce their names properly.

After touching only two or three of the shiny pins, Eleanor pushed the drawer shut and launched herself away from the dresser.

Suddenly she felt the need to talk to someone. Only pausing to get minimally dressed—underwear, jeans and one of her mother's soft, cotton, long-sleeved blouses—she dialed Jackie. Then she remembered that her friend would be in the Caribbean by now, visiting Thomas's relatives in Turks and Caicos. Nice place for a family reunion. Much better than southern Wisconsin in March.

Ending that call before voicemail, Eleanor thought of Virgil. Was he really next in line after Jackie? Today he was. Though that may not last.

"Hello?" Apparently, he hadn't saved her contact information to his phone. Or was this the church phone number?

"Virgil. This is Eleanor. Do you have time to talk?"

"Eleanor. Sure. Just give me a minute. Hang on." He seemed to set down the phone or maybe covered it with his hand. She heard no voices, just slight rustling sounds.

She waited and forced herself to stop speculating. That self-imposed discipline reminded her of the crazy chain of thoughts she had indulged when she saw Virgil with that beautiful younger woman the day before. That mental cliff dive was probably David's fault. David and Amanda. Her friends. The professor and the student he married.

"There. Thanks for hanging on. How are you doing?"

Virgil's hasty shift to caregiver mode annoyed Eleanor briefly. She discarded her annoyance, however, with the realization that she had called him *because* she needed some care.

"I am needing a confessor. Are you available?"

"Uh, on the phone or in person?"

She wanted to see him, but she was suspicious of the heat that came with that desire. "Phone is probably best."

"Yes. Of course."

What did he mean by that?

She pressed on. "I unfairly judged my mother. I carried a grudge against her, based on youthful ignorance and hasty teenaged judgment."

"Hasty teenaged judgment? I suppose you see a lot of that from your students."

"Ah. Yes. The indignation of historical distance, judging those who failed so badly in past eras, failed so egregiously that they didn't even know they were failing."

"American history?"

"Yes. That's my field. Slavery comes to mind, of course."

"Right. Just what I was thinking."

"Though, self-righteous undergraduates generally don't require so big and obvious a target as slavery." She sniffed. "But I can't blame them, because I'm one of the ones who's feeding their fire."

"You and other faculty?"

"Yes. We generally agree with their judgments, but we've learned to cloak ours in academic propriety and feigned neutrality."

"I think I've taken you off topic."

"It wasn't hard, was it?"

He snickered, perhaps. A small breathy noise. "You judged

your mother unfairly."

Standing alone, those words would have been an accusation. But his voice accompanied them with an offered pat on the shoulder, a sympathetic tilt of his head, perhaps a small smile. She was picturing him as she listened to his slightly gritty baritone.

"I did. That is my confession."

"There was a particular incident?"

"How did you know?"

"I think there usually is."

"I suppose." She calculated how much to say and then realized that this hadn't been a calculated call. Confession should never be calculated. Right?

"I saw them together one night when I was home for break, freshman year."

"Still young. Still a girl."

"Yes. In fact, it was my first trip home from Amherst, where I went to college."

"Ah. Massachusetts. A long way away."

"It was far. But I thought I would always come back to them here in Wisconsin, at least to our home near Milwaukee."

"That changed?"

"It did. That night changed it. As it turns out, my foolishness changed it."

"Can you really call it foolishness for that eighteen-year-old? What did she know?"

"Oh, Virgil. That's just it. I didn't know." The sound of her own breath rasping against the phone warned her to slow down. "But ... maybe I should have known something. I should have seen my father more clearly, understood my mother more sympathetically."

"It's really not up to the child, even a teenager, to figure all that out, to know what to do with it. And most people didn't do family therapy in those days."

She laughed. "You sound like one of the psych professors I know. Yes, clearly we would have all benefited from some therapy." She inhaled deeply. Was this going well? She wasn't feeling the tearing that she had anticipated from a true confession, a rending of her sinful soul.

"You believe in the soul, I suppose." She let her darting thoughts turn the conversation again.

"I do, of course. Though I suspect many people are unclear what they mean by 'soul.' I've often heard people confuse soul and spirit, two different concepts in biblical thought. The soul is what we call the psyche these days, the same root word."

"Ah. So, my soul is what it is. My personality. Something to be shaped in therapy. But beyond saving."

"Beyond saving? Well, I can see why you say that. But I wouldn't minimize the value of healing a soul. I've seen plenty of evidence of the significance of a wounded soul. It's real, and it's painful. And I'm not just speaking of *other* people."

She allowed half a beat. "You have a wounded soul?"

"I think most of us do. Everyone I know well seems to have some sort of soul wound."

"But then there's this thing called a 'spirit?'"

"I believe there is. The part of us that's eternal."

"I don't know if I believe in that." She had no idea what she wanted him to say about her doubt. Did she want him to convince her? To convert her? Before she met Virgil, her lack of interest in conversion was unequivocal.

He didn't go in for the kill. "Well, we can certainly talk about that sometime. But, right now, I think you need to forgive the eighteen-year-old who saw her parents doing something she really didn't understand."

"Forgive her? Forgive myself? For ... for not understanding."

"I know it sounds like we should never have to forgive

someone for that kind of thing. But Jesus seemed to think it was necessary. 'Forgive them, for they don't know what they're doing.'"

"That sounds familiar."

"Even without that reference, I'm confident that almost anyone can see that letting yourself off for a crime of ignorance is healthy. Judging your teenaged self is a lot like those undergraduates harshly treating people from earlier centuries, I think."

"Ah. Hoist by my own petard."

"Ha. I haven't heard that phrase for ages."

"Shakespeare. Sort of."

"Yes." He hesitated. "Maybe you want to do this privately, after we get off the phone. But sometimes it's helpful to say it aloud so someone else can hear it."

"This is standard confessional protocol?"

"Your option."

"Umm-hmm." She paused to wonder at her frequent swerves away from the topic at hand. But that, too, was a distraction.

"Okay. I forgive the eighteen-year-old me, Lenny, for not understanding, and for judging her mother, my mother, far too harshly. I forgive you." A spurt of emotion popped in a sob and then a spontaneous laugh.

"Ha."

"Yes? That felt good, didn't it?"

"It did."

"I could feel it all the way over here."

"You could?" She stopped herself from investigating yet another rabbit trail.

"Your nickname was Lenny?"

"Yes. I may have to revisit that, too. My dad called me that, and my mother went along with it. I'm wondering how that affected me growing up."

"A boy's name, you mean?"

141

"Yes. Clearly, there were some gender issues going on with my dad. Did he try to convert me to his ways? Or was there any intentionality to it at all?"

"That would probably be a good thing to pursue in the future. But I think you just covered some very important ground. Maybe you don't need to go for another one right away."

"You do this sort of thing all the time, don't you?"

"I would like to. But you probably won't be surprised to hear that folks around here are hesitant to go that deep into their emotional past. I don't think our church members are keeping the counselors around the area in business."

"Oh. Hmm. That's interesting." Abstractly, it was interesting. But she was glad to let it go for now.

"Well. Take some time to be quiet and listen to your soul. Let the change settle in. I expect you will notice a difference before long."

After their call, Eleanor tried to follow Virgil's advice. But scurrying around the house distracted her, including answering a phone call from David. His condolences were personal and careful, just like him. She almost told him about her breakthrough confession with Virgil. But she held back, inexplicably shy about letting him into that experience.

It was when she sat across from Candice at a steel-topped table in The Caboose, that Eleanor noted what seemed like the first fruit of that breakthrough.

"I loved your mother. So many people around here did. As an artist, she was loved and respected, of course. But, as a person, she was so full of life, like she always had more to give. I always felt like it was me that was limiting our relationship. I was so wounded after my own mother died."

Here was a young woman confessing to Eleanor. It was so easy to see her as Virgil's daughter. Eleanor had to peel back the urge to assemble a little movie of those father and daughter interactions. She stayed with Candice's confession.

"I suppose that reserve is the sort of thing you can see in retrospect. But the very fact that you studied with her was an opportunity seized."

Candice nodded and attended to her salad.

Eleanor could imagine Candice enjoying the attention of Connie. And she welcomed that picture. She welcomed the maternal link between this lovely young woman and her mother. No hint of jealousy. No drag of resentment against her mother. This was new, wasn't it? Eleanor, so free with her mother's affections?

In place of resentment, Eleanor rose on a bubbling giddiness. Not wanting to explain herself to Candice, she tried to point her thoughts in a different direction.

"I'm so excited to hear about my mother teaching. I knew only very vaguely that she did some of that. It makes me feel more connected to her, as a teacher myself, of course." She manufactured that out of the air, air laden with Italian spices, sweet soda syrup and beer. She glanced toward the sunny windows and hoped Candice wouldn't notice her rapid breathing.

Candice laughed. "I see her joy in you." She seemed to be restraining her own giddiness now.

Probably blushing, Eleanor turned toward Candice before bowing over her lunch.

Toward the end of the meal, Candice's eyes shifted shyly. "I have a confession to make."

"More confessions?"

"What?"

"Nothing. Go ahead."

"Well, there was another reason I wanted to meet with you." She raised her eyebrows apologetically. "You know my dad has been single for a long time." She fiddled with her fork, abandoned by her plate. "And I know I'm meddling. But I just wanted to say that I ... I saw him light up with you ..." She checked for Eleanor's reaction. "I saw it in a way that I haven't seen, not since Mom died." She sat up straight and looked candidly at Eleanor. "I hope that's not just too weird for me to say."

Eleanor held a deep breath, straightened her back, and blinked with her brows raised. "Well. That probably is a bit strange. But I'm guessing you saw something in my responses to your dad that emboldened you to say this to me."

Candice laughed harder. "I did. I thought I saw you light up in the same way, though it was clear that you were hurting." She paused to sip her water, gripping and releasing the clear plastic straw. "I thought it was worth taking a chance. I didn't know if anything would come of it, but I hoped you wouldn't mind a daughter's well-meaning interference."

"Ha. Yes. I think old single people probably need some well-meaning interference now and again. It's easy to just settle in where you are."

"Right. That describes my dad. I don't want to say more about him. But I just think you two have some ... possibilities, at least."

Eleanor nodded slowly. "Yes. Maybe some possibilities."

CHAPTER EIGHTEEN

Her delay at getting out of bed on Tuesday had bumped her trip to the bank to *after* her lunch with Candice.

In the safe deposit booth inside the holy of holies at the bank, she sat by herself. Perhaps this would have felt lonelier without her conversations with Virgil and Candice that day. They both remained with her in that dim, little room, under the tiny, canned lights illuminating the black table and the broad metal box set on it.

There were no grand secrets revealed in that box. No keys to a covert villa in Tuscany. No gold bars. No clues about the location of the lost treasures of past civilizations.

There was a marriage license. The title to the house. And titles to a pair of cars. Those car titles reminded Eleanor that she should decide what to do with the old silver Honda parked to one side of the driveway. The other car had been sold for scrap a long time ago, as far as she could remember.

There was also a birth certificate for one Eleanor Elizabeth Petersen. She was still thankful Connie had resisted giving her the middle name Roosevelt, as her father had wanted. Or maybe that had only been a joke between her parents.

She pulled a leather-bound volume off the bottom of the box, assuming it was a ledger of accounts. She had found nothing like that in the house, only bits and pieces of data and documentation.

But this wasn't a ledger. It was a scrapbook. An ancient scrapbook. More accurately, a newish book of ancient scraps.

How long she sat there turning pages, reading newspaper clippings, studying photographs, she couldn't say. She instinctively pondered the authenticity of birth certificates, marriage licenses and death certificates from a hundred years ago and more. But here was a family heirloom that was a historian's dream.

"Thank you, Mom. Thanks, Dad."

When Eleanor coasted up the driveway to the farmhouse, she had to steer clear of a white minivan. A woman she didn't recognize was speed-walking away from the house. The stout woman slowed and visored her eyes from the high sun to watch Eleanor's approach.

Climbing out of the little hybrid car, Eleanor attempted a friendly smile that forced away the curious scowl natural in a situation like this. Every stranger she had met in the last few days had been welcomed. She had no reason to assume this one was different.

"Are you Mrs. Petersen? Connie's daughter?" She spoke with a moderate Hispanic accent.

"Eleanor." She reached her hand in greeting and wondered if it was fair to assume that this was Consuela. She knew of so few Hispanics in this area.

"Hello. I work at The Dove's Nest. Your mother used to volunteer there. I brought some of the things she left from when she used to spend the night. It had been a while, but she still had those things there."

"Are you Consuela?"

"Oh. Yes. I forgot to say. Sorry. Yes, I am Consuela. Your mother called me that. Everyone else calls me Connie. You know why."

Eleanor smiled and released Consuela's hand. "I know why." She gestured toward the house. "I was wanting to talk to you about something else. Do you have a moment to come inside?"

"Uh. I guess so. Just a few minutes."

"It will only take a few. I want to show you something and ask your advice."

Consuela seemed impressed, perhaps that the older woman was seeking her advice. She followed Eleanor up the front walk.

Leading her guest to the front door so she could pick up the brown paper bag left next to it, Eleanor protected herself from looking inside that bag. Only later would she sample the poignancy of her mother spending nights at the house where Yvonne lived. She smiled minimally at Consuela as she unlocked the door.

"I met Yvonne in town the other day. I recognized her because my mother used her as a model for some paintings."

Consuela was nodding like a person waiting for the point of these opening comments. But then she stepped from the sunlight into the living room. Her eyes must have adjusted more quickly than Eleanor's, because she gasped sooner than her hostess anticipated.

"Oh, Dios mio! It's her. Oh, how beautiful."

Feeling no more need to explain, at least for the moment, Eleanor closed the front door and settled the paper bag on top of the wide bookshelf. She sluffed off her wool coat and dropped her purse on the floor.

"My mother mentioned these portraits in her will. I think there might be more, but I haven't gone through all of the paintings in storage. They would all be around here somewhere. She wasn't showing these in galleries." Eleanor was probably saying things about which this woman didn't care. So, she hastened to land on the real point. "My mother *gave* these to Yvonne, to do whatever she wants with them. On the market, they could be worth a lot of money, especially shown all together. But whether they are shown or sold is entirely up to Yvonne."

Consuela was frowning at Eleanor. "How can Yvonne decide? She is not sure what is real most of the time. How will she know what to do with these?"

Clasping her hands in front of her, Eleanor shrugged. "I

147

don't know. I only spoke with Yvonne very briefly, and that was before I heard the reading of the will." She remembered now that the will included a sizable donation to The Dove's Nest. She wasn't sure Consuela would have anything to do with that and set that thought aside. "Even if they just go into storage somewhere, I have to offer them to Yvonne. Can I meet with her?"

Looking now at Eleanor as if she had just asked her to dance, Consuela seemed to contemplate the options. Eleanor suspected the caregiver might be including running from the house as one of her options. But maybe she was misreading the smaller woman's body language.

"I can arrange that. You could meet with her at the house. Or you could take her to Roger's Diner. She likes to have people take her there. It makes her feel normal, I think."

It was Eleanor's turn to stand speechless. What was she getting herself into?

"Okay. So, should I meet her at the diner? Or pick her up at the house and take her to Roger's?"

"You can come get her at the house. I can have her ready. You would have to be on time. She gets nervous if she has to wait."

"Okay. Can I buy her supper?"

"Yes. She eats at five-thirty."

"Oh. Okay. Pick her up at precisely five-thirty? Or a few minutes before?"

"Five-thirty will be okay. Just be on time."

Though she came across as a bit gruff, Consuela's conversation style had probably been affected by hours and days dealing with people like Yvonne. Eleanor looked past that brusque manner to the point of her admonitions. She would arrive on time.

And she did. At 5:25 she pulled to the curb in front of a beautifully painted Victorian house, deep gray with cream trim and touches of dusty rose. A pleasant place, at least from the outside.

Eleanor slowly stepped out of her rental car, trying to guess if she was expected at the front door or just by the curb. She paced slowly up the front walk in indecision, glancing at the wood-frame houses on either side. Would she cause trouble by being early? Consuela's cautionary tone had clearly left an impression.

The front door opened at what must have been a minute or two before five-thirty. Consuela led Yvonne onto the covered porch. "Good. You are on time. Yvonne is all ready for dinner. She understands now that you are Connie's daughter. And she understands that Connie has passed away." She turned as if to wait for a reaction from Yvonne.

"I didn't go to the funeral. But she told me Connie was dead." She nodded toward Eleanor. "That really happened."

"Yes, it did." Consuela seemed satisfied that a sort of obstacle had been safely navigated.

Eleanor was relieved that she wouldn't have to remind Yvonne of Connie's death. Addressing that once had been enough.

Instead of the odd walk Eleanor had witnessed Yvonne doing before they met, her dinner guest stalked toward the car with her hands slightly raised at her sides, a bit like a character in a horror film expecting werewolves or vampires to break from cover on either side. Eleanor looked to Consuela for some clue about how to think about that eccentricity. Consuela was watching Yvonne, but she offered Eleanor no interpretation of her behavior.

Instead of continuing to critique Yvonne's gait, Eleanor turned toward the rental car and reached for the passenger door. Yvonne arrived and stopped. She seemed to be waiting for something more. Then she ducked her head and crawled onto the seat. Eleanor had to wait for Yvonne to resituate herself with her feet flat on the floor.

Resisting a glance at Consuela, who seemed determined to

leave Eleanor on her own with Yvonne, she walked around the car and reflexively pressed the unlock button on the remote. Of course, the car was already unlocked, so that only caused the horn to honk once. Instantly, Yvonne stopped pulling on her seatbelt. She grabbed the door handle instead, as if prepared to dive onto the curb.

Eleanor stood with the driver's door opened. "Sorry. I hit the button an extra time. I didn't mean to do that." But explaining seemed to settle nothing.

Yvonne remained vigilant.

"You should buckle up, otherwise the car will make more noises."

"You heard that? That beep? There's no other cars here. I heard a beep."

"I'm sorry. That was *this* car. It was a mistake. Please buckle your seatbelt."

Without looking at Eleanor, Yvonne landed her upper back against the seat and reached again for the seatbelt, as if this spaceship was about to blast off.

Eleanor considered praying at this point. But she suspected God would recognize the hypocrisy and she didn't want to tempt him to more judgment. This thought led to wondering what Virgil was doing for dinner. He would probably be helpful in such a cross-psychological encounter as this.

"Okay. Here we go." She started the car, which made little noise at first, just humming sounds, followed by a singing, like an angel choir in the distance. Yvonne was plastered to her seat with one hand still gripping the door handle.

Eleanor did pray then. "Help me, Lord." But she kept that to herself and hoped for divine mercy regarding her past silence.

The drive to the diner and a very normal walk from the car to the restaurant offered Eleanor some hope that Yvonne's odd behavior stayed within a modest range, one that allowed her to get out of the house and into the community without crises.

Eleanor was still recovering from Yvonne's hasty flight after hearing the news of Connie's death. But she could hardly blame someone for an extreme response to that news. It had upended *her* life ever since she received the first call from Paul. Right now, she was looking forward to dinner with him the next night. That would be a vacation compared to this.

Yvonne stopped inside the front door of Roger's Diner. "You know that I'm with you. You want me here, right? I didn't ask you?"

"Yes. Of course. Roger will be fine with it. He knows me. He knows that I know you, too. He knew my mother."

"Everyone knew her, of course." Yvonne led the way through the inner door, having completed that preliminary confirmation process.

Eleanor followed without further comment. Once inside, Yvonne yielded to Eleanor in choosing a seat. The woman behind the counter was unfamiliar. She spoke without looking squarely at the two, who now stood assessing the restaurant.

"Sit anywhere you like. I'll be with you in a minute."

After trying to calculate the optimal place without knowing all the issues that should direct that decision, Eleanor lurched toward the window booths. She landed next to the one where she sat the last time she saw Yvonne. Perhaps caught by surprise at Eleanor's sudden step toward the booth, Yvonne remained standing just inside the entryway.

"Yvonne. Over here. Is this all right?"

"All right for me or all right for you?"

"Well, for both."

"Okay." She sat down and took her knit cap off and stuffed it in a side pocket. Her coat was a burgundy quilted winter jacket of a fairly recent style. The hat with the animal ears on it was the sort of thing Eleanor had seen undergraduates wearing at

Carlisle for years—quirky, cute and edgy all at once.

"Consuela is called Connie, too."

"Oh. Yes. I discovered that. My mother's friends call her 'the other Connie.'"

"I don't."

Eleanor nodded, not sure she wanted to find the end of that unraveled string.

"I wanted to talk to you about the paintings my mother did of you. I've found seven of them." She accepted a menu from the waitress and studied Yvonne for a response to this introduction. What she saw silenced her.

A girlish glow began to emanate from her face, as if the version of Yvonne that Eleanor had met was just the cocoon. A butterfly began to emerge now before her eyes.

The waitress backed away and retreated to the counter.

Yvonne was languidly lifting her right hand and brushing the back of her fingernails gently up her cheek, her eyes half closed. "I was beautiful. Stunning. Gorgeous." Then she seemed to alight back in that booth. And she opened her eyes to fixed them on Eleanor. "Connie said that. The painter. Not Consuela."

"My mother."

Yvonne stared at Eleanor. Then she leaned forward and squinted slightly. She squeezed her eyes more intensely. "Are you sad?" She relaxed a little but didn't pull back. "I was very sad. I thought it wasn't true." She sat up straight. Her voice rose. "Just one of their lies." Then more calmly. "But I already knew. She came to say goodbye." Turning toward the window. "She was laying on the ice. That made me sad."

It had happened to Eleanor once before. This silent suspension of all motion. This captivity in a moment. That first time was during the call from Paul Wasser. "I'm so sorry to tell you, your mother has died."

In that instant, Eleanor had waved a stunned farewell to her past life, to the recognizable places and times, and to any hope of ever finding her way out of the capsule of that revelation.

She was captivated again.

Connie had visited Yvonne to say goodbye? Literally? Physically? Or ...

For a second, she couldn't recall exactly what Yvonne had said. But then she knew that was denial. She tried to advance her thoughts out of that stall. Restart. Step forward.

"You saw her? She came to you?"

Yvonne's voice rose again. "You can't ask me that." She shifted her eyes side to side. "It might encourage my ... it might encourage the ... the things ..." She resorted to a whisper. "You're not supposed to encourage that."

That warning clarified what Eleanor had heard. Yvonne wasn't describing a literal physical visit. She was describing something her psychiatrist would consider a delusion.

Yvonne couldn't say more. Eleanor wouldn't ask her to. And Eleanor would just have to believe what she believed. To tuck away what she had heard.

"Okay. I understand. We don't have to speak of it again."

"Then we understand *each other*."

"Yes, we do. We both loved Connie. The painter."

"The painter." Yvonne stared at the tabletop as if they had finished a liturgy. Head bowed. A moment of silence.

Perhaps it would serve as grace before dinner.

Eleanor picked up her copy of the menu.

CHAPTER NINETEEN

Arranging to bring Yvonne to the house required a personal consultation with Consuela and a phone conversation with a younger woman who would be covering for Consuela on Wednesday morning. Eleanor drove to The Dove's Nest again and arrived exactly at nine-thirty. The appointed time.

"I know this car now. I've been in this car before." Yvonne pecked the air in front of her before climbing in, as if punctuating her declarations with her nose.

"Yes. You have been in this car. I left it unlocked this time, so it won't beep at us again." Eleanor walked around the car but slowed as Yvonne seemed delayed by her comment, a moment of consternation written in scrunched eyebrows and the slightest nodding that could qualify as more than a palsied tremor.

Eleanor restarted her trip around the car to the driver's side. She settled into her seat without staring at Yvonne. But her left hand shook visibly as she pulled the door shut. Yvonne was just now settling into the passenger seat.

"I can see the paintings. They are at Connie's house?"

Eleanor paused before answering, wondering what manner of statement this was. A question? Was Yvonne questioning the nature of reality again? The actual visibility of the paintings? Or was she clarifying their destination? Eleanor opted for a complete reiteration. "I found some of the paintings in her barn and brought them into the house. They each had your name on them. There are eight of them now. That might be all of them. Connie said that you can do what ..."

"I know. I remember."

Too much information, apparently. It was, of course, repetitive, except the part about the eighth painting. That one had been hanging on the wall in the basement, next to the flat-screen TV. Her mother's media room was crude, a recent development. Eleanor would never have hung a painting so close to the TV. Had the painting been hung first? Or the TV?

Yvonne seemed to have an information capacity that Eleanor was prone to overfill, given her tendency to lecture and clarify.

"How did you know that Connie was dead?" Yvonne was once again pressed back in her seat with a hand clutching the contoured door handle. That handle seemed appropriately designed for just such an anxious grip.

"How did I find out? Paul Wasser called me. He found her."

"Paul Wasser is not her husband."

"No. Connie's husband was Darrel. He was my father."

"How did Paul Wasser know that Connie was dead?"

Again, Eleanor struggled with that wording. Was it the event of discovering Connie that Yvonne was seeking to understand? Or was it the perception of the reality of death?

"He found her lying on the ice one day, when he went to her house to check on things. He fixes things around the house."

"He was a handyman."

"Yes. And he still is."

"And he was sure that she was dead?" Her intonation wasn't quite right for a question, but Eleanor adjusted for Yvonne's generally wooden tone, dull and emotionless most of the time.

"He was sure. But he called an ambulance just in case. Maybe he was hoping they could revive her, since she was frozen." A bubble of pain swelled into Eleanor's throat. Oh, if only it had been true. Why couldn't they warm her up? Bring her back?

Yvonne sighed audibly. Eleanor glanced at her.

"I am so sad." Yvonne addressed the windshield.

Eleanor chirped a small sob and bit it off. She was so sad, too. But she was driving.

155

Yvonne turned toward her. "It's all right. I can't feel things. Don't worry." She paused as if she were dissatisfied with her own words. "I mean, I'm sorry to make you sad."

Squeezing the steering wheel, as if to choke the car with her bare hands, Eleanor shuttered her emotions again. "It's okay. I'm sad all the time. It's not your fault."

They drove for another minute, up Main Street.

"Whose fault is it?"

Eleanor eased in a big breath as she signaled for the left turn onto the highway. "I think it was really no one's fault. I don't really think I want to blame anyone. I've been blaming ... Connie for too many things in my life."

"I had a difficult relationship with my mother."

Eleanor snorted and then sniffled sharply. She needed a tissue. "Mothers can be difficult sometimes." Then an implication of Yvonne's revelation expanded. "Was Connie like a mother to you?"

Glancing quickly at Eleanor and then away, Yvonne re-gripped the door handle as they accelerated up the hill toward the farmhouse. "Don't make me more sad."

"Of course. I'm sorry."

Okay. No more therapeutic questions. Not even historical inquiries with emotional implications. Was it even possible to meet those standards? Eleanor turned the car up the driveway. She climbed out and Yvonne did the same, following her to the back door. Eleanor would, of course, not point out the spot where her mother had been found by Paul Wasser.

As Eleanor fumbled to unlock the back door, Yvonne was looking at the Honda Accord parked by the barn. Yvonne must have ridden in that car a few times. Connie had bought that car to replace her husband's beloved Cadillac. She had never liked the big car. "An old man's car," she called it. The only drawback of the Honda was its limited size, given her need to haul canvases.

Tugging her focus back to the task at hand, Eleanor pushed the back door open. In the house, she led Yvonne directly to the living room. She had stacked all eight of the paintings against the bookshelves across from the couch, facing away. All the other paintings in the room had been carefully propped in corners. A simple presentation seemed best, given Yvonne's limitations.

"Do you want anything to eat or drink?"

"Can I see first?"

"Of course." Eleanor dropped her coat on a dull beige stuffed chair. "Do you want to take your coat off?"

Yvonne complied without moving her focus. She was staring at one of the piles of paintings, not the ones of her. Eleanor took Yvonne's coat and slung it over a chair.

"Over here. These are yours." She lifted the first one and spun it around, setting it gently on an old dining room chair next to the shelves. That was her plan for how to display them. The plan was a work in progress.

The absolute stillness that settled on Yvonne arrested Eleanor into a similar state. Then a smile began to grow on Yvonne's face. She reached first one hand and then the other up to her shirt front, a blue plaid flannel shirt half tucked in. Delicately perusing the tips of her fingers over the clothes she was wearing, Yvonne remained enthralled with the painting.

Eleanor tried to imagine pulling out a second painting. The animated response elicited by the first seemed to warn of overload at the next step up.

"Why do they call it a pair of underwear? It's just one."

"Huh?" Eleanor couldn't pretend to take that stray inquiry in stride. "What made you think of that?"

"Connie didn't know. She thought it was funny." A pained smile remained on her face as she turned it briefly toward Eleanor. But Yvonne's eyes remained cabled to her portrait. Her head rotated back.

Eleanor chuckled from the back of her throat. "That *is* funny. It makes no sense. But that is what we all say."

"See."

"Yes. I do." Eleanor relaxed a bit. "Do you want to see more of the paintings?"

"I want to see all of them."

"Of course." Still, Eleanor hesitated to overwhelm her guest. She lifted one painting and carried it to the couch, turning it around and propping it on the seat in the way she had displayed three of the paintings before.

"More." Yvonne turned from one painting to the other. Her dull intonation obscured the meaning of that one word. Was she reiterating her call for seeing them all? Or was she celebrating the addition of another exhibit?

Eleanor accommodated her previously stated wish, even if she doubted Yvonne's capacity to take it all in.

By the time all eight paintings were visible, Yvonne was spinning slowly around and around, a gleeful grin on her face. Her eyes were brightly lit for the first time that Eleanor had seen. Instead of overwhelming her, the display of her own beauty, shown through the eyes of someone who clearly loved her, pulsed life out through Yvonne's formerly frozen face.

It was Eleanor who was overwhelmed by this pageant. And not the display of the paintings. She had already warmed herself with sips and gulps of the vision revealed on those canvases. She was overwhelmed now by the joy that spun Yvonne and radiated around the room.

* * *

Sitting across the table from Paul Wasser later that evening, Eleanor tried to recount the experience for him. "I was afraid. Her emotions seem so cut off. And I had seen her sort of blow up over hearing that Connie was dead." She shook her head. "I could never have believed what a transformative effect those paintings would have on her."

"But you think it wasn't just the paintings, it was remembering Connie?"

"I do. Yvonne spent a lot of time touching things in the studio, before she left. She seems to have trouble knowing what's real and what's only her imagination. So, she was touching everything—the easels, the other paintings, the tubes of paint, the brushes. She must have been remembering my mother, and not just making sure that the things were real." Eleanor had to catch her breath, pausing to sip water.

Paul signaled for the waiter to refill her water glass. She had refused wine but found that she needed lots of water. They were in the third restaurant in town, one she and her mother had visited a several times—The Excelsior. The grand name may have been more appropriate in its glory days, fifty years before. On a Wednesday night, it wasn't crowded.

In the midst of the meal, Eleanor decided to face the most obvious pending item between her and Paul. "Virgil Meers walked me through a process of forgiving myself for some of my mistakes in my relationship with my mother. It was stunningly effective." She leaned her elbows on the table, wondering if she should be so bold. "Are you still blaming yourself for my mother's death?"

Paul set down his knife and fork, nearly finished with the thick porkchop on his plate. He wiped his mouth with the white cloth napkin and reached for his water. Perhaps he would have preferred beer. But he was driving and had been the first to order only water. "I *am* still blaming myself." His eyes traveled over the table, up her arm to her face. "But you think I should somehow forgive myself?" He didn't sound skeptical, as much as shy about accepting the offer.

"Well, it feels like unfinished business between us. Am I

right?"

"I guess so. Sure." He took a deep breath. "I know how people are, though, especially around here. You know, they just don't wanna get into hard things, afraid of offending. So, when you say you don't blame me, I worry that you're just saying it to be polite." He contemplated that pork chop now, as if to measure whether there was room for it alongside these fears he couldn't digest.

"I do know what you mean. But I'm not like that." She smiled. "I'm not really from around here. I may not be from New York City, but I *am* a New Yorker now, and I've been one for thirty-three years. I think that has made me generally more direct. Not so polite in the way a Wisconsin housewife might be." She waited to see if he accepted her credentials. One raised eyebrow seemed to imply an opening. His hands still rested next to his fork and knife.

Eleanor returned to cutting her salmon with her fork. "I would confront you if I thought there was something to confront you about. You're not so scary as to stop me from speaking up." She paused and looked at him. "I don't blame you, Paul. I don't even blame Connie." Slipping a morsel of fish into her mouth, she was trying to appear nonchalant. Fortunately, the salmon was tender and wouldn't be difficult to swallow, even down her half-constricted throat. She reached for her water again.

He was nodding. His voice seemed renewed. Almost excited. "I can just imagine Connie with this burning idea about a new painting." He paused as if for Eleanor to catch up. "Maybe she stopped in the middle of another one she was doing. And she just had to get out to the barn to find exactly the right-sized canvas. She couldn't just use one of the ones sitting right next to her in the studio. It's the way she was. The way her art was for her. She just had to go out into the cold night to find the perfect canvas." Paul was almost grinning, looking past her, his eyes round.

Then he adjusted his gaze to take in Eleanor more directly.

She couldn't speak. But she could see. She could see her mother driven by an artistic inspiration to trek out to the barn in the cold.

Paul's voice broke into that imagining. "You're not exactly like her. But I can sense something of her in you, maybe like her spirit or something."

That might have prompted a denial from Eleanor a few weeks ago. But the joy she had discovered in the lives of the people in this little town, joy inspired by her mother, made Paul's words a generous compliment.

"I hope so. I hope you're right."

In the rising and strolling and driving back toward her mother's house, Eleanor welcomed a clarity about her and Paul. She had never actively considered the prospect of romance between them, but she had worried that he might have wanted that, or something like it. Now she felt certain that the sort of leaning toward her that she had detected, or at least suspected, had been from his desire for forgiveness, for a *convincing* forgiveness. Whatever existed between them now seemed purified by her pardon offered and apparently accepted.

"Thanks for dinner, Paul."

"Thank you." He looked like he might say something more but turned his head toward the darkness outside the storm door. "I'll keep an eye on the place. See you in the summer?"

"Yes. I'll be back before the end of May."

"Good."

And he left her there alone in her mother's house, which was gradually becoming more her own, with every passing day.

CHAPTER TWENTY

"So, you have my email address, as well as my phone number?"

"I do. Yes. I have them both on my phone now."

She fiddled her thumb over a sharp corner on the nail of her index finger. A professional manicure was overdue.

"No need to say anything about the unfortunate timing of leaving so soon, I suppose."

"No. It won't help. And we can start by corresponding. We're both good at words."

She laughed. "Yes. We are both good at words."

He laughed with her.

She resisted a melancholy tug and tried to project energy. "Good. We really will stay in touch. Not just saying that."

"Right. Not just saying it."

"That's good."

"Goodbye, Eleanor."

"Goodbye, Virgil."

She wanted to swear.

"Damn."

That didn't help.

Other words, more profoundly profane or blatantly blasphemous, wouldn't help either.

She forced herself to stand up from her mother's desk chair. "Get up, Eleanor." She glanced at the window. "I'm not Lenny anymore." Those who had called her Lenny were no longer in the land of the living.

Eleanor.

That long conversation with Virgil had ended in a commitment to stay in touch. Not just a generic polite promise. A real covenant based on possibilities, even intentions.

The sky outside the lone window in that office was un-marred blue. Pure and wide open. This was one of those days where everything felt poignant, even if purely mundane.

She hated days like this. All trips should start at five a.m., to avoid the breathless waiting that filled everything with longing and sorrow. She was stuck in that place waiting for the drive to the airport.

Rosemary would pick her up in Syracuse and drive Eleanor to her townhouse near the university. Her graduate student had ignored spring break in favor of working on her thesis. Eleanor tried to think about Rosemary's thesis now. Doing so would surely transport her back to her real life, her permanent life.

Was her life back in New York really permanent?

What was she thinking about?

Eleanor was turning sixty-five this summer and had been considering retiring in the next few years. What about the next few months? This was the first time she had allowed that question to stretch to its full height. She would have options after retirement— traveling, lecturing and publishing. Why not take advantage of those opportunities while she was still mobile and energetic enough to enjoy them? She could break free from the politics of heading a department in a modern university. And that would leave her to her research. She could explore more places, absorb the context, the context of her studies in American business and the role of women in developing it.

Was all this just preflight panic? She wasn't afraid of flying. But the tension of making travel connections always erased some measure of her rational capacity.

She forced herself again through the checklist required before leaving her mother's house. Her house. Her Wisconsin house. She had a Wisconsin house now. And she had all those paintings.

No dog, however.

Turning away from the window, Eleanor glanced around the office. She walked out to the hall where two stacks of paintings required a careful step. She was still debating moving them back to the barn. But, with no one living here, the paintings could just as well benefit from the environmental controls of the house. The conditions for storage in the house had to be at least as good as the barn. She would come up with more permanent storage priorities when she came back for the summer.

Down the stairs she swept, unable to stop herself from walking straight ahead into the living room. There, a portrait of Yvonne glancing over her shoulder invited Eleanor to join her.

Yvonne's gaze was an invitation to investigate.

What is that? Who is that? What's back there?

This was Yvonne, still in Eleanor's house.

Yvonne had gone home with seven of the paintings. Eleanor had helped carry them up the stairs to Yvonne's room. Patricia, the caregiver on duty, had stared dumbfounded when Eleanor explained what she was doing. But the young woman eventually agreed to see that those seven portraits would be hung in Yvonne's room. Patricia seemed to be calculating whether there was space to fulfill this commitment when Eleanor left.

But one portrait remained here.

As they had begun to gather them up, Yvonne had held one out to Eleanor. "This is for you."

"For me? Why? Connie gave them to you."

"I can give them. She gave them to me. I can give it to you. This one."

"But, why?"

"So you can feel it too."

"Feel what?"

"Being beautiful."

Eleanor took the painting and stood staring at the woman in

the white blouse and the red skirt. She held onto it for a while. Setting it down seemed rude, inappropriate.

Yvonne released her. "You can put it there." She pointed to the couch.

That was where that painting of the joyful and beautiful woman still sat on Thursday. Eleanor stood in the middle of the room with an arm crossed over her chest. She caught herself fingering her hair where it hung around her right ear. Like Yvonne might do.

Her mother had given Yvonne something priceless. And it wasn't only paintings worth a hundred thousand dollars or more. She had given Yvonne her own beauty. Connie had given her a view of herself that no mirror could provide. The reflection in Connie's eyes was truer to the beauty inherent in Yvonne.

Eleanor pressed her fingers to her lips, holding a tearful spasm inside. That encapsulated emotion wasn't actually painful, where it lodged there at the top of her diaphragm. It felt okay. Maybe good. Connie had given that to her. She had given Eleanor an assortment of emotions, some too big to pass with a breath or to release with a shower of tears.

Impulsively, Eleanor turned her loafers toward the basement, where she had seen a painting Amandar—a black box, hard-sided with strong nylon straps. She would try to take that painting onto the plane, checking her carry-on bag, if necessary. She would take Yvonne home with her. Yvonne's gift to her. Yvonne's gift of beauty.

The flight attendants stored the painting in the back of the plane, unfazed by the request, and Eleanor's carry-on-sized bag arrived on the luggage carousel in Syracuse without incident. Rosemary found her at the arrivals pickup. And then Eleanor was back home, her real home, familiar territory. It was the place where she had lived a life separated from her mother.

She had been to her mother's house at least twenty times in

the last ten years. This last time, however, Eleanor had so entwined herself with her mother that Connie's presence lingered
more intensely than after any visit when she was alive. This time,
Eleanor brought much more home with her. It included the
scrapbook from the safe deposit box, substituted for a travel bag
of toiletries which she could replace before her next trip. Of
course, she had taken heirlooms home before, memorabilia from
grandmothers and great-aunts, grandfathers and great-uncles
whom she had never met. On her bookshelf, she had an early
translation of *Les Misérables*, leather-bound and ornate. It had
belonged to her great-grandfather. He had been an avid Jean
Valjean fan, apparently.

But what Eleanor brought back from her mother's funeral
was much more substantial than books and paintings.

"You *have* changed. You have definitely changed." Jackie
had arrived back from her vacation the day before classes re-
sumed.

The second half of the semester awaited. And Eleanor was
feeling unprepared. In fact, she was teaching little that she
hadn't taught before. But she was unprepared to get back into
academic mode, back to that emotional neutrality. Or, at least,
that's what she feared.

"Recovery is a long process. Recovery from your mother's
death could take years. Healing from that resentment toward
yourself, like that pastor helped you with, that could take a
while, too." Jackie patted her on the cheek. "Don't worry. Lots of
people here have your back. Just ask if you need help."

Eleanor was grinning dumbly at her friend. She was thinking that Jackie had become like a mother to her in recent years,
more than Connie at times. And she was thinking that her relationship with Jackie was one thing that would keep her from retiring any time soon.

"Okay? You okay?"

"I am. Thank you. I will definitely be calling on you for rescue and for crying on your shoulder again and again."

"Then I'll be sure to wear washable clothes."

Eleanor's favorite seminar was offered in conjunction with the Women's Studies program. It was being attended exclusively by young women this term. Of course, male students weren't excluded from signing up for the course. But none had registered for this semester. It was only the second run of this particular syllabus. The subject matter tracked closely with her last book, and would help her focus on her next one, a biography of Madam C. J. Walker, reputed to be the first woman to become an American millionaire by owning her own business. Eleanor and Jackie would be writing that book together, alternating chapters.

On that Monday afternoon, in the Carter building—an ancient three-story structure that was probably a smoldering fire hazard—Eleanor entered the seminar room to the waiting faces of bright young women. Most of those faces were wearing a question. They had certainly heard about the death of her mother. Eleanor surrendered to their unspoken need.

"As you have probably heard, I have just returned from my mother's funeral. My mother was an artist who lived in southern Wisconsin, in a big farmhouse by herself. She outlived her husband by ten years and left one daughter. But she also left dozens of people that she generously loved and blessed. And she succeeded at establishing herself as a painter. You may come by my office sometime and see one of her portraits, a painting of a woman that I met this past week. I'll tell you about her if you come by."

The breathless silence in the room was mitigated only by the sound of the little fans in laptop computers around the tight formation of rectangular tables. Eleanor had seldom spoken about her personal life with these students, certainly nothing so expansive as this little obituary for her mother. But she was feeling free to acknowledge the large gathering in the room, the crowd of unspoken questions from her students, and even more questions from within herself.

"Professor Petersen?" In her office, a girl's voice broke Eleanor out of her consternation over the latest email from the academic dean. She wasn't even sure what the dean was trying to say, let alone whether she accepted his decision. She felt the obligation of her chairmanship, as well as her seniority, to oppose wayward policies introduced by the academic dean. Maybe he had obfuscated his position in that email to avert a confrontation. It would be hard to challenge something so convoluted. The language reminded her of an American conglomerate spinning confusion into its accounting practices in order to avoid effective audits.

"Tiffany. Come on in." Eleanor had office hours this afternoon and her door was standing open.

Stepping through the massive oak doorway, Tiffany glanced to her left and did a double take that landed her eyes on the portrait of Yvonne. Eleanor had regretted that the painting was dwarfed by the high walls and heavy woodwork. The thick gold frame she had selected for it was meant to battle back against those opposing forces.

"Is that it? Your mother painted that?"

Eleanor gripped the arms of her chair and stood up. She needed to stretch her legs anyway. Doctor's orders. She walked around the end of her desk and posted herself approximately in front of the portrait. Tiffany joined her there, shoulder-to-shoulder.

"She did. My mother painted eight portraits of Yvonne that I could find. She bequeathed them all to the woman in the painting. But Yvonne insisted that I take one of them."

"Why did she do that?"

"She said I needed it. She said that it would give me beauty. I think she said that because seeing herself in that painting made *her* feel beautiful. She has had a hard life and had a difficult relationship with her mother, she told me." Eleanor was glad to release all that. It was like having an idea for a chapter in her book and needing to get to the computer to compose a draft.

"Wow. That is so ... profound. So, it was like she was taking care of you. Was it 'cause your mother died?"

"Probably that. And maybe something deeper. She has schizophrenia and doesn't seem to feel emotions the way most people do. Maybe because of medication. But she seemed to intuit something about me, at least she thought she did."

"Well. The painting is beautiful. And I can see why it would make her feel beautiful." The slender sophomore was wise enough to stop there. She might have recognized the psychological implications of what Eleanor had admitted so far.

They turned together back toward the desk. They transitioned to discussing the topic for Tiffany's oral presentation in the seminar.

And Eleanor was back. She had been teaching for decades. She could easily find the autopilot switch and allow her instincts to fly her through the rest of the semester. Maybe that had always been a temptation. But the hungry young women and young men that entered her office and sat in her seminars insisted that she remain current and present, engaged with ideas and feelings outside her personal struggles, including grief.

Eventually, she hoped to face into the questions about her future. Questions that seemed to linger still on the prairie, east of a town inexplicably called Dove Lake, Wisconsin.

CHAPTER TWENTY-ONE

Dinner at David and Amanda's house, along with Jackie and Thomas, was a familiar event. But it had been so long since they had gathered that it felt a bit nostalgic. Eleanor opted not to bring a date this time. This gathering promised to be too intimate for her to introduce a wildcard, some man with whom she had only a tentative friendship and little history. She wasn't really dating anyone now.

"Are you still talking with that minister in Wisconsin?" Thomas was a man with a theatrical career that enriched even a simple question over dinner. She had first seen him in a large theater in Albany, where he had played Othello. That role might have influenced the way Eleanor heard his voice from then on.

"So, has that movie deal come through, Thomas?" She jumped to the most obvious diversion from the subject. But it wasn't a serious attempt.

"Am I sensing some reticence about discussing your long-distance relationship?" David stepped easily into faux therapist mode.

Eleanor grinned and reached for her wine. Was that one of her mother's little grins? She warmed to the idea. "What makes you say that?" She prolonged her sip to drag out the dramatic timing of this scene.

"She is keeping her intimate, long-distance, celibate relationship with a fundamentalist minister private from her friends for the time being." Jackie was playing along, but she brought out longer barbs than Eleanor would have expected.

Trying not to choke on the long sip of wine sliding down her throat, Eleanor shot a look at Jackie. "He's not a fundamentalist." She stopped there to consider the intriguing potential of a partial denial. It seemed a good place to let it lie.

At least three of the others laughed. Jackie seemed to be checking for open wounds on Eleanor's face. Was she afraid she had jabbed too hard? Eleanor smiled reassurance toward the other side of the table. That elicited a relieved smile from her best friend.

Then she took a leap. This was a high-powered collection of counselors that she would exploit while she had them gathered in one place. "I'm considering retiring after this year and going to live in the farmhouse, so I can focus more on writing." She only glanced at them before devoting her attention to buttering a dinner roll. Was that real butter?

"What?"

"Retiring?"

"You can't be serious."

Maybe they won't be willing counselors. But she would persist with this impromptu brainstorming session. Topic—Eleanor's life.

"You *are* serious, though, aren't you?" Amanda did the full-faced eye contact that was part of her winning charm. No one wondered why David had married her, against the weight of controversy over marrying a student. They all loved Amanda. Her intense sensitivity was so pure that one might easily doubt its genuineness, if that one didn't know Amanda as well as Eleanor did.

"I am at least half serious. I want to at least begin considering the possibility of retirement and not just fantasizing about it."

"Are you fantasizing about that minister?" David was probably not teasing.

"He is part of the picture. We've been keeping in touch. We aren't even beginning to discuss our relationship, though."

"So, you want to stop just thinking about retiring and start

171

talking about it." Thomas nodded sympathetically.

"Talking about it with dear friends who know me well."

"Although we may not know you as well as we used to." Jackie popped the last bite of one of those rolls into her mouth. They were the sort of sweet dinner rolls that Eleanor never bought for herself, because she knew she would eat the whole package in about two days. Maybe one.

She knew what Jackie was saying. "The things I learned about my relationship with my mother might really be transformative. So, I guess you're right that maybe I'm not the same person you knew earlier this year. I'm wondering if I really know myself now."

"Does everyone know about your father's confession to your mother?" Thomas glanced around the room. Of course, *he* knew something. Jackie had told her husband.

"My mother knew he was homosexual from early on, as far as I can tell. By the time they were old and retired they seemed entirely reconciled with it. She consciously chose to stay with him. My only question about that has been whether that makes her a heroine, a martyr or a drudge."

"Surely not a drudge." David was sitting up straight, fully focused on Eleanor.

"A drudge, in the sense of a woman oppressed by men and accepting of it?" Amanda was the one most likely to check on the definition of vocabulary in a discussion among these friends.

"My mother was a feminist for her day. A liberated woman of the seventies, if not a radical. So, I guess the real question is how *I* feel about her choice, and how it reflects on me."

"How could it reflect on you? You had no part in those decisions." Jackie was still eating at her usual pace. Certainly, this was all less startling to her.

David interjected. "It reflects on you, of course, because our parents teach us things subconsciously. They are key to forming our identity." The others seldom complained about his expert opinions on the human psyche. David wasn't a practicing therapist these days, only a professor. So, it felt like his psychological analysis was allowed. He wasn't doing therapy on Eleanor, just offering an informed perspective out of his field of study.

Eleanor was interested in his point. "That is important, I think. At least it raises an important question. Did I stay single all this time because I was uncertain about my own identity, or even my orientation? Did I inherit something from my parents somehow?"

"Does it really matter?" Thomas tossed back the last of his wine.

"It matters if I'm deciding about pursuing a potential relationship with a man."

"Is that what you want to do?" Amanda stopped herself in the process of rising from the table. She was probably going for more wine.

"Part of me *does* want that. The inconvenient thing is that I probably have to decide about retiring before I make a real try of it."

"What about a sabbatical? That would be less permanent, in case things don't work out in Wisconsin." Thomas glanced at Jackie. He might have been wondering if she and Eleanor had already discussed this. Jackie probably didn't tell him *everything*.

"I have thought of that. But I'm late in starting that process. Which is not the case with a retirement announcement." She weighed the facts. "But maybe there is still an option there."

"You still have some hesitation about the retirement?"

"I do. Some significant hesitation."

The next afternoon, Eleanor sat in her living room with one foot propped on the corner of her glass coffee table, the sole of her leather slipper protecting her foot from the sharp edge. She held her cell phone out in front of her, on speaker. "I want to ask you something, with the proviso that it is entirely preliminary. Purely in the testing phase. But I know I have to make arrangements immediately if I'm going to go ahead with it."

"Are you thinking of retiring?"

"I am. But I'm also weighing the option of just taking a sabbatical at first."

"That's two different things, two different processes." Gerald Grossman, the academic dean, had never been Eleanor's friend. As a colleague, he had been prickly at best. Getting him to cooperate with her sudden shift to a break from teaching was the most unattractive part of her exploration.

"I understand that, and that you oversee both. So, I'm coming to you to float the possibility."

"Possibilities."

"Yes. Possibilities. I would need to apply for either option right away, I know."

"Technically, it's too late for the sabbatical to begin in the next academic year. You can retire any time you want. You would receive a full pension." Was he promoting the retirement option?

"I would really prefer the sabbatical, if its available, so as not to lock myself into retirement so hastily."

"I hope you don't mind me asking, but is this because of your mother's death?"

"That has something to do with it. And I now have a farmhouse in Wisconsin. I need to take some time to decide what I want to do with it. I might like to live there, at least in warm-weather months." She wasn't going to dig deeper into her continued need for mourning her mother. Not with Gerald.

He released a heavy sigh over the landline in his office. He was working on a Saturday. No surprise to Eleanor. No matter how much they butted heads, she recognized that Gerald was hardworking.

He held a long pause. It was certainly his turn to talk. "I will discuss the sabbatical with the rest of the committee. That's all I can offer you for now. It *is* late. But I will give it a try for the coming year." Gerald had never been her advocate for anything. She hadn't needed him to be.

"Thanks for considering it. I very much appreciate it."

"You are welcome. I'll have an answer in a few days, I would think."

"Okay. Thanks again."

Her discussion with the people at dinner the previous evening had clarified one thing for Eleanor. Her urge to get to know Virgil wasn't the primary motivation for her prospective retirement. The value of that monumental change didn't depend on starting a relationship with him. So, she didn't mention her explorations to him, waiting until she knew something for sure.

"How is it different? Being back to work after your mother's passing?"

"Actually, I'm a little annoyed at myself for how easily I can just go right back into it, into this academic flow, and sort of set aside what I learned about Mom and what I still have back there at the farm."

Virgil made that knowing sound that often began his response. "Ahhh. So, it's more than your mother, it's something about the house as well."

"As much as I tried to talk her out of living there by herself, I was always sympathetic. The place has undeniable charm. I could see myself writing there. I've even thought that I could turn her bedroom into an office. It has the best view, unless I converted her studio. But that would feel like a sacrilege this soon."

"Well. I can see that you've put a lot of thought into this already." He paused.

She jumped in. "I'm probably conflating all these things together. I mean, the wonder and joy that my mother brought to people there is something seductive for me. I want some of that. I want to experience it and to spread it around. I can do that, to some extent, with her paintings. But that would require considerable focus. And I can only imagine doing that with the paintings around me." She paused this time. "And, of course, this is all still about mourning her, mourning my loss."

"Yes. Of course it is." His voice rose to a slightly higher note. "You wouldn't consider just shipping the paintings back East?"

"It would be interesting to see the reaction of East Coast buyers to mother's Midwestern rural art. The rustic appeal might be winning. I know she has some patrons around Chicago. But that's different, I think."

"Sure. Midwest versus East Coast, not just urban versus rural."

Virgil's agile intelligence warmed her in a way that she liked to savor, even during a phone call. It was so easy to understand him and to be understood by him.

"Well, I should get some sleep. Thanks for talking."

"I always enjoy talking with you, Eleanor. Thanks for calling."

"Good night, Virgil."

"Good night."

CHAPTER TWENTY-TWO

In the middle of her second week back at school, Eleanor sat in the small conference room near the academic dean's office. Gerald was there with Beatrice Smith and Lon Woodley. Eleanor felt like she had been called to the principal's office. But really, she had requested this meeting.

"Eleanor, how are you holding up after your trip to Wisconsin?" Beatrice introduced the subject of Connie's death without naming it, without naming her.

"I'm fine. Back to work. Keeping busy." It was a political answer, of course. What personal struggles was she willing to reveal to this committee?

"The reason we ask is because of the lateness of your sabbatical request." Gerald skipped right to the point. "It is technically too late for us to grant it for next year, unless there is a hardship." He paused as if waiting for her to get the translation. "The death of your mother qualifies as a hardship, in our opinion." She could almost imagine Gerald using the royal plural even with no other committee members involved in the decision.

A hardship? Was she a hardship case? Eleanor didn't want to be anybody's hardship case. She blinked back that thought for a few seconds.

"It would probably be a good idea for you to take some time. Perfectly normal and healthy, I'd say." Beatrice was a biology professor, elected to the academic dean's faculty committee, along with Lon and two other members not present.

Lon spoke up. "We're all in agreement." He flipped a thumb toward Gerald and Beatrice. "And we consulted the other members of the committee." Lon taught computer science classes, an associate professor these days.

Eleanor had asked for this break. But now she felt ashamed for asking. Her mother's mute grin presided over this meeting. Connie would never have allowed herself to be a hardship case. Dying as suddenly as she did had suited Connie. No one would ever have to wipe her chin or help her take a bath.

Grieving, processing her mother's exit from life, had happened entirely in the context of Eleanor and Connie, with occasional accompaniment by her father, and sympathy from her closest friends. This committee wasn't welcome inside the tight-lipped space created by Connie Petersen and her frozen death.

Shaking her head for just a moment, Eleanor managed to push past these hesitations, like pushing her head through the tight neck of a sweater. "Thank you. Thank you for granting my late request." She would *not* thank them for thinking of her as a hardship case. No thanks for that.

"So, you and I should meet again next week to discuss your scheduled classes and the parameters of your sabbatical. In the meantime, I will start the process of locating another history instructor to help fill in. Who would you recommend for acting chair of the department while you're gone?"

She shifted from supplicant to administrator. "Dierdre would be good at it, but I'm not sure she would accept. Peter might be more likely to accept. It might be a stretch for him. But I think he could grow into the opportunity."

"Good. I'm glad you've thought that through. I will approach Dierdre first and Peter after. Good choices, I think."

A scene from *It's A Wonderful Life* came to mind here. The one where George Bailey suddenly sees himself shaking hands with Mr. Potter and considering the old miser's job offer. Gerald was taking Eleanor's side, praising her choices. When had he ever been this agreeable? Was he anxious to usher her toward the door? Was he hoping the sabbatical would serve as an anteroom on her way out of the university?

But that was her original motivation. Moving away from her current responsibilities was her plan. Not a bad plan, just an uncomfortable one when Gerald endorsed it. She shook free once again.

*   *   *

"They said 'yes.' So why are you grumbling?" Jackie sat behind her desk, a modern black lacquered desk, more like what you might see in an architect's office than the old banker's desk Eleanor used. Eleanor's desk was more historical. Jackie's desk was more ... black. That had been the joke between them, years ago.

Nodding and sucking in a purging breath, Eleanor denied nothing. "You're right. It was just a shock to find myself under the sympathetic gaze of the academic dean. It was hard not to interpret his smile as malignant, his willingness as hope for a future free from me."

"I doubt he spends that much of his time scheming ways to get rid of you."

"It took him very little time. I handed him the opportunity."

Jackie leaned back. "You *do* need a break, Ellie. I think this waffling is proving that fact."

"Am I waffling? I'm just concerned that I may have made more of a decision than I intended. I gave Gerald an opportunity too easily."

"Gerald has aligned himself against some of your opinions, and you against many of his. But that doesn't mean he's out to get you."

Stretching a tightness in her neck, which she could still trace back to her father's old bed, Eleanor found that her worry had lost its satisfaction. No more energy to ruminate on regret remained.

"Okay. I'm done venting my spleen."

"You'll have to go to Beatrice and the Biology department

179

for that anyway."

"Huh. Hmm." She stood and looked past Jackie, toward the window behind her. "I haven't even started to get excited about having the time to read and travel and write. I hope I get around to that part."

"You will. Of course, you will." Jackie stood with her. "I always said you were a born writer. History professor is just your alter ego. What do they call it in the superhero movies?"

Eleanor snickered. "I don't know. Ask your husband. He would know about that."

Jackie rounded the desk. "You probably haven't stopped to think about how much I'm gonna miss you." She slid a hand down Eleanor's arm to her elbow.

"Oh, but I have. I've been daydreaming about you coming out to visit me for a week or two during the summer." She grabbed her friend's hand. "Get away with me, Jackie. Thomas has that movie shoot, doesn't he?"

"Hmm. I *was* planning to do some of my writing during that alone time."

"Come out and do it on the farm. We'll turn off our phones and just write for hours."

"That sounds very enticing." Her broad grin and glistening eyes confided just how attractive she found the offer.

"Good. We'll set the dates as soon as you know Thomas's schedule. My plans are fluid at present."

Eleanor spent the next few weeks solidifying her plans. She persuaded her colleague Dierdre to take the stint as acting department chair. She interviewed for an additional history instructor. A young man working on his PhD at Princeton looked like a good fit for the survey courses. And a couple of her seminars could be postponed for a year. A pair of them could be taught by Dierdre, including a joint seminar with Jackie.

"You know she'll drive me crazy with all her Britishisms.

That's why you're sticking me with her."

"Briticisms, I think, is the term."

Jackie popped Eleanor in the rear end with the palm of her hand. They were walking briskly around the track in the stadium, early on a Friday morning. They were back to the warm-weather exercise routine that matched them up one day a week.

"You could start a scandal with sexual harassment like that, you know."

"Probably all kinds of scandals." Jackie puffed and chuckled at the same time. "Speaking of scandalous behavior, have you talked to your pastor friend this week?"

"Yes. But with no scandalous content for you to worry about."

"Oh, I'd only worry if you never had any scandalous content passing between you."

"For a church lady, you seem curiously invested in me corrupting a clergyman."

"I think he's already gone on you. I'm just getting all the vicarious enjoyment out of it I can."

"That makes it sound like you have designs on defrocking some man of God."

"Actually, Thomas and I have this little scenario we like to play sometimes ..."

"No. No." Eleanor put her hands over her ears. "Don't tell me. Don't tell me. I don't want those images in my head. I'll never be able to look Thomas in the eyes again."

Jackie laughed so hard that she veered off course and slowed her pace considerably.

Eleanor turned to look at her. "You don't really ... No, never mind. I don't wanna know."

This stopped Jackie in her tracks. Two younger women jogged past and grinned at the unhinged laughter of the renowned professor. She was clutching her side with one hand and leaning the other hand on a knee.

*   *   *

"So, you have all the arrangements made, then?" Virgil sounded tired at the end of the day, perhaps more so than during any previous conversation.

"Is my sabbatical making you weary just thinking about the arrangements?"

"Ah. No. No, just a long day at the hospital with Mrs. Mendelsohn. The family had to decide to take her off the respirator."

"Oh. I didn't realize it had gotten to that point." Virgil had been sharing some of the challenges from his work at the church. Mrs. Mendelsohn, ninety years old, had been failing for the last few weeks.

Virgil rallied. "I drove past your house the other day. It looks good. I get the feeling that Paul is taking pride in keeping it looking fit for you."

"He's probably still feeling guilty about Mother."

"I haven't seen him in church for quite a while. He may be attending elsewhere."

"Or maybe he's hiding from God and from you."

"God and I would only offer him grace and forgiveness, and permission to let himself off the hook."

"Does he know that?"

"Well. I can't say, of course. But knowing and doing are not even in the same department much of the time."

"What is it, theology department versus the pastoral care department?"

"You've been looking at seminaries. Interested in attending?"

"Ha. No. Just trying to imagine what your graduate education would have been like."

"Most of the time, I think it only prepared me for getting this job, not so much preparing me for actually doing it. But that's what I've been busy at for the last thirty-some years, figuring out the job."

"Humility becomes you."

"Well, humility is about realism. It took me about two decades to establish a realistic notion of what I can and cannot bring to people, for example grace and freedom to those that aren't ready to accept it."

"Like Paul."

"Well. I can't speak to what Paul needs. But, in the abstract, yes, people who have suffered loss and feel some guilt."

"Guilt? Suffered loss? Now you're talking about me."

"Am I? Hmm. How did that happen?"

She snickered at him. She held her cell phone in her palm, the speaker phone activated. Leaning back in her leather recliner, she bent her knees and pulled her feet up a few inches to get them under the red fleece blanket. Evenings were still cool in New York in late April, and her furnace had just now kicked on, late to this party.

Virgil seemed to seek cover from her long pause. "I promise I won't psychoanalyze you and pastor you when you come out this summer."

"You think that would scare me away?"

"We don't have that kind of relationship, whether it would scare you or not."

She shifted the topic. "Have you given any more thought to retiring from pastoring?"

He paused, perhaps over the quick change of subject. But it wasn't entirely out of the blue. "I actually looked at the numbers. They don't look so bad, now that the kids are fully independent, and I have the option to receive Social Security benefits."

"When is your birthday?"

"May."

"Just curious."

183

"When exactly will you be back here?"

"Commencement is the last Sunday in May. Will I miss your birthday?"

"Looks like it."

"Are your kids coming out this summer?"

"I don't know if Candice can travel again so soon, after coming out for Connie's funeral."

"If she comes back out, I want to give her one of Connie's paintings."

"Oh. Well. That would be wonderful. But those are quite valuable, aren't they?"

Eleanor laughed. "Did I tell you about the big scuffle over Yvonne hanging her paintings in her room?"

"About the board members worrying that someone would steal them?"

"Yes. I told you about the new locks and everything?"

"Yes. Connie's donation was more than enough to pay for a few new locks, as I recall."

"That's right. I guess I told you."

"Uh-huh. And you changed the subject again."

"Did I? Hmm. So, how's the weather out there these days?"

They laughed together, his chuckles joining hers in the small dome of light over her chair. She looked forward to joining his laughter in person.

CHAPTER TWENTY-THREE

The commencement ceremony braided together a heavy cord of medieval European academia with the living strands of young lives twisting toward their future. Eleanor paraded with other faculty members in their colorful doctoral robes. Her regalia, from her Brown University PhD, was in fact brown, with black and red stripes at the sleeves. She wore her soft, black tam with tassel. And she openly envied Jackie's University of Chicago maroon.

"Oh, I'm looking forward to upgrading to the princess version." Jackie deflected Eleanor's jealous admiration. "That should come out about the time this current generation of students finishes grad school."

Their annual jokes about the faculty playing dress-up obscured Eleanor's anxious obsession with her travel plans. Her townhouse rental arrangements had been completed weeks ago, and the academic arrangements had coalesced in time for the fall catalog. So, all she had left to worry about was going west. Those fears included travel connections, of course. But they also included uncertainty about her relationship with Virgil. They would get an early start. He was meeting her at the airport in Milwaukee.

She thought about Virgil during most of the graduation ceremony, while she hunkered comfortably in the auditorium seat. Dierdre sat next to her, the History department faculty packed together. Dierdre assiduously searched for her bachelor's and master's students in the list of graduates. She commented on the destination of each one that she could remember. For Eleanor, it was pleasant background music. She admired how much Dierdre knew about her students. But Eleanor didn't envy the interpersonal energy required for Dierdre's level of acquaintance.

"Law school, graduate school, law school ..." Dierdre was still scoring undergraduates and their destinations, as the graduate students were being introduced. Perhaps she was simply working harder at coping with the boredom of the event.

But Eleanor did share some of the pride behind that tally of Dierdre's students. As the graduate students rose to be recognized, she watched Rosemary Kepler turn to smile at a friend. Rosemary caught her academic advisor watching and waved in Eleanor's direction, before joining the line at the edge of the stage.

Ardent, idealistic, responsive and conscientious, Rosemary had been an obvious choice for her graduate assistant. As chair of the department, Eleanor got first pick. She tried not to monopolize the best talent every year. But Rosemary was a natural match for the classes Eleanor taught and the writing she was doing. Young feminist historians like Rosemary helped Eleanor stay current with social and political trends. And Eleanor probably succeeded at moderating her graduate students' youthful militancy on occasion. Rosemary, particularly, needed none of that. If anything, she had needed Eleanor to affirm her bold declaration of herself: "Look out world, here I come." She probably didn't convince Rosemary to literally say it. But Eleanor did help her get an article published in a journal at a large American university.

"Here she comes." Eleanor said it to herself as Rosemary strode across the stage to receive her diploma. Dierdre patted Eleanor's hand. She probably wasn't reading Eleanor's mind, but she certainly knew how proud the department chair was of her graduate assistant.

Receptions, more and less formal, followed on that graduation Sunday. But Eleanor stuck around only long enough to attend the History Department open house. Hosting that small event was the first act of Dierdre's tenure as acting department chair.

Eleanor excused herself early. "I'll not stay and hover over your shoulder. It's all yours now, dear."

They hugged briefly. The most affection Eleanor expected from her British friend.

"I want to hear from you as often as possible. Don't just wait for my distress calls." Dierdre hung on to Eleanor's arms for a few extra seconds, as if to extract a commitment.

"Of course. I'll call and email. You'll be fine."

Dierdre gripped her a moment longer. "You *are* coming back, aren't you?"

Eleanor paused over her friend's dark blue eyes, noting little wrinkles around them, more lines than she had observed before. "Right now, that's the plan."

"Right now?"

"That's all I can talk about. Right now."

Dierdre released the sleeve of Eleanor's tan suit jacket, her change of clothes after hanging her academic robe in the small coat closet in her office. That office would remain empty while Eleanor was gone, as far as she knew. Gerald didn't control that level of logistics within the department, so she trusted he wouldn't have her books and papers boxed and stored while she was away.

But she was apparently worried about even that unlikely scenario.

For thirty-three years, this had been her place of employment. Only twice before had she taken a sabbatical, not following the seven-year schedule implied in the name. But this one was different, of course. There had already been that question about when she would retire, a consideration that escalated with each passing year. Now it seemed that everyone in the department knew that this sabbatical could possibly turn into the first year of Eleanor's retirement.

The fact that she had only taken two breaks before meant that even if she did opt to retire at the end of the coming academic year, Eleanor wouldn't have to refund the university for the cost of this sabbatical. They owed her one. At least, that's what the faculty guidelines stated.

The next day was Memorial Day. She stood in the Syracuse airport, headed for Wisconsin once again. This time, she would fly *through* Chicago to Milwaukee, to make it easier for Virgil to pick her up.

She tried to distract herself from some of her anxiety by watching a movie between Boston and Chicago. The movie streamed to her laptop wasn't good enough to hold her attention, and she probably lost what little it had to offer by revisiting her worries during what must have been a crucial scene.

She barely made her connection at O'Hare, after forging off in the wrong direction from her arrival gate. She was more used to a straight arrival or departure at that huge airport, not connecting to another flight. She *had* connected through there once recently, to visit a friend in Seattle, a former student now teaching at a university out there.

This recollection detoured her to thoughts about Candice, Virgil's daughter who lived in Portland, not far from Seattle. Fortunately, that mental detour happened only after Eleanor had boarded the plane for the quick hop to Milwaukee.

"Hi. I'm Fred Baker. Are you headed to Milwaukee for business or pleasure?" The rotund man taking up more than the seat next to her clearly had in mind a convivial little flight.

"Oh. Well, that's hard to say."

"If you can't tell the difference then you must have a pretty good job." He grinned, showing gold caps in the corners of his generous mouth.

"I do have a job I love."

"What is it? Wait. Let me guess." He pointed at her. "You're a teacher."

Eleanor looked down at what she was wearing. A navy-blue linen suit jacket over a white scoop neck t-shirt, and comfortable jeans. There was no name tag attached to her lapel. "How did you know? I'm trying to figure out how I'm so easy to read."

"Oh, well the hint was the way you said you loved your job. Teaching has to be right up there near the top of most-loved jobs, don't you think?"

"I suppose you're right. What is it that you do?"

"Sales. Computer hardware and communication equipment for larger organizations and businesses. I'm going up to Marquette University for a meeting."

"Flying from Chicago, or just passing through?"

"From St. Louis. Just connecting here." He turned to look out the window next to him.

Eleanor had wanted the window seat but couldn't find one available in the economy plus section when she booked this flight. "You must travel a lot."

"I do. But not as much as I used to. I can do some meetings remotely these days and email is good enough lots of times. Our products are all on the Web now, too, of course."

"Of course."

"What about you? You teaching classes or something up this way? Or is this summer break?"

"Summer break. I'm going to do some writing. I actually have the next two semesters off as well."

"Oh. Right. What do they call that? There's a word for it, right?"

"A sabbatical."

"Sabbatical. Sounds like sabbath. But it's not a religious thing?"

"No, my sabbatical is not especially religious, though a pastor friend *is* picking me up at the airport." As far as she knew she was simply improvising, bringing Virgil into the conversation as an ironic element. But, once she said it, she realized she may have been using Virgil as a shield from certain ideas this salesman might have about his time in Milwaukee.

Her deflection, however, didn't seem to impact Fred Baker at all. He proceeded to chatter on about his schooling, his travels and his church attendance, as well as about his ex-wife. "She was a Lutheran. I tried it, but just couldn't make the transition from Catholic."

"Ah. That's interesting." And, in a way, it was interesting to her. But Eleanor wasn't planning to delve deeper into Fred's personal faith journey. Not on a full plane from Chicago to Milwaukee. She wondered how much the slender young woman on the other side of her was catching from this conversation. Her white headphones might have blocked all of it. Eleanor was only a little jealous.

The short flight included all the same departure and arrival announcements, so there was very little quiet time between questions from Fred and turning the topic back on him again and again.

"Well, I hope you have a productive time writing, and ... ah ... blessings on your pastor friend, I guess would be appropriate." Did Fred resist crossing himself at that moment? Maybe Eleanor just imagined that.

Virgil met her by the curb after they exchanged a few texts. He had been waiting in the cellphone lot not far away.

"Hello." He reached an arm around her and kissed her on the cheek.

She forced half a smile. She paused a moment before returning his greeting ... though not his kiss.

"Hello. Thank you so much for coming to get me."

"Oh. Glad to do it.

She climbed into the passenger seat after helping Virgil slip her two suitcases into the trunk of his Toyota Camry—not new, but not very old either.

Her evaluative observation started her thinking about cars. "I'm hoping my mother's old Honda is still usable." She said it after Virgil started the ignition.

"I thought we could stop somewhere for lunch."

He didn't comment on her mention of the car. Was he nervous? It wasn't like him to ignore something she said.

"It *is* that time, especially for me." She made the leap.

"Not too late? You didn't eat already?"

"No. I'd love a good lunch."

"I found a decent Mexican place, I think. Interested?"

"Oh, sure. That sounds fine. You're making me hungry. I hope it's not far."

"No. Less than twenty minutes. You have to promise not to gnaw on the upholstery for that long."

"After that it's okay?"

"It'll be on me after that."

"Deal."

"Oh. Paul dropped your car off yesterday. Or maybe it was today. Oh, wait. This is Monday. It must have been Saturday." He was checking his mirror, intent on his driving.

She noted that Virgil had not missed her comment. And then she remembered the holiday.

"Monday is pastors' day off, isn't it? Does it matter that it's a holiday? Or maybe you have Memorial Day obligations?"

He paused, slowing the car for braking traffic. "I don't have anything these days. I used to share responsibilities with a few other area pastors for a Memorial Day service at the cemetery. But we don't do that anymore."

During the following pause, Eleanor decided not to pursue

the history of that civil and religious ceremony. The questions that came to mind felt too much like work. She hesitated over initiating a new topic of conversation. And she scolded herself for struggling with what to say next.

"How are your kids?" That was safe.

"I heard from William yesterday evening, in fact. We had a good talk. He just switched jobs recently, pursuing a dream that he only hatched a couple years ago. But it fits him very well, apparently."

"What's he doing?"

"Well, there in San Jose, he's been working for a software company, doing tech support for clients over the phone. He has years of that kind of experience. But now he's transitioning to software development."

"Really? I thought his background was in music."

Virgil chuckled. "Yes. He studied music at Stanford, on scholarship. But he missed the cut when it came to symphonic work in percussion. There aren't many of those jobs around."

"Or jobs teaching music?"

"I don't think Will ever considered teaching, especially not little kids."

"Ah. Yes. It's definitely not for everyone. I wonder how many music majors work in software development these days."

"Probably more than most people would guess." He grinned at her and then signaled to change lanes.

After a while he asked. "You had graduation ceremonies yesterday, didn't you?"

"Yes. I escaped right after, anxious to start the next chapter, and not fond of goodbyes."

"No time for a farewell party, then?"

"Oh, some of my colleagues tried to make the graduation reception in the History department into a going-away party. But I think my ambivalence about returning took some of the air out of it."

"Ambivalence about whether this is just a sabbatical or the beginning of your retirement?"

"Yes. Most of them seem to know about that dilemma."

"That sounds like a cozy working environment." He maneuvered the car into the right-hand lane.

"Yes. It has been quite cozy. And I supposed I've shaped the department to fit me, in lots of ways."

"How long have you been chair?"

"Well. Let's see. Fifteen years? That sounds about right, give or take."

"I expect that reflects the respect your colleagues have for you."

"I'm sure there is some of that. But chairing the department is political and administrative work that not all scholars welcome. So, it's also a measure of temperament."

"And aptitude."

"Yes. And availability. Some departments rotate the responsibility. Only recently have I found someone else with the skills to shift into the position."

"She or he is taking your place this year?" He was exiting the thruway now.

"She is. It took some arm-twisting. But she agreed."

He slowed to stop at a light.

She turned her head left and right to assess the surroundings. "How often do you get to the airport? You seem pretty comfortable around here."

"I pick up the kids when they fly in at least once a year. Probably twice, between the two of them. And I try to take in a play or concert at least once a year, downtown. So, I've made a few dozen trips this direction by now."

Within a few minutes, Virgil pulled the car off the arterial road into a restaurant parking lot, following the blue line on his phone's display. Eleanor congratulated herself for sitting back and trusting his driving and navigation.

When the car rolled to a stop, she released her seatbelt. "You've been in Dove Lake for how many years?"

"Twenty-five, almost." They each pushed their door open.

"Before that, where did you serve?"

"We were in the St. Louis suburbs before that, for six years."

"Oh. I met a gregarious man on the plane who was from St. Louis."

"Gregarious as in overly talkative?"

"It was a short flight. I wouldn't have gotten much reading done anyway." She was following Virgil now into a small, stand-alone Mexican restaurant. Most of the booths and tables were empty. It was certainly late for lunch.

When they sat at a table, looking over the menu, Eleanor tried to get ahead of the argument that would come at the end of this meal. "I know you're not going to let me reimburse you for the gas or anything, but you must let me pay for lunch."

Looking up from his menu, Virgil frowned briefly.

She returned to perusing the lunch choices.

Without looking up again, Virgil commented. "I better order something really good, then."

She chuckled at his response. But his ready acceptance stirred suspicion. She almost started a supporting argument for her offer, just in case he was only pretending to agree. Instead, she decided to leave it untouched.

No filet mignon on the menu, and he didn't even go for the skirt steak. But Virgil did order a full meal. "It'll be my big meal for the day."

"I guess I'm not sure how much cooking you do."

"Enough to survive. Lately, I've developed a habit of cook-ing a big meal once a week and eating the leftovers through the weekend. I usually get a dinner invite or two, a lunch here, a breakfast there, with people from the church."

"I suppose you could eat out for a living."

"You, too. Don't students and faculty invite you to lunch all the time?"

She nodded. "Yes. I get to eat the lunch I pack myself about once a week." She smiled at him. "And they say there's no free lunch."

"Right. Clearly the people who popularized that saying were in the wrong line of work."

"Clearly." She grinned at him over her sangria. He had encouraged her to order that drink. He settled for iced tea, since he was driving. That was his explanation, but she had yet to hear him mentioning drinking alcohol.

When the check arrived, Virgil reached for it. But Eleanor fixed him with a scolding stare that slowed his hand and gave her the advantage.

"Sorry. Force of habit."

"Really? Don't your church members insist on paying the bill?" She pulled out her credit card and slipped it into the little folder with only a glance at the receipt.

"Not all of them. And I can expense some meals." He leaned back in his seat. "It's a legitimate expense, in my mind, when I can meet with a single woman in a public restaurant, for example. It's better than a meeting in my office in some cases."

"What if you have to discuss a private matter?"

"I have a part-time secretary, of sorts. A retired administrative assistant comes to work in the office several hours a week. We can coordinate my counselling schedule around her availability some of the time. She can sit in the reception area while I meet with someone in my office."

"Have you ever had trouble with that sort of thing?"

"What sort of thing?"

It was an awkward, half-baked question. Jet lag or sangria?

She tried to laugh off the clumsy inquiry. "Oh, I'm not sure what I was asking. But it is good to know that you take precautions against improprieties and the appearance thereof."

"Yes. Including the appearance thereof."

"That's a phrase from our faculty guidelines. Advice for avoiding entanglements with students."

"Have you always been able to avoid tangling with your students?"

She laughed as the waitress carried her credit card away. "I have restricted all tangling to the intellectual plane. None of that other kind."

"Good for you."

"And you? You've avoided tangling with your congregants?"

"I have." He nodded as if deciding what more to say.

Eleanor was looking at the way his upper lip curved to a prominent point in the middle. It reminded her of Michelangelo's statue of David. But, of course, Virgil was fully dressed.

Perhaps the sangria had been too much. She allowed that thought to cloud her face. "I'm glad you're driving. That sangria made me loopy."

"Not a hearty drinker?"

"No. A little wine now and then. What about you? I think I recall that Martin Luther cherished his beer."

"I've heard that he did. But I think most Lutheran pastors avoid using old Martin as their guide for a balanced life."

"Really?" She signed the merchant's copy of the receipt and calculated a 25% tip for the waitress, always a generous tipper as a matter of economic justice. "You will have to fill me in."

In the car, Virgil did regale her for a while with the life and times of Martin Luther. He probably talked longer than she knew, for she fell asleep for at least an hour before they reached her farmhouse.

"Oh, my. I'm so sorry. I must be more tired than I realized."

"No apologies needed. You said some very revealing things in your sleep. It was worth it."

"What? I said ..."

His grin gave away his joke before she could sputter any further.

"Just teasing. You slept peacefully."

"Oh, good." She regarded him for a few seconds. "I used to trust you."

"Ha. Well, I will try to earn that back in the days ahead."

"Hmm. That's something to look forward to."

CHAPTER TWENTY-FOUR

After Virgil had left her largest suitcase on the floor at the bottom of the stairs and departed to the refrain of her gratitude, Eleanor allowed the silence of her mother's house to sidle up to her. Would it ever become *her* house? No longer her mother's? Perhaps Eleanor could only hope to join her mother in owning this house, even if she decided not to sell it in the months or years ahead.

She could tell that Paul had been in the house since she left, not just mowing grass and pulling weeds outside. The paintings were more carefully stacked, with cardboard slipped in between. They were pressed closer together, perhaps to prevent warping. Certainly, Paul would have learned about this with her mother, if not *from* her mother. Connie had seemed generally unconcerned about little things like that, evidenced by the piles of stuff filling the house.

Now Eleanor noticed that the place had been dusted and vacuumed. She could see stripes embossed on the old living room carpet by a vacuum cleaner. Paul would probably give her a bill for the crew that did this heroic task. He *should* give her a bill.

Virgil's departure had lacked some of the drama that she had anticipated when she was still wide awake. She had wondered if she should ask him to stay for a drink. Was that appropriate? Would he refuse? Would his refusal mean it was inappropriate?

But he must have counted her obvious weariness as a firm indicator of his soon departure. A good call. She had been combining the eye-straining work of final exams and final papers with packing up her personal items from her townhouse. Three large cardboard boxes should be arriving Tuesday, with books, clothes and her laser printer, among other valuable items.

Taking off her jacket, she expelled the exhaust of finals week and graduation, as well as the trip west. And her brain wandered toward the westward journeys of previous settlers in Wisconsin, the European pioneers who arrived here a hundred and fifty years ago. Her flight from Syracuse couldn't compare to such an odyssey, even if theirs was only a wagon ride from the frontier town of Chicago or Galena. Her parents had settled in Dove Lake after a station-wagon trip from a bedroom community of Milwaukee.

Eleanor was tired. These random fragments of historical musing proved that.

Her delirious mental stagger led her up the stairs, bumping her biggest suitcase up one step at a time. Virgil hadn't even offered to make the climb up the stairs. That probably was a matter of propriety. He certainly could have guessed that the contents of those bags would ultimately be unpacked on the second floor. He had abstained from a trip deeper into her house, deeper into her life.

Eleanor was still determined to convert her mother's bedroom to an office. That would start her on the giant project of clearing out her mother's accumulated belongings. Those excavations would be her recreation between research and writing.

She stood on the upstairs landing contemplating the use of the various rooms, thinking about which mattress was best for long-term use. She stepped into her father's room to test his bed again.

She woke when it was dark.

Crickets and frogs signaled for mates and reminded her of summer visits to her parents in this house. Certainly, these nocturnal critters were the descendants of the chorus that had sung her mother to sleep on warm nights. Eleanor sat up and tugged her cotton top free from her jeans. Then she unbuttoned the jeans and slipped them off. A hovering friend was advising her to get up and get something to eat, to get a start on ... a start on what? That was, perhaps, not the voice of a friend in her head. And it was probably okay to ignore whoever it was.

She did ignore them. And she slept until deep into the night, when she rose for a trip to the bathroom and returned to fall instantly asleep again.

Her father's bedroom had one tall window, in the style of old prairie farmhouses. This lone window was why her mother's room would make a better office, both a north- and a west-facing window. It wasn't ideal, not as bright as the studio downstairs, with four windows facing north and west, one a bay window that caught some southern rays. But that much light seemed excessive for her writing. The lighting requirements for writing history weren't the same as for painting.

Toward the eastward window in her father's room Eleanor shifted her head on the pillow and strained her neck for a hint of the hour. She had unplugged electrical appliances, including the clock opposite the window. Reaching her phone would probably be easier than seeing anything out that window. The fact that she saw little there meant that it was still early. But the morning songs of robins, redwing blackbirds, sparrows and mourning doves assured her that dawn was near, and the day had begun already for the smaller residents of this farm.

She wondered if the crickets from the night before were so much quieter now because so many birds were up and active. She was neither a biologist nor a naturalist. She had listened to her mother describe the creatures she observed around her farm, during late-night phone calls through the years. Now Eleanor wished she had paid closer attention. Those critters were *her* neighbors now.

That thought, and the energy stored from a long sleep,

levered her to a sitting position. She sat in the bed surveying the room. If this was to become her bedroom, it would need a complete overhaul. Every room in the house constituted a project. She would need help. Paul Wasser? And maybe some young people with strong backs and lower hourly rates?

Breakfast. Eat first, and solve the issues of the old farmhouse after.

*   *   *

"So, what are you doing now?"

"You mean, where do I start? I think I'll do one room at a time. First setting up an office in my mother's bedroom."

"Renaming the rooms has to be high on your agenda." Jackie grunted lightly as if she was working on something as she spoke, probably gardening.

"I'll find a local printer to make me new room nameplates."

"There you go. You'll need help. This is gonna be a big project."

"I was beginning to think of it as half a dozen discrete projects, so as not to be buried under the idea of one gigantic ordeal."

"Good. But best to leave the word 'ordeal' out of the planning, I think."

"Good point." Eleanor slurped the last of her morning coffee. "My next call has to be the handyman."

"You never told me how attractive this handyman is."

"I didn't want to feed your fantasies."

"Oh. That good-looking, huh? And younger?"

"It would be hard to find a handyman older than me."

"Right. How handy could he be? You're ancient."

"Hmm. Thanks." She sighed. "I miss you already."

"Go for a walk on the prairie and imagine I'm there with you."

"Will we both be able to avoid all the goose poop and cow

pies on that imaginary walk?"

"It's *your* imaginary stroll. Feel free to improvise."

"Thank you, I will."

"Okay. Call me again whenever."

"I will do that."

When she cleared the flotsam off the top of her mother's dressing table—a dozen small paintbrushes, two hairbrushes, a tube of black acrylic paint, scores of old bills, one squashed Cubs baseball cap, numerous books, and so on—Eleanor finally succeeded at connecting her laptop to the wireless network. That allowed her a better view of the email Paul Wasser had sent with a monthly bill attached. That bill included the cleaning service in the itemized list. Tamara Keeney appeared to be the name of the industrious cleaner. That name didn't sound like an agency, and the hourly rate wasn't nearly what Eleanor's New York maid service charged.

"Hello, Eleanor. I assume you're in your house." Paul sounded energetic.

"Yes." She hesitated. "My house. Thank you so much for looking after it. I appreciate the cleaning and such. Very good of you. I'm wondering about the cleaning service you used. Do you think I could get them to help me move some things around and help throw stuff away?"

"Sure. It was my cousin Tammy. I can give you her number."

"That would be great. I'll also want to move some heavy furniture. Do I contact you about that?"

"Sure. I can bring a guy with me to haul some furniture. I'm assuming anything that's in there is small enough to move up or down the stairs and out of the house, if needed."

"That seems likely. I doubt my mother built any of these things inside the house. She wasn't *that* kind of an artist."

He paused, perhaps to chuckle at her joke. "You see that I

restacked some of the paintings? I didn't wanna take them out to the barn without asking you."

"Good. That works. I need to figure out what to do with them. And they're keeping me company, right now." She was looking into the hallway, at a painting of clothes drying on a line in front of a weathered farmhouse. It may as well have been a portrait of her mother.

"That makes sense. That's why I didn't move them to the barn. If you keep the house comfortable for you, it'll be fine for the paintings."

"Right. I'm not going to store them in here forever." She swiveled her chair back toward the dressing table. "So, you learned about protecting art by helping my mother?"

"Yes. She wanted to preserve things but hadn't really looked into how best to do it. So, I did some research."

"Google is pretty handy, right?"

"And YouTube." He laughed lightly.

Collecting the phone number of his cousin and thanking Paul again, Eleanor said goodbye. A fragmented echo of Jackie's jokes about the handyman prompted an eyeroll for no one's benefit but her own.

"He's far too young." As she walked out of her new office, toward the stairs, she glanced around the hallway. "And then there's Virgil."

Through the rest of that day she surveyed each of the rooms and wrote herself notes on her laptop. She had once assisted with the sorting and preservation of a house in Schenectady, the former home of a woman who had been a prominent crusader for women's voting rights. That was the closest Eleanor had come to this kind of project. But this one was, of course, more personal.

After lunch, and finishing her To-Do list outline, she sat down in her mother's former bedroom, her new office. "I'm taking over, Connie. I hope you don't mind."

She imagined a sparkling smile and friendly nod from her mother. At least the part of Connie that she had internalized seemed satisfied with the arrangement. Maybe even happy.

But even as she piled magazines, sorted old mail, and boxed up ancient bottles of perfume, lotion and hairspray, Eleanor had to press back against a swelling inside her chest, a rising sadness like bread dough waiting to be punched down.

"This place smells like you, Mother. Maybe that's too much for me to bear." She shook her head and wiped the back of her hand over the itchy tip of her nose. A breeze tossed the thin, white curtains. Outside air was being invited in to help purge that provoking aroma.

Her phone buzzing, where she had set it on the dressing table, pulled her out of that downward spiral.

"Hello, Virgil. How are you?"

"How am I? Well, I'm fine. Ensconced in my routine. But I imagine you are having a day like none you've ever navigated before."

She nearly allowed that pressure below her throat to escape. Sitting down hard on the chair by her computer, she rested her eyes on a photo of her parents leaning into each other in some subtropical location, perhaps twenty years ago. Her breathing steadied. "You have a very sympathetic imagination. I'm impressed."

"Hmm. How is it going? Just getting organized?"

"Yes, one room at a time."

"I'd be glad to help, any time you want. My schedule is quite flexible, and I'm usually not very busy."

She twisted her mouth to the side. "I suppose you should be careful who you tell that last part."

"Oh. No worries. My supervisor is never breathing down my neck. And the folks in my congregation really have no concept of what it takes to be a pastor. So, I mostly just have to meet my own expectations on a day-to-day basis." He paused. "But maybe that was too much information. You were probably just joking."

"Probably." She stood up, pulling herself away from the smiling faces of her parents. "But I really would like some help. Some of it's just lifting and toting. But there are some decisions to be made."

"Each difficult in its own way, I suppose."

"Yes. I plan to get some young hands in here for the lifting."

"I'd be glad to help with any of it, including sorting through the memories and the accumulated stuff."

"Have you done that sort of thing before?" She didn't know much about his parents.

"Similar. Folks in my congregation have needed a sympathetic ear as they justified giving away or throwing away things accumulated by elderly or deceased parents. I was in one house in which an entire room had been devoted to plastic jewelry purchased from a TV shopping channel."

"Oh, my. And the family needed permission to get rid of it?"

"Actually, in that case, they needed other kinds of reassurance. They were afraid that their mother's hoarding reflected badly on their care and attention for her. And maybe there was a bit of fear that her obsession was embedded in their DNA."

"Well. There is nothing like that over here. At least I'm sure of that much."

"Nothing as obvious as that?"

Eleanor flipped through a quick list of vague fears about what else she might find about her parents. She rested on the reveal that she was certain to see—that she hadn't known them as well as she now wished.

Virgil interrupted her long pause. "Perhaps there's something else I can help you with."

"You have something in mind?" She winced at the leading

tone in her reply.

"I can help you remember to take a break now and again. A sabbatical is meant to be something of a vacation, isn't it? And you just finished a stressful school year. You need to take care of yourself."

She was grinning and looking at the pond, her forehead just clear of the glass. "Are you *trying* to impress me? Because you are excelling at it."

"Not trying to impress you, just trying to entice you to go for a walk with me this evening, after dinner, perhaps?"

She hadn't thought about dinner yet. What did she have to eat? Maybe a can of soup. Lunch had been a box of instant beans and rice. There wasn't much in the fridge. She side-stepped that for now. "A walk is a wonderful idea. Should I meet you somewhere?"

"I could come by and show you around your own neighborhood. There are some hidden walking paths around you."

"Oh. All the better. Okay. What time?"

They settled on a time and ended the call, Eleanor still grinning out the window. Certainly, Virgil was still interested in her. Just friends? Maybe. But he had demonstrated such sensitivity with other things. He must know how she would receive his persistent attention.

He had missed his chance with dinner, however. So, he wasn't perfect.

Thoughts about Virgil accompanied her sorting and piling and hauling for the rest of the afternoon. That combination nearly led her right past dinner time. She rushed her can of soup, before quickly showering and primping in preparation for their walk.

CHAPTER TWENTY-FIVE

She recognized Virgil's arrival by the sound of plastic grocery bags crinkling at the screen door. Paul had switched out the storm doors. When she saw the bulging shopping bags straining Virgil's hands, she knew that there were two men helping her take care of herself.

"You brought me groceries."

"Yes. Let me know if any of it isn't useful. I'm not totally familiar with your eating habits. So, I got things that were organic and non-GMO and all that, but not necessarily low sodium or entirely fat free." He was panting a bit as he hauled the stuff into her kitchen and lifted the bags onto the butcher block island.

"Oh. I'm not so picky. I doubt I'll be sending any of this home with you. You probably didn't get me deep-fried curds or whatever that stuff is."

"You don't like those? Well, I'll just put those back in my car then." He faked a search past the carrots and apples on the way to the fried cheese curds.

She laughed, careful to contain a girlish giggle that threatened to despoil her dignity.

They found places for all the healthy food he had bought her. The nearly empty refrigerator made stowing the groceries easy. But there remained one issue.

"I don't want to sound ungrateful, Virgil. But I want to be honest with you right from the start."

This prelude caught his attention. He stood up straight and slipped his hands into the pockets of his jeans. "What are you worried about?"

She faltered for a second. "Worried? Well, I guess I *am* worried." She crossed her arms over her chest. "I just want you to know that I am ... I am ... set financially. My mother left me something. She was very successful. And I have ... well, I just don't want you to feel some male obligation to *provide* for me, to spend money on me."

The corners of his mouth tightened briefly, and he glanced downward, away from her face, scanning the floor, her shoes and her jeans. "I won't try to buy your affection, Eleanor. And I won't insist on taking care of you. This was just a one-time gesture. I actually felt bad when it occurred to me that I should have invited you out to dinner. I realized too late that you probably hadn't gotten to the grocery store yet."

What he was saying was important, of course, but she was trying to read his face as well. When he was looking squarely into her eyes again, she found him as trustworthy as ever, and showing no signs of being wounded by her cautions.

That emboldened her. "We can have a ... relationship free from old gender expectations, right? I mean, I can pay for things. I might buy *you* a load of groceries or take you out to dinner."

He nodded and then tipped his head toward the back door. "Wanna walk and talk?"

"Sure. Lead the way." She brushed her bangs off her forehead before considering how she might look. Had she remembered to brush her hair during all the running around? Well, too late now.

As he held the screen door open for her, he continued the conversation. "Are you just concerned about gender roles or about an income disparity?"

Eleanor released a full laugh. "You are so insightful. Are you reading my thoughts? You seem to know my mind at least as well as I do."

He smiled at her when she turned toward him. Then he gestured toward the opposite end of the barn, and she followed.

208

"I basically read people for a living. And I spend a lot of time trying to understand what motivates them. That goes into my sermons and into counseling. And I feel like I understand a lot about you. But I certainly don't know your mind." He was leading her around the back of the barn, where a sort of deer path opened into the trees.

She discarded a comment about him taking her behind the barn. They were having a serious adult conversation. Jackie would just have to stay out of it.

"But you seem to anticipate so many of my thoughts."

"So, it *is* the wealth gap that concerns you?"

"Wealth gap? I don't know. I think it's a combination of gender roles and the disparity in our positions. But here I am, making assumptions about *your* finances. Maybe that's not fair."

"No. I think it is fair, because I believe you're thinking about it out of concern for me. You don't want me spending too much on you if I have a more limited income. I get that. I would feel the same way."

She snorted a laugh as she shook her head. Even as she did that, she considered how often Virgil had inspired this same re-action.

Her steps along the narrow deer path paced her words. "To tell the truth, probably part of it is me just trying to get my head around what my mother left me. I've been so preoccupied with trying to get to know her all over again, and with arrangements to spend this time on the farm, that I haven't really stopped to appreciate the inheritance she left me."

"I suspect that you had a pretty secure financial situation before the reading of your mother's will, right? Pension and such."

"Yes. I was already in a position to retire pretty comfortably, after thirty-three years at Carlisle." She stepped over a small log that lay across the path. The evening light was sending spotty shadows from the small poplar and sumac trees to her left. Virgil was headed north over what must have been the land attached to her farmhouse in decades past. "And then my mother left me with more than I expected, after she made substantial donations to charity, and the church. The fact is, I still don't really know the full value of everything she left me."

He bypassed her mention of Connie's bequest to the Lutheran church. "That can, of course, be exciting. But it can also be stressful. Do you have a good financial adviser?"

Eleanor stopped walking and set her hands on her hips. "Maybe the issue I'm worrying about is you taking care of me. I feel like you're sort of pastoring me."

"Too much advice?" He was turned back toward her, his hands in his pockets again.

"You're certainly not heavy-handed about it. But I'm adjusting to how much you seem to know and care about me and my life. It's not an inherently bad thing, of course, but quite unfamiliar, especially from a man."

"You have women friends who would ask you about having a financial adviser and things like that?"

She followed when he turned to resume the walk. "I do. At least one. Maybe the issue is whether I can get used to a man being that kind of friend." She took a deep breath, beginning to feel the strain of their brisk hike. "There are a couple of men who might ask that question, now that I think of it."

"So, the issue is not getting advice from a man. Is it me, in particular?"

She had caught up a bit, walking now just behind his right shoulder. The path was generally too narrow to allow them to be side-by-side. But they emerged from the tree line, and he nodded toward wheel ruts that seemed little used in recent years, a tall hump of grass growing along the center. Now they could walk next to each other more comfortably, treading between the medium length grass outside the tracks, on the scruffy weeds struggling to fill in the old tire marks.

"I like you, Virgil. But I must admit that I'm concerned about our differences in faith. How far can this relationship go with you a pastor and me an agnostic?"

He tipped his head away and shaped a pucker. "I've thought about that. Spiritual things are rarely black and white, at least with most people. I'm hoping that your agnosticism is more compatible with my faith than you think."

"How would that work?"

"Being agnostic means you're uncertain, you're not dogmatic. That uncertainly sets you apart from lots of people who count themselves as Christian. But not all Christians are dogmatic on all issues, not all of us are certain about every answer."

"Of course, it's no surprise that it's not as simple as two conflicting categories."

"I don't think it is."

"Then, we could take some time to explore the things I have doubts about and see if those are okay with you? And I can listen to the things you're dogmatic about and see if those are okay with me?"

He slowed, turned his shoulders toward her and grinned. "I would like to do just that. And we can move slowly in our relationship while we explore those questions."

"I think I can do that."

"I can too, as long as we can just enjoy being with each other from time to time, not always having to be deep in theological discussion."

"A friendly walk? A dinner out?"

"Yes. We can explore some of the restaurants in surrounding towns."

"And we can go slow."

"We can go as slow as a farmer driving his tractor from one

field to another." He raised his head and pointed his nose across the low field of beans, where a monstrous vehicle lumbered along a county road.

"Handy object lesson, Pastor."

"Yes. I worked hard to arrange that one."

She laughed. This time not so tempted to giggle. The uncertainty of the future stunted some of her humor.

They followed the wheel ruts toward that county asphalt in silence. A redwing blackbird clung to a tall stalk of sedge grass in the ditch they passed and ratcheted a metallic call into the dimming light.

"Where are we? Are we trespassing?"

"This used to be the land owned by the farm family who lived in your house. That was before my time. But if you talk to local people for a while, the conversation is likely to get into who's buying whose land, and who owned it before that." He stopped and looked up and down the narrow road. Then, leading her across, he continued his answer. "This section is now owned by the people to your east. They're church members and probably wouldn't shoot me if they saw me on their land."

"Probably? And what about me?"

"Oh. That's a different story, of course." He raised his eyebrows and widened his eyes to show white all around his dark irises. But he continued to walk that straight line toward another stand of trees, and a relaxed smile returned to his face.

"You've walked here before?"

"I have. I've walked here with Elmer Jennings, the farmer who owns it. And I once walked this way with your mother."

Eleanor stumbled slightly over a clump of weeds. She had lost sight of the track beneath her feet. "You went on walks with my mother?"

"Not very recently. I think she was getting less mobile. At least less active outside the house. I suspected she was having some health issues that slowed her. She didn't share any of that with me. I was just observing and guessing."

"But you walked with her before that?"

"We probably took half a dozen walks together over the years. Not frequently. The first few were clustered soon after your father died. She seemed to need someone to process that loss with. But I also felt like she was needing to walk and talk with a man, as if it was a transition away from having your dad around."

"I suppose that's common for widows, right? Used to talking with a husband and suddenly being without him."

"Your parents were closer, I think, than many couples I know. I've talked to women who hardly noticed that their closed-mouth man wasn't there anymore. Not exactly 'good riddance,' but no great loss."

"That's a bit shocking."

"Yes. As a young minister I was very concerned. It didn't seem right. But I decided that I shouldn't focus on being scandalized by a wife's blasé reaction after the old man dies. Instead, I've worked to encourage communication between the couple while he's still alive. That's why we have marriage seminars on a regular basis."

"Did my parents attend any of those?"

He shook his head slowly. "Your father was a Sunday-only church member. Your mother got much more involved after he was gone."

"I could tell that by what she told me. Even then, she didn't insist that I attend with her."

"She was a gentle believer."

Eleanor snickered at the apt description. "She was gentle about everything she did." That prompted a vulnerable question. "Did she talk about me? Did she ask you to pray for my conversion?"

Virgil kept his eyes on the copse of trees they approached now, gesturing with his left hand to indicate the path into that small woodlot. "She mentioned you, of course. I could certainly see how proud she was of you. As a parent, I could appreciate her satisfaction at what you'd accomplished. And I could sympathize with her concerns about your happiness."

"She talked about my happiness?" Eleanor ducked beneath the tendrils of a willow tree. A damp moldiness in the air hinted at a creek or drainage ditch to her right.

"She did. And she did pray for you and asked others to pray. But she never said anything really personal about your life. I could guess that you weren't a believer like Connie was. But I didn't know much more, besides your academic accomplishments."

Eleanor stepped over what looked like a fallen squirrel's nest, perhaps dislodged by a storm. "I remember an old woman from my childhood. I suppose she was in her fifties at the time. Fifty used to be old, you know. She would regularly ask for prayer for her husband. But it was always an 'unspoken request.' That was the phrase as I remember it, though I think it should have been 'unspecified request,' more accurately."

Virgil nodded thoughtfully. "I've heard of that practice, that way of putting things. We don't use it, but effectively there have been requests over the years that remained unspecified. Perhaps an alcoholic spouse or a child in trouble with the law, shameful things best not mentioned in church."

"But they do share those with you privately?"

"Sometimes. Shame is a powerful thing, though, and it often keeps people from getting the support they need."

"Have you ever thought of doing some writing? I'm not an expert, of course, but it seems to me that you've accumulated some wisdom that you could pass on to new generations of pastors."

"That's an interesting proposal from an agnostic." He lowered his head and looked at her over his glasses, his eyes wide.

"Well I believe in *some* things. I believe in the wisdom acquired over a life well-lived. And I believe in *your* skills, and your wisdom."

He stopped. "That's one of the best compliments I've ever received." He seemed truly astonished, standing there at the bend in the path that would lead them back out of the trees.

Eleanor cocked her head. "I don't know whether to be proud of having delivered that compliment or sorry that no one has told you that sort of thing before."

He started walking again. "I've received meaningful compliments over the years. But I particularly respect your opinion."

She didn't know what to say to that. Instead, they walked in silence, heading south now, back toward her mother's house.

Toward *her* house.

CHAPTER TWENTY-SIX

Eleanor stared at Tammy Keeney much longer than was polite. "Oh. Hello. Sorry. I was just startled at how much you look like Paul."

Laughing, Tammy entered when Eleanor pushed the screen door open. "I get that all the time. Our mothers are twins. And we both look like our mothers."

"That explains it. Of course." Eleanor was stepping slowly up the stairs into the kitchen. "I don't think I've ever witnessed it before, but that must be common for twins."

"I guess." Tammy stood in the middle of the kitchen surveying the scene. She seemed anxious to get to work. Or maybe just anxious to get off the topic.

"So, like I said on the phone, I need you to help me pull some light furniture in and out of my office and my bedroom upstairs and to help me sort and bag my mother's clothes and her magazines. Iris, at the library, has agreed to take some of the periodicals—art publications the library doesn't carry." Eleanor led Tammy through the dining room toward the stairs as she spoke. "How long can you stay?"

"I have all day. I can put in eight hours."

"That would be great. If we finish with those two rooms, then there are plenty of other things to do."

Tammy smiled admiringly for a moment as they neared one of the stacks of paintings still in the upper hallway. The visible painting was a pair of kittens climbing in and out of a basket. It was one of her mother's "precious" paintings, as Eleanor categorized them in her head. Not her favorite, but she had propped it in front of the stack, for a change from the winter landscape that had been visible for the first week back on the farm. Tammy followed Eleanor into Connie's bedroom after pausing over the painting.

"I have some things organized in here, already. And I think if we can just clear out some of this furniture and stuff, then the sorting and moving will get easier." Eleanor used a toe to nudge aside a cardboard box with just two pairs of shoes in it so far.

Beginning at nine in the morning, Tammy helped Eleanor to transform the two upstairs rooms that she would use daily. This included switching her mother's mattress and box springs for her father's. She and Tammy stood the older set against a wall in her mother's office, as a deposit on converting that room to a guest bedroom.

"Too bad you couldn't just use this as your office." Tammy's voice carried no real bite to what might have sounded like a criticism. Her easy attitude reminded Eleanor of Paul almost as much as the shape of her big eyes and the scooped nose that led to her full lips.

"Yeah. My mother and I have different careers. I think the office was where she did the business stuff that she *had* to do, not a place she spent creative time. It looks like it was a sort of receptacle of things she didn't want to deal with. That's what business was for her." Eleanor didn't mind explaining. It offered her a chance to think through her plans once again. "I like the light in her old bedroom better for my writing."

"What are you gonna do with the studio downstairs?"

"I'm thinking of using it as a gallery in the short-term. Maybe bring in some of my favorite paintings still out in the barn and line the room with them. I did that with the house the day of Mom's funeral. I like the way that made me feel."

"I could help you set that up."

"I would love that. Yes, I will definitely give you a call for that, and a bunch of other things that have to get done around here. I haven't even begun to assess the basement."

When Tammy left that late afternoon, with two hundred-dollar bills, Eleanor joked with herself about employing all of Paul's family. He had mentioned his father helping with some of the electrical and plumbing work in the basement. And she suspected the moving guy Paul was bringing the next day might also be related. But this thought soured in her stomach. It reminded her of plantation owners and the sharecroppers that worked for them. She wasn't interested in being *that* kind of landowner.

But she *was* a landowner now. She had a barn and a stand of pine trees and a pond. The honking of battling geese was coming from the pond. Still standing at the back door after Tammy's departure, Eleanor decided to follow that racket. On her circuit around the house, she paused to pick up small branches that had fallen from the old maple trees guarding the front of the house. She tossed the sticks up next to one wizened trunk and slowed to look at the pond. From where she stood, the surface mirrored the trees and sky. The cranky geese were all on shore now, the glassy water settling from the last of their ripples.

Maybe if she had grown up on a farm Eleanor would have thrown off at least some of her sweaty clothes and dived into that water. She could imagine kids from centuries past boldly running off the little dock which tilted slightly at the near edge of the pond. She opted, instead, for her own version of that visceral relief. She climbed onto the short dock, sat down, pulled off her sneakers and lowered her feet into the cool water. The baggy blue shorts she wore had belonged to her mother, disposable clothing for dirty work.

She contemplated her bony ankles and feet, maybe bonier than she was used to. She had been doing more manual labor since she moved into the farmhouse, and eating mostly salads, except when she and Virgil went out. How much weight had she lost? The fact that she didn't know the numbers wafted a vacation breeze her way.

Very little progress on her writing, and just the first attempts at accessing her mother's financial accounts, marked a slow start to those aspects of her sabbatical. Sitting on the dock now, she admitted to herself that her mother's death did require that she take time off, and not only for the logistical challenges.

That sent her thoughts toward the old letters she had found bundled in the bottom drawer of her mother's dressing table. Why in the world did she keep those in the back of that drawer? Had Mom known they were still there? Had Dad known they existed at all?

"Dear Constance,"

That's how they all started.

"Yours, Linus."

That was how they ended. At least it wasn't, "*Love*, Linus."

She couldn't help picturing the letter writer as the adult version of Charles Schulz's cartoon character by that name. Had the *Peanuts* cartoons even existed back then, in the early sixties? They must have. Eleanor could remember the first Christmas special on their black-and-white TV from when she was a girl.

"Huh. I suppose this Linus had outgrown his blankie." She exchanged glares with two mallards who seemed to be wondering who she was talking to.

Eleanor stood up, obeying a sudden compulsion to look at those letters again. Now she regretted dipping her feet in the water without a towel handy, grass and dirt adhering to her skin as she shuffled quickly over the yard. She stopped by the back door and ran her feet through the two-inch grass next to the sidewalk, the place where her mother fell.

"Did you fall before that, Mother? Did Dad's 'preference' drive you to seek comfort elsewhere?" She sighed hard and waved one frustrated hand at her still damp and dirty feet. The first towel she found inside was probably one that her mother had used for the dog, when he came inside from a walk. A long pause over that thought ended with shaking her head and wiping her feet with the dog towel. Monet had been gone for months.

She had seen Monet once since she arrived back at the farm. Paul had asked for permission to bring the two dogs for a walk down that same path Virgil had shown her. The old cocker spaniel seemed excited about being around his former home. But Eleanor hadn't been tempted to invite him inside. She was just starting to turn the tide in the battle against dog hair on the carpets and furniture.

Setting aside this menagerie of distractions, she left her sneakers by the back door and thumped through the house toward her mother's old office. The letters were in the bottom drawer of the big desk, transferred there when Tammy had been out of the room.

If her father knew that her mother kept those letters, did he understand? Now Eleanor was keeping them. She was wondering if she should talk with Virgil about what she had found. Maybe he could settle her turmoil.

She pulled a chair next to the desk and sat down, unfolding and spreading one letter in front of her on the old green blotter.

"You know you can count on me, dear Constance. You know I would do anything for you."

Was this Linus married? He doesn't mention a wife. But his pledges of devotion implied that he would abandon whomever— wife, kids, everyone. Had that happened? Had *anything* happened?

The letters weren't all dated. Not all of them were in envelopes. Her mother wasn't an archivist. No matter which letter was the last one, Eleanor could find none that contained any hint of an ending to the correspondence. Had her mother written him back? He doesn't mention any letters from her. Had she written the final letter, the one that ended the ... the whatever it was between them?

"Mother, Mother. What did you do?"

Eleanor sat now with sticky itches interrupting her obsession. Sweat between her legs, under her arms and around her neck was scratching at her. Bits of grass tickled where they still clung to her ankles and calves. She stood abruptly, slowed to allow the blood to rise to her head, and then headed for the hallway and a shower.

"It doesn't mean she had an affair." Jackie reassured her early that evening, the letters completely co-opting their conversation about Jackie's visit later that month.

"The words are so intimate, even if they're not sexual. The relationship was clearly out of bounds, even if they didn't consummate it."

"So, what? What does that say about your mother? And what does any of it say about you?"

"I was just a kid still. I was going to Sunday school in the church where they met. I must have known who he was, even if I can't remember him now. It feels as if I *was* involved, or at least as if it involved me."

"I guess when there are kids around, it does involve them. A parent's life involves the kids."

Jackie's daughter had graduated college the previous year and was entirely on her own now. With Thomas, Jackie had done a good job of raising Raisa, as far as Eleanor could tell. Jackie knew something about parenting. More than Eleanor.

Eleanor ruminated for several seconds. "Just get out here. I need to see you. I miss you."

"I miss you too."

Virgil had invited her out for dinner that night. His turn. He was taking her for Chinese food in Janesville. She chuckled with relief at discovering Chinese food so close to the farm. Her mother had never taken her for Chinese. Connie's dining choices leaned toward steakhouses and Italian American restaurants.

In the shower, Eleanor debated telling Virgil about the letters. "Why *wouldn't* I tell him? We're going slow, of course. But that doesn't mean I should withhold a troublesome issue like this. This is exactly the sort of thing he can help me with."

She turned off the water with a squeak, pushing the shower curtain back and reaching for a dull forest-green towel. If she was going to live here long-term, she would have this bathroom updated. The clawfoot tub and wrap-around shower curtain were quaint, but impractical.

"Okay. So, update the bathroom and tell Virgil everything."

"Check."

"Did you get a lot done upstairs?" Virgil was standing in the doorway between the kitchen and the dining room. He could see the living room clearly from there. Certainly, he could see the opposite of progress in there. Regress?

"Yes. Upstairs is transformed. At least two rooms are usable for what I want. Paul is coming to move the big desk tomorrow, to complete my new office. My mother's old office is still a mess. But my dad's bedroom is becoming mine. It's almost there."

"You sound upbeat. But I notice that you're not inviting me up for a showing."

She smiled at him. "None of it is ready for public viewing."

The way he was looking at her erased some of the weariness of her manual labor. Virgil appeared to be restraining a cheer, his eyes smiling at her in her light blue sundress. It was the girliest outfit she had brought with her. When she had bought it, she knew it was cute. Jackie had called it sexy. But Eleanor was avoiding such thoughts when it came to Virgil. Or trying to. The summer dress was merely a cool, comfortable option at the end of a sweaty day. That's what she would argue, if pressed.

Virgil's smiling eyes insisted that she own the cuteness, and perhaps the sexiness. "You look great." He raised both hands. "That's all I'll say, in order to avoid gender stereotyping and inappropriate behavior."

"Your restraint is commendable." She slipped past him toward the back door, restraining her own smile.

Virgil's proposal to slow-track their relationship wasn't just something with which Eleanor would passively comply. She didn't want to get too deeply involved with him if they couldn't become something serious and lasting. For him, of course, that would mean marriage. Anything short of that might lead to scandal and even Virgil losing his job. She would never allow herself to be the cause of that sort of destruction and sorrow.

"I discovered another secret." She was seated in his Camry, appreciating the air-conditioning. The evening air wasn't so hot and humid as earlier in the day, but she had straightened and curled her hair into a reasonable shape, which wind and humidity would contest at every opportunity.

"Oh. A secret about your parents?" He had turned the car around already, so he put it in drive and eased toward the highway.

"A secret at least about my mother. I don't know how much my dad knew about it."

"Romance?"

"Of course. You know me so well."

"Well, I can't picture Connie being part of a terrorist sleeper cell, so I went for the next possible option."

"Understandably." She welcomed the light beginning. It didn't diminish her concern but seemed to keep it in perspective.

"So. What was it?" Off her county highway, he turned left at the road south to Janesville.

"I found letters from a man named Linus, pledging his undying loyalty to her. He avoided saying he was in love with her, in so many words. But the sentiments all added up to that."

"No letters from her back to him, I suppose."

"No. That would be too convenient." She was watching a

fallow field out her window. "Letters from her might have helped me to sleep tonight." She shifted her right foot in the new sandal she was wearing. Hopefully some wear would soften it up. She assumed shoes were required at the Chinese restaurant, though there was that Eastern tradition of removing shoes at the door. Maybe she would explore that option.

"Any idea where she met this man?"

"I remember his name from that church in Milwaukee, where I grew up. And he says a couple of things that make it clear that he knows her from there."

"So we're left with mystery and speculation, without letters from your mother, or closure from that man."

"Yes. None of his letters are clearly the end of his corre-spondence, the end of the affair." Eleanor paused over recalling who wrote the novel by that name. But she decided not to allow that diversion into focus.

"So, it clearly has you stirred up. What's the worst part, the most disturbing part?"

Eleanor tried a thoughtful pause, but she knew the answer immediately. "The idea that my mother was unfaithful to my father."

"Was there any indication of that in the letters?"

She did allow a pause, here. "No. Nothing solid. The only thing it establishes is that she had an admirer. But I also have to consider the fact that she saved these letters from the 1960s to her death."

"Yes. There is that. I wonder if she remembered that she was keeping them. Maybe she kept 'em for a while and then for-got about them."

"Maybe. But I'm not sure how much difference it makes whether she cherished them for one decade or for five decades." She weighed Virgil's conjecture. "She might have just put them away and forgotten them immediately. Who knows?"

They had merged onto the highway leading into the big town. Eleanor was only vaguely tracking their progress. They exited at an arterial road and then had to slow when a car pulled out of an industrial parking lot and into the slowing flow of traffic. It was a Thursday night, after rush hour, if there was such a thing in this part of Wisconsin. Virgil demonstrated only patience with the traffic. If anything, he was a bit distracted by his conversation with Eleanor, perhaps allowing their discussion to slow his driving.

His voice elevated, as if aiming at a more distant audience. "On the other hand, I've seen times where people cherished what *might* have been, even where nothing significant really happened. The dream was never pursued or fulfilled. In some ways, that's more seductive. It stays pure, free from the encumbrances of daily reality and its consequences."

She watched him in fascination. "You really should write about your experiences, Virgil. You have some extremely valuable insights into things like this."

He might have blushed. It was hard to tell with peachy orange sunlight glaring through the front window. "Well, I have you fooled, at least."

"Oh, there's no chance of that." She sat back and smirked. "You're talking to a tenured professor with a storied career of busting freshman attempts to recycle term papers, of discerning all kinds of concocted evidence of undergraduates completing reading they never even started. I'm not easy to fool."

He snickered. "No. I bet you're not."

CHAPTER TWENTY-SEVEN

The sound of wood splintering in the basement set her teeth on edge. Eleanor rested both forearms on the dining room table, working on her laptop. She was updating a spreadsheet she had found on her mother's computer, a list of paintings. Most of the paintings had been labeled with colored pencil on the back. The others Eleanor marked, and she was adding them to the spreadsheet.

Her third week on the farm, she had also done some online research for her next book. She had discovered that her internet connection was too slow, considering the impending hours of perusing electronic publications in libraries all over the country. The installer from the internet service provider was downstairs now.

It was quiet down there. Perhaps nothing major had been destroyed.

Ten minutes later the technician had left through the back door and was headed to his truck. And Eleanor was clicking through a much quicker connection to the World Wide Web.

"Nice." She was searching a collection at Northwestern University. Much faster load times. "Very nice."

She had thought of Northwestern today because of an email she had received from a professor there, an invitation to deliver a guest lecture to history students and faculty in the graduate school in the fall. Eleanor was still thinking about whether she could compose a satisfactory lecture while pursuing so many other projects. Maybe she could recycle an existing lecture. Or maybe she would speed through her work now that the internet was streaming into her house, and not just chugging in.

Her phone buzzed. It was Audrey.

"Hello, Eleanor. Did I catch you at a bad time?"

"No. I'm cataloging paintings. Glad to take a break."

"So, you're serious about me coming over to choose a painting?"

"Of course. Can Debbie bring you over?"

"Yes. Is tomorrow morning okay?"

"Perfect. After nine, please. I've gotten into the habit of sleeping much later than when I was teaching."

"Oh, well, you're entitled. This is a sort of vacation for you, isn't it?"

"Sort of. Okay, Audrey. I look forward to seeing you tomorrow, then."

"Yes, we'll be there after nine."

Denise and Gretchen had already visited. Eleanor had taken them out to the barn to look at some of the paintings out there. Sorting those canvases to show to her mother's two old friends helped Eleanor decide which ones she wanted in the house, to display in the studio.

Gretchen had cried all the way to the car, clutching a painting of a girl and a puppy and sniffling harshly. Denise held one arm and Eleanor the other, in place of the walker Gretchen had abandoned on the driveway.

"I loved your mother so much. This means the world to me, Eleanor. It really does."

Eleanor had no doubt. She appreciated the way each painting represented a piece of Connie. When those two visitors had left, she considered how an art dealer would regard their two gifted paintings. Dollar signs, certainly. Lots of dollar signs.

She and Tammy and Paul had worked on arranging easels, hanging paintings on walls and propping some canvases on shelves in the studio. It was intended as a temporary display, just rearranging what was in the house by then. The surprising number of easels her mother had owned was just one example of her hoarding tendencies. For now, some of that clutter would be useful.

Helping her locate paintings stored in wooden boxes in the barn, Paul had also showed her how to check for damage to the canvases. They found no mold or mildew on any of the paintings. And Paul's relief was palpable. She suspected he had been holding his breath during their digging, sorting and assessing. She still wondered if he was trying to redeem himself for her mother's death.

It was a struggle each time she tried to pay him, with Paul minimizing the charges with the same persistence that a dishonest tradesman would have applied to inflating the bill.

The next morning, Eleanor was on the phone with Jackie when Audrey and Debbie pulled into the driveway.

"Will I get to meet some of these folks when I'm there?"

"Of course, you will."

"Will your black friend scandalize you among the natives?"

"Oh, I doubt it. Not with these folks. Connie was allergic to racists."

"Ah. I've never heard of *that* allergy before."

"No worries, dear. Besides, they know you're from New York. That'll be the scariest part for them."

"Oh. Well. I feel better now."

Eleanor laughed and then said a hasty goodbye when Debbie knocked at the back door.

Once inside, Audrey slowly climbed up to the kitchen, her back curved in a way that implied that she might be there to inspect the quality of Eleanor's sweeping and mopping. Tammy was taking care of all that, these days, so Audrey's inspection wasn't so intimidating.

"I always liked her sunsets. Do you have any of those still around?" The three of them moved slowly through the dining room.

"I'm sure I do. Let me just run upstairs. I think there are two or three in one of the stacks up there."

"Oh. Don't rush. I don't want you hurting yourself for me." That seemed a consistent theme from Audrey: "Don't let me put you to any trouble."

"I'll just be a minute. Make yourselves at home." Eleanor gestured toward the living room and withheld an apology. Finding a place to sit in there would require logistical creativity. She hoped Debbie could help her mother free up a comfortable seat. It did only take Eleanor a couple minutes of flipping through the stack in her mother's old office, the new guest room.

She carried three sunset paintings downstairs. "I think there might be a couple still in the barn." She glanced toward the studio door, just out of sight in the living room, wondering if she was remembering rightly. "If these aren't what you had in mind I can go look there." Instantly, she regretted offering Audrey another chance to insist that Eleanor not go to any trouble on her behalf.

But her guest was distracted from any such considerations. "Oh. Look at those." Audrey was seated on the couch, looking up at the paintings in Eleanor's hands. Debbie was standing behind her. The daughter had been looking at a small display of paintings arranged in the corner of the living room.

When Audrey struggled to stand, Debbie stepped forward. "You can see them from there, Mother."

"Yes. Just rest there. I'll set them at eye-level for you." Eleanor scooted a box of books with one foot, propped a painting on it, and then set down the other two canvases while she collected two more cardboard boxes as platforms. Those were full of clothes that Eleanor planned to donate. She was wearing a pink cotton button-up blouse of her mother's that she had decided to keep.

"Oh. Okay. I can see those from here."

Once the paintings were standing at an advantageous angle, Eleanor stepped to the floor lamp just past Audrey's seat to shed more light on the display. She considered opening the front door to add more natural light. But Audrey's tone ended Eleanor's fussing around.

"Oh, so beautiful." Audrey crooned in a way Eleanor had not heard before. "I so love that one. Such a glorious way to think of Connie and remember how much she loved sunrises and sunsets." Her voice dipped lower. "Though I can't say I saw any sunrises with her."

"That was my father's specialty. He used to wake her up early if there was a good one to see."

"Yes. I think I remember her saying something about that, one of the things she missed about Darrel after he passed."

Eleanor inhaled a purging breath. "How well did you know my dad?" She hadn't yet thought of asking her mother's friends for insights into her father.

"Well, I played some bridge with him back in the day. And we all went out to dinner when Harold was still alive. Your father was a gentleman. Actually, a very gentle man, you know, in the literal sense of the words."

Eleanor stood staring at Audrey who continued to stare at the sunsets. The one in the middle had captured her especially.

"I've heard others say that about him. Did you know anything about Mom and Dad's marriage?"

Audrey glanced at her. "Oh, you know, we didn't talk about those sorts of things in the days when I was coming up. And your mother and I weren't part of the tell-all crowd that gets into each other's bedrooms. We were just bridge friends and dinner companions." She leaned back and considered Eleanor before returning her admiration to the paintings. "Can I see that one a bit closer?" She pointed a gnarled finger at the largest canvas, the one in the center of the three.

Eleanor lifted it and brought it close.

Reaching out and brushing her fingertips over the deep ochre and burnt umber in the foreground, prairie grass and a farmyard outlined but not detailed, the old woman sat silently. Was she lost in that farm scene or in a memory of Connie? She quivered slightly.

Eleanor could see tears now on Audrey's cheeks.

"She was a good woman. She never would have said anything bad about her Darrel. Nothing to shame him in any way."

The air in the living room stilled, a moment preserved, as if in a pricey gallery. What was Audrey saying? Did she know something? Perhaps she had sensed something. Even though they didn't talk about every intimate detail in those bridge circles, her mother's old friend might have intuited something about Eleanor's dad.

But maybe all that Audrey had seen was the love of a woman for her husband and the commitment encrusted on their marriage, like diamonds permanently set.

Eleanor stood up straight. "Yes. She was good. She was good at letting my father be himself, and at letting me be myself. She *was* a good woman."

Audrey craned her neck slightly, her eyes visible above her glasses. "I'd like to have this one, Eleanor, if you don't mind."

A sob escaped Eleanor's mouth. "Yes. Of course. I don't mind. It's yours. It was yours all along."

A sniffle from Debbie confirmed that there was not a dry eye left in that living room.

Eleanor carried the canvas to the car, cardboard tied with twine to the front of the oil painting. Debbie was helping her mother step over the bumps and cracks between the house and her sedan. The three women said little to each other on the driveway. Eleanor's thoughts didn't lend to interruption by words just then.

Standing with her arms crossed, the air cool in the shade of the house, Eleanor watched Debbie back her car in an arc so she could drive forward onto the highway. Audrey waved weakly as she passed Eleanor's view.

When they drove away, Eleanor thought of the barn and recalled leaving the door unlocked yet again. She slowly shook her head at herself and headed for the side door, intending to reach around and turn the lock on the knob. But then she thought of that question about where she had seen the other sunsets, and she pushed through the door, flipping on the light in the narrow corridor.

It was warmer inside the barn than out on the drive, the air stiller than that in the house. She paused at the first door on her left. Unpainted canvases were stored in there, along with tubes of paint, brushes and cans of gesso for preparing raw canvas. There were still two easels in there. Eleanor stepped in and pulled out those thin wooden easels, apparently unused before, resting them on the door frame. She would take them with her when she headed back to the house.

She continued down the corridor and opened the door to her left. This room was probably empty now. No. There were those racks of her mother's early paintings. Eleanor didn't know what to do with those. She was certain that the decades-old paintings were worth little commercially. Their primary value for Eleanor was their origin. They were her mother's work. It was crude in some ways, experimental in others. Amateurish. Even Eleanor could see that. And maybe that impression had been encouraged by Connie during her early days, her hobby days.

Eleanor left those older paintings and opened the door to her right, the largest room in the barn. She paused again, wondering whether there was anything of value in the attic, the upper level of the barn, open above the corridor. She had never been up there. Maybe Paul would know if it was worth the climb to those warm heights.

In that largest storage area, a few dozen paintings remained. Maybe as many as sixty. Paul had helped her unpack many of them, returned from a gallery in Madison, or in Springfield, Illinois. Here was a box from Evanston, Illinois, only a few paintings remaining. Among them was one of those sunsets Eleanor had thought she remembered. She slid it out of the tall, rectangular box in the low light and wondered whether Audrey would have preferred this one. But, of course, she wouldn't torture the deferential woman with another choice.

Grabbing two more barn paintings, along with the sunset, Eleanor headed back to the house, struggling to include the two thin easels in her load. This time she did remember to lock the door behind her. There were still hundreds of thousands of dollars' worth of her mother's art in there. Priceless, really. For the first time, she thought about checking the locks in the house, the latches on the windows. But maybe that was a New Yorker looking at Wisconsin in a way that was unduly cautious.

Taking her time getting the three paintings and the easels in from the back door, Eleanor chased away a fear that she was behaving like a packrat. Or maybe she was more like a crow, gathering shiny things to line her nest. Why not just leave these in the barn, while she thought about what to do with her mother's work?

The answer to that question was probably irrational. That was how it felt to her. A firm indication that she should ignore the self-criticism, for now. Jackie would be here in two days. She would help Eleanor find that "why."

She contented herself with rearranging easels in her mother's studio and finding space for the sunset she brought in from the barn, as well as one of the other paintings she had hauled in with her. Her gallery was a rough draft, at best. But it would be fun to show all this to Jackie. Surely, her friend would feel the overwhelming awe of so much Connie.

Even if she couldn't paint like Connie, Eleanor appreciated beauty in much the same way as her mother. Even after her education and her exposure to the East Coast art scene, Eleanor still favored her mother's style, her mother's Midwestern aesthetic.

Connie had laughed at words like that.

"You gotta get used to it, Connie," her dad had said once. "You gotta think about marketing. Folks want to buy paintings by an artist that calls them to transcend their own way of seeing the world. Part of that is the artist's language, transcending ordinary people's way of saying things, too."

"Transcending? Marketing? Pshaw. It's not some magical new soap."

Maybe Connie hadn't said it exactly that way. Maybe that memory wasn't from one conversation, but fragments of many back-and-forths between her parents. Her father, the sensible money guy—the engineer. And her mother—ever the artist.

Eleanor stood in the crowded studio gallery. "No, Mother. These are not soap. They're more than that. You were right."

CHAPTER TWENTY-EIGHT

"Your friend is coming tomorrow?"

"Yes. Jackie. She's my best friend. We've known each other for decades, teaching together at Carlisle. We've been through a lot together."

"And now she's coming to share in this next phase of your life?"

"Yes. And to get away from New York for a bit, to get out where the breezes run free." Eleanor laughed at herself. "You've been reading the Wisconsin tourist board literature, obviously."

She squinted at Virgil across the little table at The Caboose. It was becoming her favorite place to eat in the area. And Virgil didn't seem to mind it at all. How many times had *he* eaten here? Had there been other women? She hadn't voiced questions like that with him. Not yet.

"Jackie's saying she's gonna be like one of those Fresh-Air kids that gets a sponsor to take her out of a gritty urban environment, for an escape into rural America."

"I remember that program. Does it still exist?"

"I don't know. It was Jackie's joke."

"But isn't Carlisle in a small town?"

"A small city. The whole area, near Albany and Syracuse, is pretty urbanized. At least suburbanized. The town is old and built close, not wide open like my farm on the prairie."

"I just heard you say, 'my farm,' did I not?"

"I believe you did. You're hearing is pretty good."

"Yes, most of my parts still work as intended."

"I think I'll let that comment go unelaborated."

"Good idea. I didn't realize how that would sound before I

put it out there."

"Yes. Anyway. Jackie will be at O'Hare tomorrow. I'll go get her. The Honda is running fine. And then I hope the three of us can have dinner sometime. Maybe dinner out a couple times. The house still isn't ready for hosting anyone, I think."

"I doubt Jackie would be more judgmental about that than I would. And you know I wouldn't complain about visiting your house while it's in transition."

"I thought we were avoiding eating in, for the sake of the potential temptations."

He pursed his lips and nodded before sitting back to allow the waitress to set his plate in front of him. Once the young woman checked with them about needing anything else and turned toward the kitchen, Virgil responded. "I think that is a good precaution. But the three of us will be less scandalous."

Eleanor decided to bypass another off-color response, feeling proud of her restraint. "That brings up something Jackie is worried about, having never been here before." She lifted her fork and poked at the little salad beside her Tuscan chicken.

"What's that?" Virgil was cutting into a fillet of trout that looked good to Eleanor.

"She's African American, of course. And she's sensitive to her extreme minority status around here."

"Yes. That's a real thing. But I think folks around here are as various on race relations as they are on everything else. Some are open-minded and some not. Part of the dynamic around here might be the extreme rarity of people of color, especially African Americans, which sort of reduces the pressure. Where minorities are more populous is where there's the most resistance. Around here it's most likely to just be awkward."

"I think you're right." She sipped her wine. "I've been mostly treating Jackie's questions like a joke but trying to listen for real concern on her part. I assured her that Connie's old friends are open-minded folks."

"That's probably generally true." Virgil had a mouthful and was chewing with his eyebrows raised. "Good trout."

"I'm glad."

They had met late on Thursday night. Virgil had attended a board meeting that ended at seven-thirty. After finishing their dinner, they lingered a while. They shared a small dessert of chocolate cake. And then they stood together in the parking lot for a few minutes, squinting in the rising breeze.

"Have a good night, Eleanor." He brushed a hand down one bare arm.

She consciously resisted the urge to lean toward him. It was late. And they were still going slow.

"Good night, Virgil."

Eleanor drove herself home from the restaurant, the last twilight in her rearview mirror when she hit the county road east. She rode with her windows open, allowing the night air to rush over her and toss her hair.

She noticed a faint smoke smell that reminded her of a fireplace in winter. But no one would light a fire on this warm June evening. Not intentionally. Unless it was a bonfire.

As she approached the farm, the smoke smell seemed to be intensifying. A question was flitting around the periphery of her mind. As she slowed near her house, the faint glow of late twilight defined a low cloud in front of her. But there had been no clouds that evening.

She found her driveway, even as she jolted at the fact that the billowing cloud was smoke. Smoke rising from her place.

Eleanor slid into a sort of numb trance. The world around her paused.

It was the barn.

Eleanor cursed and then thanked the heavens that it wasn't the house.

Slamming on her brakes, she jumped out of the car. There were still paintings in the barn. She stumbled on high heels toward the side door of the barn but then realized she had left her keys in the car. She had added one barn key to her main key ring. Kicking off her high-heeled sandals next to the car, she swung around the driver's door and reached in to extract her keys.

As she ran toward the barn, she heard sirens in the distance. That was good. "Lord, bring them fast." Her hands shook violently as she hit and missed and hit the doorknob again. Finally, the key zipped in and she turned it, pushing the door at the same time.

The most valuable paintings were in the room to her right. She ran down the corridor, forgetting to turn on the light, feeling her way until she reached that door. Orange flames glowed against the beams of the roof, far above her. That glow helped her find the light switch in the big storage room. She seized the box from Evanston, slipped two more paintings into it and dragged it out to the corridor. The wooden box rasped heavily on the plywood under her feet, the raucous scraping chasing her toward the side door.

Smashing out through the screen door, she let the box of paintings fall over. Those were safe now. She jerked the door open again, aware of a truck coming up the driveway as she ran back into the barn.

A distant voice was telling her this was dangerous. Crazy. Let someone else do this insane thing. But she was too busy rescuing her mother's artwork to listen.

Clenching six canvases between two hands and backing out of the storage room, she heard the screen door slam. The sound of the fire was intensifying. She couldn't hear what the man was saying until he grabbed her.

"Eleanor. Get out of here. This is dangerous. It's not worth it." It was Paul Wasser. He was dragging her with one hand and supporting the stack of paintings with the other. Something above the other storage room fell with a ripping crash. Opaque smoke had filled the building down to her level now.

Coughing and crying at the same time, Eleanor let Paul haul her out the side door. They dropped the canvases onto the black plywood box from the Evanston gallery. Instantly, Eleanor calculated. Twelve saved. Maybe thirteen. There might be fifty more, plus her mother's old paintings in the other room.

When she stepped back toward the door, Paul intercepted her, grasping both her arms very firmly. "You can't go back in there. It's not safe." He looked into her eyes. What he saw there seemed to awaken something in him. "I have an idea. Get away from the building. Come over here." He was dragging her with him to the driveway.

Her feet yelped in pain as she stubbed toes and stepped on sticks, winter rock salt, gravel and rough asphalt. She ignored those complaints. Sirens commanded the night now. Sirens close at hand.

"Come here." He released her near her car, near his truck. "Wait here."

Paul ran and jumped into his pickup. Eleanor stared at him as he started the ignition and roared in low gear toward the barn. He was sitting up tall as if looking over the front of his hood, over the black rhino bars. He nosed his truck right into the white slats in front of him. Wood cracked and a sliver of darkness opened in the side of the barn. His wheels spun. His truck stopped. A billow of gray smoke escaped from the gap and rose toward the sky.

Another pickup was arriving on the driveway. Doors slammed and men yelled. One woman's voice was calling instructions. For a second, Eleanor thought it was her, her own fears being expelled into the chaotic air. But that sound was outside her. Everything that was happening now was located well outside of her. Including Paul crashing his truck into the barn and jumping out after backing it up.

He ran toward the tall gap he had opened. That must have been the old barn door. He had broken the old barn door open. Now he was pushing aside insulation, kicking at studs and climbing through the slim gap. He would be climbing directly into the large storage room. His father had built that room. Paul had arranged the painting storage in that room. He knew what he was doing.

When he reappeared in the tall gap, shoving several canvases out, Eleanor woke from her stupor. She ran toward where Paul was dropping those paintings. She stepped on something sharp. "Ow!" She would have to look at that later.

The paintings.

She gathered the rough stack of canvases and limped to the back of Paul's truck. She lifted them over the side and dropped them onto the plastic bed liner.

By the time she turned back, Paul was setting more paintings on the ground outside the barn. Others had seen him and were grabbing the artworks. A person with a helmet and fireman's coat pushed through the gap after Paul. A woman dressed in the same uniform lifted several paintings and dashed to the back of the pickup. She looked down at Eleanor's feet.

"Ma'am. Get back. You need medical attention. Paramedics are arriving now. Get to their truck. Your feet are injured. Ma'am?"

Eleanor stared at the woman. She looked familiar. A waitress from somewhere she had eaten? Maybe.

The driveway was full of vehicles now, full of noise. Someone was attaching a hose to the spigot on the house. Eleanor wondered if she should help them. It was her house. Was that her hose?

"Ma'am, I'm Helen Burchard, I can help you." A different woman. "Come with me." Strong hands pulled her away from her house. Away from the barn. Away from those flames now shooting through the roof.

A bigger hose was aimed at the barn. Lots of shouting. Who was shouting? She was stumbling away from the barn, but she turned back again to look over her shoulder. That was Paul leaning out of the opening in the barn, the old barn door.

Then he was down. Paul was down. A firefighter dragged him clear. Another had an armful of paintings, dropping them into the back of the truck.

Eleanor wanted to shout instructions to them, about those paintings. Those were her mother's paintings. But that woman. What was her name? That woman was helping her sit down on the grass by the driveway. Eleanor had never sat out here before. Not on this hill, this grass behind the sign that said, "The Dovecote."

A car swung into the driveway. Another stopped on the county road. That one had flashing lights. Sherriff's police, maybe.

A gush of water was pouring onto the roof of the barn now. Where did they get that water? Where was there a fire hydrant out here?

"Eleanor. Are you all right?" It was Virgil. He fell to his knees next to her.

"She'll be fine. Maybe some stitches in this foot, but I don't think there's anything still in there." The woman wore a headlamp and was working closely with Eleanor's feet.

"I'm fine. But the paintings. There were still some paintings. And Paul. How is Paul?"

"They've got him. He looks okay. A bit shaken up. But he looks okay."

"How did you know? How did you get here?"

"They called me when the volunteers got the alarm. They usually do that for house fires, call clergy. But they knew I knew you. They called me before they got here, I think."

"And Paul?"

"It's a small town. They probably called him too. Or maybe he's part of the volunteer department. I don't remember." Virgil was hunched toward her, intent on her. He was there for her. He was okay. She was okay. Paul was fine. But, what about the paintings?

Another crash and more flames swung her attention back to the barn. Someone backed Paul's truck further away from the fire. Then Eleanor saw a stack of paintings still leaning against the side of the barn.

"Look. There's more. More paintings."

She tried to stand, but Virgil rested a hand on her shoulder as he stood. "I'll go. You stay here. Your feet are hurt. Don't move." And then he was striding away. Running. Almost running. He was waving his hands and shouting at a firefighter. Then they both ran to the barn and grabbed paintings.

How many more was that? She strained to look toward Paul's truck. How many were in there? The truck was parked in the dark now and she couldn't tell whether she could see paintings sticking up from its bed. What about the ones she had left lying on the ground by the side door? "Oh, Lord. Help. Please take care of those, too."

Virgil was gone for longer than she had expected. A sort of sleepiness was settling over her. Now a blanket was around her shoulders. It wasn't really cold out, but that blanket felt good. She suddenly felt like sleeping. It was hard to breathe.

Then Paul came to her, something wrapped around his wrist.

"Are you okay, Eleanor?"

She nodded drunkenly. "I think they gave me something. I

feel sleepy."

"That's shock. Stay awake. You can stay awake. You don't need to go to sleep. We got lots of the paintings out, most of the ones in the big storage room. I had them move the ones you pulled out around onto the front porch. The house will be fine. The wind is blowing away from the house." He stopped at the sound of another siren moaning to a stop at the bottom of the drive. Firefighters were dragging another hose and more people were shouting. "I'll keep an eye on things."

Paul stumbled and then righted himself, gesturing and shouting to a man in a helmet. He pointed to the house. Eleanor watched him, believing that he had given her an assignment. Stay awake. Stay awake, Eleanor.

That woman was back. Where had she gone? "Okay. We should take you to the hospital in Janesville. I want them to look at your feet. I gave you a numbing shot in your right foot, but they can do more and do a better job at stitches than we can at the clinic in town."

Virgil returned before Eleanor could reply.

"We're gonna take her to the hospital in Janesville."

"I'll come with her."

"Okay."

They were settling things, taking care of things. That was good. Eleanor didn't feel like handling anything. She was just too tired.

"I feel like sleeping."

Virgil looked at the young woman with a question on his face.

"It's okay. No head injury. She can sleep if she wants. She's just overwhelmed. Probably a defense mechanism. We'll get her hooked up to oxygen, in case she inhaled too much smoke. I wouldn't worry about it."

What was that woman's name?

243

The two of them helped her onto a bed on wheels, and the young woman pulled the gurney into the ambulance with the help of a young man who appeared out of nowhere. It was dark. Most of the illumination came from flashing emergency lights and an orange glow off her barn. Her mother's barn. Her mother's former barn.

Virgil climbed into the ambulance. Eleanor rested her head on a small pillow. And she let everything fade away.

CHAPTER TWENTY-NINE

They didn't keep her in the hospital overnight. Just some stitches and a day's worth of pain meds. She was awake and numb when they rolled her out the door, Virgil walking next to her.

A man that she didn't recognize stood by a big, blue sedan. "How's the patient?" When he spoke, she knew she had seen him at church and at the funeral. "Kevin Miller, in case you don't remember me. It's been a hard night, I know."

"I do remember. Thank you for picking us up."

"Thanks, Kevin." Virgil helped Eleanor into the car. He spoke to Kevin the way one would to an old friend with whom much more is being left unsaid than the words needed in the moment.

Getting her feet up onto the back seat of that big old American car helped. The pill they gave her was helping as well. Now that overwhelming need to sleep was coming back. She rested the side of her head on the back of the seat. She didn't see him do it, but she could sense Virgil turning to check on her. Everything was going to be fine.

When she awoke, the clock in the dashboard of Kevin's car said 1:39. She didn't know if that was right. Car clocks are the hardest to set, aren't they?

There were no other cars in the driveway, except the Honda. Something had happened to it, but she was too tired to investigate. And the silhouette of the eviscerated barn—no longer a building, more of an overcooked carcass—prevented her from seeing anything else.

"Are you gonna be okay?" Virgil was propping her while she searched for her keys. They weren't in her pockets. Where would they be? She thought of the door to the barn. Then she leaned on the back door of the house. It was unlocked. How had that happened? She couldn't stop to worry now. Small worries need not apply for her attention. She was occupied.

"I'm fine. I just need to rest."

"You sure?"

She was too tired to change course. She was sending Virgil away and heading to bed.

"Thanks, Virgil. I'm fine."

"Call me when you wake up. I'll rearrange some things so I can drive you to O'Hare."

She stopped in the dining room, next to the stairs. How did he think of that? She had forgotten Jackie. "Oh. Yeah." She looked down at her feet in the disposable slippers from the hospital. The stitches on her right foot would prevent her from driving for a while.

She looked him full in the face. "Thank you, Virgil. Thank you for everything."

He smiled, patted her shoulder and watched her climb the stairs, slowly, steadily. Imitating steadiness. Imitating composure.

By the time she reached her bed, Eleanor was sobbing. How had that started? Maybe the drugs were making it happen. Or maybe the medication just provided the cover under which those overwhelming emotions had been sneaking up on her.

She sat on the edge of the bed and kicked off those silly slippers. She unzipped her skirt and fiddled with the button. She should have started on that button while standing up. No good. Too hard.

Using her last withered energy to lift her feet onto the bed, she lay down on her side and felt the cool pillow against her cheek.

She woke in the dark, a damp spot on her pillow where she

might have sweated or cried or drooled. Limping and hobbling to the bathroom and back, she thought she should probably take another pain pill. But she didn't know where they were. She lay back down and fell asleep, wondering where she had left the pills.

The regale of songbirds rose to a racket. Her brain engaged the bright world in which she lay. Her eyes still closed, she could tell that the sun was up. And she could tell that her feet were swollen. One foot was practically yelling at her.

"Where did I put those drugs?" She pressed herself to a sitting position, but double clutched on the way up, finding that her right wrist hurt. And then she decided the drugs were messing with her mind, which explained why she couldn't remember where she had left them.

"I shouldn't take any more of those." She stepped onto the floor and swore at herself. "Whoa. Oh, my God."

In the bathroom, she pried open the medicine cabinet. It was mostly empty. But there was acetaminophen. The doctor at the hospital had recommended that.

She took four. "Compromise. I'll overdose on over-the-counter drugs instead."

Her voice sawed at her throat, like it was scratched and scabbed. Not literally, right? She didn't remember hurting her throat. But it was stinging harshly.

"Smoke. I breathed in that smoke." She ran the water and sat on the lid of the toilet. Knocking the plastic cup into the sink, she retrieved it and filled it full. One long drink and her throat felt better. But then she thought she might throw up.

She took a few deep breaths and relaxed. "You're a mess, Lenny. Get a grip."

Why was she calling herself that?

The clock on the nightstand said 10:20 when she arrived back from the bathroom. That wasn't so hard to believe, assuming Kevin's car clock had been right. As tempting as the bed seemed, she turned away from the bedroom door and slowly eased down the stairs. She should eat something. And she was curious.

She was curious where she had left those pills. She was curious where she had left her keys. And where were the paintings they had rescued from the fire?

A three-foot-high pile, neatly stacked in the middle of the living room, on top of a black plastic garbage bag or two, answered something about the paintings. There must be at least thirty there. That was something. That was good. She stood staring at that stack for half a minute, seeing a hint of another stack just past it. Then she urged herself toward food, at least some juice. And a place to sit.

When she pivoted away from the living room, she saw her keys on the dining room table. Next to them were the pain pills in a prescription bottle, lying on its side. Unopened. It would stay that way. That stuff was debilitating. She limped her double hobble to the kitchen. Her left foot was banged and cut. Each step on it hurt. But her right foot was yowling at her. "Caterwauler. That's the word."

She ignored that insistent pain long enough to get bread into the toaster, apple juice into a glass and a chair arranged so she could put up both feet. Where was her phone?

She stood with more speed than she should have, fueled by panic. She found her purse on the table too. Why didn't she see it there before? Because she wasn't looking for it. That's why.

In her purse was her phone. She carried the phone with her toward the kitchen, stopping mid-course to survey her surroundings. Anything else I should be looking for? Anything else I should be noticing? She bent at the waist, to see through the sheer white curtains in the dining room. She could see a slice of the barn from there. No. She didn't want to notice *that* right now.

She returned to the kitchen to rescue the bread from the toaster just in time. "I hope you had insurance on the barn, Mom."

While she ate, her phone buzzed.

"How are you?" Virgil sounded normal, like nothing unusual had happened.

"You seem to be asking me that a lot."

"I care about you."

"I know you do. I'm fine. I survived the night."

"You taking the pain meds?"

"Too strong. Left me totally disoriented. It felt dangerous."

"Okay. Probably not the best fit for you." He paused. "What time is Jackie's flight coming in?"

Had she forgotten that again? Eleanor switched to the texting app and found her conversation with Jackie.

"It comes in at 2:25." She gave him the flight number.

"Good. I'll check to see if it's on time."

"You rearranged some meetings?"

He laughed. "Well, about that. Do you mind if the Larsons come along with us? I have a counseling session scheduled with them. I thought we could do it in the car on the way to the airport."

Not until the end of that little proposal was she certain that he was kidding. She was glad she had bypassed the meds, or she surely would have missed the joke. "Okay. But I get to chime in with some advice when I feel like it."

"That should be interesting."

She snickered, all out of witty replies. "My foot was caterwauling at me."

"Caterwauling? Is it still making a racket?"

"Not so loud now. I took a dozen Tylenol."

"You didn't."

"You're right. I didn't. Less than that, I'm pretty sure."

"Okay, now I'm only a little worried about you."

"That's an improvement."

"I'll be there at 11:45 to get you. Can you be ready?"

"I'll try."

"Good girl."

"I feel like a girl. I called myself Lenny this morning."

"Injuries will do that. I have to go now. But I'll pick you up in a bit."

"Okay. Sure. Thanks. See you later."

Getting ready for the trip to O'Hare was a twisted little struggle, including a bath in the claw foot tub so she could keep her stitches out of the water. Maybe a plastic bag on her foot in the shower would have worked. But she didn't want to stand up that long. For just ten seconds, she thought she might fall asleep in the tub. But she rallied and got herself together.

She was wearing her running gear when Virgil showed up.

"You must be feeling better. Going for a jog?" He looked at her shower sandals on her feet. "I don't think those will be good on the hills around here."

"You call those hills?" She followed him toward the car, gimping and limping. The shower sandals clopped on the pavement of the back porch. "These were easy to put on. I know Jackie won't mind."

"I understand. They look good on you." He looked at her face. "How are your eyes feeling? They're pretty red."

"Smoke."

He nodded and pulled the back door shut behind them. "Lock it?"

She fished the keys out of her warmup jacket pocket. She would peel off that jacket in the car. It was too warm for that late June day.

In the front seat of the car, crossing her leg with her ankle on her knee seemed to work, elevating the stitches. She just had to be careful not to bump her toes on the glove compartment. Those toes were sore, too.

"I'm such a mess."

"You look amazingly good, considering."

"Hmmm. That's like telling a woman that she has aged well."

"You mean I shouldn't tell a woman that?"

She snorted at him and reclined against the headrest. "You shouldn't ask her if she's pregnant, either."

"I knew that one."

They rode in silence for long stretches of the eastward journey. The sun was high, and the farms and rest stops were brightly awake. Eleanor was having less trouble staying awake herself.

"You wanna talk about it?"

"About the fire? About dozens of my mother's paintings burning?"

"That many?"

"Mostly her old ones, I think, her first amateur attempts. Purely sentimental value. I bet she would come back from the grave if I showed them or tried to sell them."

"I'm sure your mom would still be polite as a zombie."

She snorted. "Probably. A zombie that says, 'Oh, bother,' when she's done eating your brain."

He laughed from his belly. When he was sitting in the car, he had a little paunch, pushed up by his belt, bulging against his yellow polo shirt. She hadn't noticed it before. Maybe bringing Jackie into the picture was alerting Eleanor to some of Virgil's superficial liabilities. If that belly was his worst flaw, then she had nothing to worry about.

Weightier matters rose to prominence. "Did Paul go to the hospital? He was in the smoke longer than me. Longer than anyone."

"Yes. But they let him go this morning. I found out just after I called to you. The fire is the talk of the town."

"That's not surprising." She remembered the volunteer first responders. "No one else was hurt, were they?"

"No. No one I know of."

"What about you?"

"I didn't charge into the flames."

"I did see you charge up there and yell at some people. You got pretty close to the flames when you picked up those paintings."

"You saw that?"

"Yes. I was still cognizant."

"How did I look? Pretty heroic?" He looked at her boyishly.

"Oh. Very. Superman-like."

"Excellent. That was the best way I could think of ending our date. Then Paul got in there and tried to steal my thunder."

She laughed for several seconds, breathy and low. "Do you think Paul blames himself for the fire? The way he ran in there? Or maybe he was just trying to make up for his guilt at Mother's death."

"Paul is the kinda guy you want on your side in a crisis. I've seen that before. He used to be a volunteer in the Fire Department. He's the kinda person that runs toward trouble."

"So, maybe it wasn't about me?"

"Not entirely."

"That makes me feel better."

"Good."

She rested her sore throat and her sorrowful soul. How much had she lost? Contemplating that was too daunting right then.

The reunion with Jackie was chaotic, so much explaining to do. Eleanor had considered texting some of it as fair warning.

But all she had sent in advance was an alert that Virgil was with her.

"Oh, my. Sit yourself back down, girl."

"You mind if I take the back seat? I wanna put my feet up. It feels better."

"No. No. Go ahead. Whatever makes you feel best."

"Hi, I'm Virgil."

"Hello, Virgil. I'm Jackie."

"You're black."

Jackie stared at him for two seconds and then cast a side-long squint toward where Eleanor was trying not to hurt herself laughing, stalled in the process of scooting into the back seat.

Scowling askance at Virgil, Jackie said, "And you're white."

He looked at his arm. "Damn. Will you look at that."

He had joked with Eleanor many times. And some of his teases were a bit outrageous. But that one was the worst. In a good way, probably. After that, they were a loose little group on the way back to Dove Lake. After filling Jackie in on the news about the barn, Eleanor managed to doze a bit while the two in the front seats conducted mutual in-depth interviews. Their laughter woke Eleanor more than once.

CHAPTER THIRTY

With Jackie in her peripheral vision, sitting on the wrap-around porch where it faced the pond, Eleanor was having a historical experience. Nothing in view had been invented in the last century. Yet she was sitting on that Adirondack chair next to her friend whose political and social liberation had only been realized within that last century. These were the sorts of thoughts that filled silent moments with Jackie, between conversations about chicken pot pie and insurance investigations.

"Paul was being very … maybe diffident about all of it, wasn't he?"

"I only worry that he's going to take too much blame on himself, again." Eleanor turned her head toward Jackie. Her friend held a Pearl Buck novel in her lap, open and ignored.

Jackie closed the book and inhaled briskly. "Well, as long as his *mea culpa's* don't slow down the insurance payout."

"Oh. I'm not worried about that."

"Does that mean you're in no hurry to sell this place?"

"Maybe that is what it means. I don't feel restless about the farm, like I did when Mother died. I'm not anxious to break free from this place anymore."

"And that's all about Virgil?"

Eleanor smiled, eyes still surveying the pond. "I'm glad you like him so much. I do, too, of course. But all I have with Virgil is a *potential* relationship and lots of unanswered questions."

"You wanna go over *The Apostle's Creed* with me to see if we can negotiate a palatable position for you?"

"You make it sound like I'm running for office."

"A candidate for marriage would do well to have her religion and philosophy platform firmed up." Jackie tossed her head from side-to-side in small shakes, probably enjoying her own attempt at running that metaphor to its useful conclusion.

Eleanor belly-laughed and then looked down at her belly. Jackie was being a bad influence, cooking up irresistible dishes from her childhood, inspired by the farm kitchen. "Speaking of 'firmed up.' I need to eat more salads."

"Did I hear you say, 'I need to eat more' just now?"

"Salads. Greens. Low-calorie healthy food with no butter, no cream and no animal fat."

"I have no idea what you're talking about." Jackie wasn't obese, but she carried at least twenty more pounds than Eleanor, and carried it well, despite being two inches shorter.

"And no sugar. Your cinnamon rolls are going to kill me."

"Yes. But what a way to die." Jackie laughed and stood up. "Okay. What about a walk?"

Eleanor rallied and stood up as well. They had done a lot of packing and moving of boxes that day, so a walk sounded great, if she could get her tired limbs to cooperate. "Finally, I can show you that path Virgil introduced me to." She wiggled her right foot, still feeling a lump where the stitches had been removed the day before.

"Not the path in that park where I walked?"

"No. This is one that starts just past the barn."

With walking shoes on and already-sweated-in cutoffs and tee shirts they started a pre-supper walk. A steady breeze from the west was keeping the summer day comfortably warm, as opposed to stiflingly hot.

Eleanor paused at the corner of the barn, looking for a way over the rubble, into the path behind the charred structure. That remnant resembled the hull of an ancient ship, burned on the beach to keep the enemy from fleeing these shores. That wasn't what was keeping Eleanor from fleeing. It was something more hopeful.

They were both glancing into what was left of the blackened interior as they found the path beyond the disaster scene.

Several of her mother's old paintings had been recovered from the fire, char marks, water warping and crashing beams sparing a few entirely and leaving others still sentimentally valuable. Only two of the remaining newer paintings survived inside the barn. But forty-nine had been pulled out before the roof collapsed and the three fire engines doused the blaze into submission.

"You given any thought to rebuilding it?" Jackie introduced a subject Eleanor hadn't explored much with her yet.

"In fact, I had this idea while I was lying in bed this morning." She lifted her head and allowed the wind to push her hair off her forehead. She needed a haircut soon. "I was imagining a gallery, featuring the works of Connie Petersen and other local artists."

"One of those eureka-in-the-sheets moments, huh?"

Eleanor was leading the way through trees that had fully leafed out now, and past taller and thicker weeds than when she and Virgil had walked here. "It was pretty sedate for a eureka moment. Just an idea."

"A Connie Petersen gallery sounds pretty inspired to me."

"Inspired?" Eleanor stepped around a thistle that was impressively large for this early in the summer. The breeze was cutting into the openings between the trees, and the sun marked a latticework on the path in front of them.

"That reminds me. When the barn was burning down, I called out to God more than once. And the whole time I was really hoping for some divine intervention."

"Seems like you got some answered prayers. I never would have expected you to recover so many of the paintings."

A chill tickled Eleanor's back. "Huh. Yeah. I've been wondering something about that." She was wondering now how much she was willing to say to Jackie.

"What's that?"

"I've been quietly marveling at how things worked out." Her breathing was accelerating. She hadn't walked this much since the fire. "I had far more of Connie's paintings in the house than she ever had. I was getting kind of obsessive about it, sort of doing it without understanding why." She stopped walking there, touching on a superstitious credulity that made her suspicious. And her right foot was starting to hurt.

Jackie looked down where Eleanor was flexing her foot. "Wait. You're thinking that maybe God led you to move paintings into the house because the barn was going to burn down?"

"I wasn't going that far." Eleanor started hiking again. "But it does seem odd that I would do that. I'm a de-clutterer, as you know. Why was I cluttering up the house with her paintings, at the same time that I was trying to clean it out?"

"Well, I was thinking the paintings were a way to have your mother close to you."

"Um-hmm. That's what I was telling myself. It was like having her arms around me, when I stood in that studio surrounded by dozens of her paintings." A small stitch was starting in her right side. "The other thing was trying to assess what I had, what paintings she left me. And, of course, it made it easy for me to give some away to her friends."

"Did you give one to Paul?"

Eleanor slowed and turned around. Jackie nearly crashed into her.

"Why do you ask that?"

"He was close to her. Don't you think he would like one to remember her by?"

Turning again, to resume their trek, Eleanor nodded. "In fact, I did hint that he could have one. I didn't offer it outright. He was quick to insist that I not give away too many, like he was protecting Connie's legacy, or something."

"Well, that's her agent's job, right? I mean, the agent controls the paintings already out in galleries. She's the one who's gonna decide how to sell and where to donate to standing collections."

"That sounds right. But, apparently, I need to keep you in the loop. You've clearly given that some thought."

"That's just because of my brother. He's still living, of course. But I could tell right away what the agent's role would be, when you told me about your mom's will. At least, that's how Ty's agent would probably see it." She had caught up and was nearly shoulder-to-shoulder with Eleanor. "But I think you should try harder to give Paul one. I think he needs a concrete expression of your forgiveness."

"I'm not holding anything against him, that's true. Even if the barn came down because of bad wiring, wiring his dad and uncle did, we saved most of the paintings. And Paul risked his life to do that. How could anyone resent *his* role in all of it?"

"*He* could, I think. Sounds to me like he's still kneeling in contrition, waiting to be released."

"Maybe I should get Virgil involved in this. He knows more about that kind of thing than I do."

"And he knows Paul?"

"It's a small town, dear. Everyone knows everyone."

"Not literally."

Eleanor turned back toward the house. "No, not literally. But that reminds me. I want you to meet Yvonne."

Jackie made a small noncommittal sound as she continued to follow. Slowing, Eleanor tried to estimate the distance back to the house. Her foot was ready for a break.

That meeting with Yvonne happened faster than Eleanor had assumed it could be arranged. It turned out that the next day, a Tuesday, was a good time to come by and visit The Dove's

Nest. Eleanor wanted Jackie to see the paintings.

On the phone, the caregiver had assured her that Connie's portraits were still displayed in Yvonne's room. "I don't think she would ever consider taking those down. It is like a drug for her. It makes her high."

Eleanor didn't know how literally to take that assessment. What were Consuela's medical qualifications, her psychological credentials? But she certainly knew Yvonne.

"Yvonne does still come out of her room. I was worried at first that she would never go for walks or come downstairs for meals. The first week she was totally obsessed."

That Tuesday, Consuela met them on the porch of the group home. She led the two visitors inside. On the way up the stairs, she dipped her head confidentially toward Jackie.

"I hope you don't mind me mentioning that Yvonne doesn't know many black people. She might say something insensitive."

Eleanor guessed that hearing it from the Hispanic woman made that warning a little easier for Jackie to accept in its best light. Jackie was remarkably secure about racial identity, anyway. All she showed in response to Consuela's caution was a smile that might have been a bit mischievous.

When they reached the top of the stairs, the door to Yvonne's room swung open. She stood before them wearing the white peasant blouse and red skirt that Eleanor had found in the studio and had brought over the week before Jackie arrived. For a long moment, Yvonne stood holding the door, as if still deciding whether to admit the visitors. But Eleanor suspected that it was a pose, a sort of performance art.

Then Yvonne broke character. "You must be Eleanor's friend. Were you Connie's friend, too?"

Jackie smiled and offered her hand. "I'm Jackie. Pleased to meet you."

Yvonne just looked at that hand.

Taking the hint in the hesitation, Jackie responded to Yvonne's question. "I mostly knew Connie through her daughter, Eleanor. I only met her once, in New York. In some ways, I'm meeting her anew through her paintings."

"Then you can meet her through these." Yvonne reached slowly for Jackie's hand just as Jackie had begun to withdraw it. With her other hand, Yvonne performed a sort of spokes-model flourish toward the fabulous prizes on display.

Jackie allowed herself to be towed into the room. She was looking at the paintings on the walls, speaking in a muted automatic tone. "Thank you. Thank you for sharing this with me. I know it's a precious thing."

Still holding Jackie's hand, Yvonne nodded. "A precious thing. Connie was like a mother to me." She settled into a kind of meditative stillness, standing now in the center of the room.

Eleanor was watching a hint of amusement and a full portion of fascination on Jackie's face. She stepped next to the two of them, as Consuela departed down the stairs.

Yvonne's room wasn't large. It had space for a double bed, a small desk painted antique white, and a tall, narrow dresser of similar design. A small bedside table and one armchair were the other major furniture items. A basket of stuffed and plastic baby dolls in one corner caught Eleanor's attention for the first time, but her interest clung to the dance between Yvonne and Jackie, the dance of the model and the admirer.

Sweeping her free hand toward the paintings on the wall again, her arm lifted high, like a gypsy dancer in a vintage cantina, Yvonne said nothing now. Her body was speaking for her. That explanation included a satisfied smile and glistening eyes. Eleanor wasn't even looking at the paintings.

Jackie stood enthralled by the portraits arranged on every wall in that room, at eye level. Almost every inch of wall space was covered by framed paintings of Yvonne.

Eleanor had contributed the frames, two at a time, hoping they were a way of honoring those paintings, enhancing them for both artist and model. Each time she had arrived with a frame or two in hand, along with the tools for setting a painting into a frame, Yvonne seemed to receive it as a sort of ceremony. It was a ceremony celebrating her paintings, Connie's art and the beauty communicated by the gift from one woman to the other. Yvonne continued to welcome Eleanor into that beauty.

This was the first time this summer that Eleanor had visited without a picture frame in hand. But bringing Jackie with her seemed to please Yvonne as much as those golden gifts.

"I would know you anywhere, after seeing these." Jackie studied Yvonne in person for a few seconds and then returned to the portrait reverie.

Something about Jackie joining in Yvonne's glory, displayed in those paintings, cracked Eleanor as if her heart were a hard-boiled egg. A disturbing feeling. What was it? A protest? An accusation? Against Connie?

Why had Connie given this to Yvonne?

Why did Eleanor's mother give such beauty to this stranger? And not to her daughter?

Eleanor knew objective reasons her mother had chosen Yvonne as her model. Yvonne was available. When had Eleanor given Connie the idea that her daughter would be available to pose for hours?

And, of course, Yvonne needed this. Connie surely knew the riches she was bestowing on this lonely and shattered woman.

Yvonne needed to be seen. She needed a mother figure. And she needed that mother to *see* her, truly and lovingly.

But didn't Eleanor need that too?

Connie had beamed over her daughter's academic accomplishments. Was that enough? Eleanor would have allowed a silent assent to that question ... before.

But now?

Eleanor's value was more than the bullet-points on her resumé. Connie should have known that. She should have seen that. Seen the beauty of her daughter.

Sensing that someone was watching her, Eleanor refocused her gaze. She had been staring at the wall, a strip of medium blue paint. Jackie was asking a question with her eyes. She was studying the expression on Eleanor's face. What exactly that expression was, Eleanor didn't know. But her dissatisfaction had come loose, come out of its box, spilled on the floor around her feet, like the pieces of a toy with some assembly required.

Then they were all back together. Eleanor smiled at Jackie, as an apology for whatever her friend had perceived on her face during that foray into regret. And Yvonne was the star in the room again.

She had finally released Jackie, standing with both hands on her hips. It was the pose from one of the seven paintings. Yvonne appeared in it from the knees up. She was looking to her right, as if anticipating a guest at her door. Her face and posture included expectation but not yet a welcome. Yvonne waiting. Yvonne hoping. Yvonne prepared to be disappointed, perhaps.

Then Yvonne, the living woman, began to cry. No sound. No movement. Just tears.

Eleanor glanced at Jackie. Jackie was standing next to Yvonne, observing the change from a foot away. Eleanor was close enough to see the shine of the tear-soaked cheeks. She was also close enough to know that she didn't really envy Yvonne now.

Blinking back her own tears, Jackie reached out and rested the palm of one hand on the peak of Yvonne's near shoulder.

Her lower lip curling and quivering, Yvonne turned toward Jackie. She shook her head. She looked at the door. And then began to sob.

"She's not coming. She's not ever coming."

That squeezed a purging flood out of Eleanor. As if she had come to visit Yvonne for this very purpose, to find a catalyst for her own grief, Eleanor lunged into sadness with full volume, before muting her catharsis from the ears of unseen listeners.

Instead of coming to Eleanor's aid, Jackie wrapped one arm around Yvonne. Even in her wretched state, Yvonne was clearly less than fully comfortable with that contact from Jackie. But she didn't resist. She didn't move away. She seemed to be as much beside herself as Eleanor was.

Finally, Yvonne turned toward Eleanor and allowed a sort of curiosity to tighten her eyes. Then she reached a hand toward her. That was all the invitation Eleanor needed. But she knew better than to wrap her arms around Yvonne. She settled for interlocking both her hands around Yvonne's offered one. Perhaps that physical contact distracted Yvonne. Eleanor could see the acid grief begin to dilute immediately.

But Yvonne's childish declaration still hung in the air. And it was landing deep in a carved furrow. A seed that seemed certain to take root in Eleanor's heart.

"She's not coming."

No. Connie is not coming through that door. Not ever again.

CHAPTER THIRTY-ONE

Virgil stood chopping tomatoes on a wooden cutting board with smooth, round corners. He was laughing at Jackie's story about her husband's latest movie.

"Thomas was perfectly serious when he compared the role to *Hamlet*. But the kid director seriously had to take a few seconds to try to recall who Hamlet was."

"I guess it was off his radar in the midst of filming a movie about invading aliens and superheroes." Virgil's laughter ended in a head-shaking smile.

Eleanor had to break herself away from watching him—Virgil being handy in the kitchen, Virgil enjoying her best friend and holding nothing back when he heard a funny story. She grinned at the phrase flashing on her internal message board. "This guy is so cute." He certainly wouldn't appreciate that label. But she could still enjoy it privately.

"So, has Eleanor mentioned her idea of building a gallery on the site of the charred barn?" Jackie cocked an eyebrow at Eleanor, even as she aimed her question at Virgil.

Eleanor read that as a defiant eyebrow. It was saying, "Ha, you can't stop me now."

Snorting and looking back at the chicken browning in the skillet, Eleanor pretended disinterest. Not a believable pretense, she expected.

"A gallery? Oh, that sounds like an inspired idea."

"What?" Eleanor let the spatula rest on the edge of the pan. "I think the operative word here is 'conspired' not 'inspired.' You two are scheming behind my back."

Virgil stopped his slicing and stared at Eleanor before checking with Jackie. "Oh. Did you say the same thing?"

"Go ahead. Feign innocence." Eleanor returned to flipping the strips of white meat and turned down the flame.

"Oh, girl, you've just been exposed, and you can't admit it." Jackie cackled. She slapped her thigh once. "You're taking direction from Heaven, but you don't want anyone else to notice." She turned to Virgil again. "Did she tell you how mysterious forces led her to move paintings into the house before the barn fire?"

Grinning at each of the two women in turn, Virgil seemed to be enjoying the repartee. Then he grew more serious and kept his eyes on Eleanor. "I *was* meaning to say something about that. I think it *is* providential that you felt drawn to move those paintings in here. It made sense to me as part of the grieving process. But, after the fire, I got a good chill out of the thought that God wanted to save as many paintings as possible."

Eleanor turned off the burner entirely, stiffening against her own chills. She scraped the chicken strips onto a paper towel folded over a medium-sized plate. "Well, if we're getting into this ..." She offered Virgil a challenging glare. "... then tell me why God didn't just fix the air-conditioner part to prevent the fire."

The insurance company was blaming the fire on an electrical part connected with the air-conditioner unit, a part that had caused dozens of similar fires around the country. They would pay Eleanor for her claim, but the insurance company would join other firms in pursuing recompense from the part manufacturer.

Leaning a hand on the butcher block and setting down the knife, Virgil seemed to rise to Eleanor's challenge. "Okay. But, why stop there? Why couldn't God help the designers make a better part? Or why couldn't God inspire the air-conditioner manufacturer to choose a different part? Or maybe God should have appeared in a dream and told the designer of the faulty part to pursue another career, say in pyrotechnics?"

Eleanor snuffled a constrained laugh, but Jackie let loose.

"Ha! This guy is good." She flipped shards of lettuce onto

the floor in her enthusiasm. They were in the middle of a cooperative salad project.

"I think we're ready to get this together." Eleanor was still grinning, but she didn't aim that grin at the others. She carried the plate of chicken toward the counter where Jackie had arranged three dinner plates.

Jackie faced her. "Are you changing the subject?"

"Would you cut the bread?"

"Yes. And yes, you *are* changing the subject." Jackie shook her head and reached for the bread knife.

Eleanor thought she saw a small conciliatory shrug from Virgil, probably aimed at Jackie. Co-conspirators, indeed.

Virgil spoke next as if into the evening air, addressing the night and no person in particular. "The interesting thing I find in lots of these discussions about why God did or didn't do something is the assumption that we humans know what's best. We ask the question 'why' because we see a failure in the system. And, of course, we look to the top of that system for the origin of the failure."

Eleanor was persisting in her food preparations, adding the chopped vegetables and chicken onto the greens. But that slowed when Virgil's voice deepened.

"I went through this when Joanne died."

When was the last time he had mentioned his deceased wife?

Eleanor stood holding two plates now, Jackie a third salad and the bread. Both stopped still.

"I had the perfect solution back then. I saw the point of failure, the fault where I could correct God. But, in the process, I realized my own failed assumption. I was assuming that God wasn't God, or at least not very god-like." His voice sharpened. "Why assume that the failure is in the only part of the system that's flawless, and not in one of the many other parts, all of which are deeply flawed? If God is just another flawed player in the cosmos, then God isn't God, but just another guy not doing his job."

In the silence that followed Virgil lead the way to the dining room. That silence grew out of the quaver that had thinned his voice. And out of the way he then reduced that voice to a whisper. And then he ended abruptly. Plates clacking together, silverware tinkling, and glass tumblers landing on the table had their say. The aroma of freshly cooked chicken and freshly grated Parmesan seemed to increase in the hiatus in human voices.

"Sorry. I guess that was too heavy for the occasion." He stood now behind his dining room chair, the sheer curtain behind him billowing with the breeze, weightlessly brushing against him.

"No. That was good. That was a good reminder." Eleanor stood directly across from him. "I've avoided seriously asking questions like that all my adult life. I certainly haven't thought them through thoroughly." She pulled out her chair. "And I appreciate you making it personal. Because, of course, it *is* personal. Which is why we even bother to ask."

He smiled at her, a grateful smile.

The salad was fresh and tasty, and the conversation easier and somewhat sedate after that. A storm blew in from the northwest. And the three of them moved out to the front porch to watch the ebbing and flowing downpour, standing just out of the wind and clear of the drenching. It had been a dry summer so far. Much of the grass had gone brown already, with most of July and August still ahead. This deluge would revive the greening of summer, at least for a while.

When he prepared to leave that night, Eleanor hugged Virgil and kissed him on the cheek. That physical farewell was more prolonged than they had allowed themselves thus far. Maybe her warm touch was safer with Jackie there. And maybe it was a peace offering, after her attempt to challenge the conjoined faith of her two guests.

She didn't really feel outnumbered by them. Jackie and Virgil surely didn't agree about everything religious or philosophical. She had also seen signals that she wouldn't have to entirely conform to Virgil's creeds to have a lasting relationship with him, just like her relationship with Jackie.

Eleanor didn't see much of Virgil during Jackie's visit, just three dinners during her two-week stay. They did attend his church on one Sunday. That was Jackie's idea.

Those two weeks felt like a break in their progress toward what lay ahead for Eleanor and Virgil. Going slow still.

When the visit was over, Eleanor drove Jackie back to the Chicago airport.

"Now you can get down to more writing." Jackie was squashing the back of her Afro against the headrest and, looking sated, as if the visit had been just what she needed.

"I can, thanks to you. We got so much stuff done. It really feels at least halfway like my house now."

"Are you traveling soon?"

"Not right away. I have plenty of online research I still want to do. If I get bored with that I'll travel to St. Louis and Denver. I'll save New York for some time when you miss me."

"I miss you already."

"I believe you. But I think you're ready to get back to your own research, and to Thomas."

"He should be back in about two weeks. I can get some chapters drafted before he shows himself back home." She lifted her head off the rest and turned fully toward Eleanor. "You gonna run into Virgil's arms as soon as you get done dropping me off?"

"I don't know. I worry that I've been holding back, keeping him at a distance. I guess I'll have to decide if that's still the case when you're gone. I'll have no excuse."

"You were using me as an excuse to stay away from him?"

"No. Not that. Just staying away from deciding how much I want to be with him."

"Did we get all the way through *The Apostles' Creed*?"

"Maybe we got through it. You would know that better than me. But that doesn't mean I'm confident that I believe everything that's in there."

"You should discuss it with Virgil."

"Yes. I know. I have to. But it feels like *the* conversation. The big one."

"Yeah. Maybe it's not time for that yet."

"On the other hand, I don't want to lead him on, if there's no way that I'll ever believe all that he believes, or all that he needs me to believe."

"Let's keep talking about it. Call me when something comes up. I still don't sense that you know what's holding you back."

"Like what are the key tenets that I doubt?"

"Maybe it's that. But I wonder if it's not still tied up with your parents and the way you blamed them when you were a teen."

Eleanor bobbed her head and then shook it. "Wow." She chuckled. "The doctor is in the house. I think I owe you about $150 for that golden nugget."

"Yes. This was a good session, Ellie. See my receptionist for your next appointment."

"Yes, Doctor."

It was hard to let her go by the curb at departures. And Jackie didn't seem any more willing to break their hug than Eleanor was.

"Thanks for coming to see me. It was wonderful. You were so much help, and more than just with packing."

"Yeah. Thanks for hosting this Fresh Air kid out in the

boondocks. Next time don't burn down the barn before I come out."

"Right. I'll make a note."

"Love you."

"Love you, too."

During the drive back to the farm, Eleanor fed and watered her doubts about her retirement. Could she really stay away from teaching? Was she really ready to make the farmhouse her permanent home?

That was when she started calculating what it would take to keep two homes. But the notion of a home in Wisconsin and one in Upstate New York seemed absurd. Why not one in Arizona? Or maybe New Mexico? South Texas? Having two northern homes made no sense, not in retirement. But what if she didn't retire? Not completely, anyway. She could drop the responsibilities of chairing the department and reduce her course load. She could spend more time on research and writing during the school year and take a break on the farm in the summer.

It was a long drive back to Dove Lake. Plenty of time to spin out the scenarios. But not enough time to settle all her unanswered questions.

And Jackie had laid a new question on her. Was there something about her resentment against her mother that was holding back her faith in God? Was Jackie the only one who thought it might be so? Perhaps Virgil had been too polite to point it out. He seemed to be pretty good at going slow. But maybe that was because he hadn't let go of his wife in the years since her death. He had mentioned Joanne just that week.

That thought uncovered something in Eleanor's memory chest.

When she was nineteen, her cousin died in a boating accident, a shocking and bloody accident with a speed boat. But Connie had provided sparse emotional and spiritual help to her daughter. She had left Eleanor to shake her fist at God by herself.

Dad had at least seemed to sympathize with Eleanor's anger. But he had averted his eyes from her, as if sending his thoughts toward the horizon, toward a place of battle in some future time.

Her parents' quiescent acceptance of the tragic death felt like another betrayal.

Lenny had probably only seen her cousin Sheri a dozen times in her life. But she had liked her from the start. Sheri was one of those girls that seemed flawless at first. And then, when you found out about her flaws you loved her even more for those. Sheri was humble. She knew her limits. And she was okay with those—okay with not being the smartest, the prettiest or the richest. She was good. Sheri deserved to live, if anyone did.

Then the accident happened the summer after Eleanor's freshman year. It had been freshman year that she witnessed her mother's Thanksgiving rebuff of her father. That connection hadn't occurred to her before this ride back from the airport. Each of those peak events was emotionally monumental in its own way. Each full of tragedy and loss.

And it was that following school year that Eleanor had started dating Gary Wilmington.

A cluster of historic events.

In the lives of the women she studied for her seminars, her lectures, and her books, Eleanor had seen this. What about her? Was Eleanor Petersen formed by a series of crucial, interlinked events in her life? Crises that shaped who she would later become?

Her phone's GPS system kept her from missing her turns. That allowed her to dive deep into those memories. There was a conversation with Connie around the time of Sheri's death.

"I didn't sleep hardly at all last night." Connie had been

sitting in the kitchen in suburban Greenfield, her hands wrapped around a cup of coffee.

"Are you angry at God for what happened to Sheri?" Eleanor remembered wanting to ask her mother that question, and saw that sleepless night as her opening, a hint that her mother was suffering the same resentful doubts as her.

"Angry at God? God wasn't driving that boat."

"So, you're angry at the driver, the one that claimed he didn't see her in the water."

"Of course, he didn't see her. Who would run right over a girl in the water? No one would do that."

Thrashing about as if she were drowning in that deep lake where Sheri had died, Lenny had tried to get more out of her mother. But what was she wanting?

"Then why couldn't you sleep?"

"It's just so sad. So very sad. She was such a sweet girl."

That wasn't enough. But was Lenny looking for something so profound that it would make sense of Sheri's death? Was there such a thing? Was she looking for something so powerful as to bring her cousin back from the dead?

Driving her mother's old Honda, she remembered the sympathy in Connie's eyes, a tired woman crumpled under her own grief, perhaps. Had Lenny seen it back then? She was not in a sympathetic place with her mother that year.

Connie had made one attempt to console her, perhaps in another conversation. "You just have to pick yourself up, Lenny." Her voice was that combination of sweet and scratchy even back then. "Or maybe you need someone else to do it. That's who God is for me. God picks me up when I feel like I can't lift myself."

Was that what she said? It was something like that. "You just have to pick yourself up." Maybe Mom had said the rest of it about God. But that first phrase was the one that had confirmed Eleanor's assessment of her mother—a cold woman incapable of deep and meaningful connection, unable to connect with her husband, clearly insensitive to her daughter's need for help.

Of course, Lenny couldn't pick herself up.

That was the crisis.

The Connie in those memories now felt like someone else, a different relative. Related to Eleanor, but not her mother. Not the mother who created those sensitive paintings. Life-giving paintings. As life-giving as Connie's compassionate generosity to her friends and acquaintances. A woman who gave so much to Yvonne.

Perhaps the revised version of her passionate mother had always been there, had always been the real one. Connie had lived with a man who couldn't love her in the way she needed. But she accepted that discovery and persisted in her life. She didn't succumb to sorrow, just as she struggled to overcome the grief of her niece's death.

Eleanor was driving into the sun now, late in the afternoon.

"I forgive you, Mom. For not having the answers I needed."

She drew a long breath. "Please forgive me, for judging you so harshly."

CHAPTER THIRTY-TWO

Her computer and her publication deadlines called Eleanor up to her office, again and again. Paul had sent a young man over to help her set up a new computer—a faster desktop with a better keyboard for extensive typing, better than her laptop. And the work was flowing, the stories coming together, a picture of a pioneering woman coalescing in her mind. Jackie's chapters were bolstering Eleanor's growing confidence in the book.

But the summer sun and the people of Dove Lake were calling her *out* of that office. Virgil most of all.

They sat one afternoon in the shade of a tall tree that he identified as a balm of Gilead tree. She suspected him of substituting that name for a more scientifically accurate one. But then she found the species of tree in a Web search on her phone.

"I should have bet you money on that." Virgil grinned under his baseball cap, sunglasses substituted for his usual black wire-rims.

Eleanor pushed up her own plastic-rimmed sunglasses. "That would be taking unfair advantage of a novice."

"A novice Wisconsinite?" He pulled his hat off. "You're not used to being a novice, are you?"

"No, it's been a long time since I took on something new. Maybe that's my hesitation about pursuing faith. I was mostly just going through the motions when Jackie walked me through *The Apostles' Creed.*"

"*The Apostles' Creed*? Really? Why did she do that?"

"I guess she was thinking it's important that I agree with the basics, if I'm gonna have a relationship with a minister."

"That's understandable." He turned toward the lake, then glanced her way. "If you're serious about pursuing that kinda thing, I would recommend a class at a church in Heeley, just twenty minutes from your place."

"Another church?"

"A friend of mine. I'm thinking it would be awkward for you to attend the class at my church. And Randy and I will be saying the same things in our Christian theology classes."

"I guess I should do that." She brushed hair free from one eyebrow. "He wouldn't pressure me to convert, would he?"

"No. That's not what the class is for. We just lay out the tradition and our beliefs about it, and we leave it for you to decide what you want to do with it."

She turned to studying the lake again, wondering if she was ready to become a religious novice.

Virgil took a deep breath, as if he had just decided something. "But, to me, the really important issue isn't agreeing with all the propositions in an abstract creed. What really matters is being willing to let God into your life. To let God give you a hand now and again, to reach out and connect. To be willing to have Jesus come alongside and pick you up when you need it."

She turned fully toward him. "Really? That reminds me of something my mother said once." Eleanor sorted through her scattered memories of those teenage conversations again.

He spoke with more force than usual, cutting through the sound of the wind in the trees. His preaching voice. "Can I tell you a story? Something I saw this past week, when I was at Starbucks?"

"A coffee-related story?"

He smiled broadly. "No. Something more to the point."

She nodded for him to go ahead, shielding her eyes from the sun.

"I often go to a Starbucks in Janesville to work on my sermons or lessons. It's usually quiet there but not totally isolated. So, anyway, I was there about ten days ago working on my sermon, which probably helps explain why I was captivated by this event I witnessed.

"I was sipping my coffee and looking out the big window next to the table where I sat, and this little Audi sports car pulled into the lot and turned toward me, into an empty parking space. But it pulled in too far and made that terrible scraping sound over the concrete barrier. You know. Screech!"

She laughed. "I get the picture."

Virgil chuckled a bit self-consciously. "And then, of course, the driver put the car in reverse and pulled back, making an even more awful sound. This one included a 'crash,' like something really broke." He winced sympathetically.

Eleanor mirrored that painful grimace.

"So, I'm watching as this very small girl gets out of the driver's side of the car. You know how, as you get older, the kids driving cars seem to be younger and younger. I mean, it was like a middle-schooler getting out of the driver's seat. And a similarly young girl got out of the passenger side. They looked at the front of the car and then the driver made a call on her cell phone." Virgil leaned forward and wrapped his arms around his knees, as if to relieve his back of some strain.

"A little while later, those two girls were in the Starbucks drinking their Frappuccinos and giggling, when another car pulls into the lot and parks next to the damaged Audi. This was a brand-new Lexus. A very nice top-of-the-line car. And a guy gets out, a bit younger than me, but old enough to be the dad. And, sure enough, the girl who was driving the Audi runs out to him. They have a brief conversation by the car, and then she comes back inside. She goes back to talking with her friend and finishing her drink.

"Meanwhile, the dad gets down to evaluating the bumper, pushing and pulling at it where it's hanging awkwardly. He worked pretty hard on it for a while. I was even wondering if I should go out and help. He was lying on the ground at one point. But then he got up and came inside.

"Of course, he goes right over to the two girls and says something to them. But he doesn't shout or say anything harsh, that I can hear. Instead, he reaches out a set of car keys. The girl who was driving the Audi takes his keys and gives him her set. And he says something more and then turns back to the parking lot. He gets in the Audi. And slowly he pulls away from the curb and drives it cautiously off the lot, like he's hoping the bumper won't drop to the ground.

"And then the two girls go back to their laughing and texting and whatever."

Virgil lifted his head, smiling at his own reminiscence and perhaps looking for signs of recognition from Eleanor.

She couldn't help but smile back. "I like it. And I see what you mean. If you weren't working on a sermon and thinking about God, you might miss the symbolism."

Virgil raised his eyebrows and bowed slightly as if asking for permission. Seeing her bright response, he finished his story with an interpretation. "I think God is like that father. We might sometimes wreck things. But then God comes to help us and doesn't scold us, even if we deserve it. And God doesn't settle for a slipshod job of fixing things up, either. Nor does the Father tell us to just fix things ourselves. Instead, God offers a whole new vehicle, a whole new life in exchange for our messed-up one."

"And that's what conversion is like?"

"Or even any time you let God address the mess instead of just doing it on your own. It doesn't require advanced classes in *The Apostles' Creed* to let God do that."

She took in a long draught of air, filled with the scent of grass, wildflowers and a hint of fish.

"After my cousin died in a boating accident, Mom was telling me that she relied on God or Jesus to come and pick her up."

Saying it aloud awakened the slammed door feeling her mother's words had provoked when Eleanor was a teenager. "But all I heard was her telling me to pick *myself* up."

Virgil clearly sensed her change of mood. "How did you react when she said it back then?"

"I was still fuming at her for rejecting my father, for being cold to him. At that point, I'd developed this narrative about my mother's coldness, her selfishness. I even thought of her painting as a selfish hobby. It was around then that she started paying for classes and doing less of the retail work she did to earn money while I was in school." Eleanor watched the wind riffle the surface of the lake and a seagull dip and swoop past. "I thought she was so selfish. But I really didn't know her."

"So, her faith became suspect? After all those judgments, you couldn't accept help from your mother's God?"

"Yes. I think so. How could I trust her to tell me the truth about God when she was so duplicitous about her marriage, for example?"

"A marriage it turned out you didn't really understand."

"What teenager really understands her parents' marriage?" She blinked hard. "But that didn't stop me from judging. I generally gave my father the benefit of my ignorance. My mother got only condemnation."

"Are you ready to let yourself off the hook for that?"

She inhaled a breath that pulled her shoulders together in a shrug. "Didn't we cover this already?"

"Clearly, it still stirs you up. And Jesus thought that some people might need to forgive 490 times before they're done."

She leaned back, with her hands behind her, flat on the giant terrycloth beach blanket she had brought from her mother's house. Turning to squint at him, where a dapple of sun evaded the leaves above them, Eleanor challenged Virgil.

"Isn't this a kind of conflict of interest for you?" She slowed, not wanting to accuse him, really. "It's like you're offering me this spiritual direction with the prospect that we can move ahead in our relationship."

"So, I'm selling my soul as a pastor to find love, you mean?" Neither of them had said anything about love. Until now.

Virgil pulled off his sunglasses and squinted back at her. "If you forgive yourself, persistently and fully, I think you'll feel differently about yourself, and maybe about God. But I've seen lots of situations where that kind of life change leads in unexpected directions. There's no guarantee for me that you forgiving yourself will advance our relationship." He lowered his head and seemed to ponder the wide stripes of that blanket. "I care about you, Eleanor. So, I do have an interest." He stopped there, as if convinced he had confessed as much as he needed.

She softened her voice. "The conflict-of-interest angle is why you suggested I go to that other church for catechism training, right?"

"I think it would be good for you to explore your faith with others, as well as with me. It would also be less awkward for you to be a student in Randy's class than in mine."

"I suppose conflict of interest is a political label. Maybe clergy have another term for it."

"Well, you are as skillful as a politician at changing the subject, I notice."

Eleanor sat up and laid her hands on the blanket in front of her. "I like that you feel free to call me on it when I do."

He nodded and then leveled his eyes on her. "Forgiving yourself?"

"Yes. That's what I was avoiding."

"It's not a feeling, remember. It's an act of the will."

She studied his eyes, a rare look at them without glasses. "So, I can just say it, just declare it?"

"Yes. And you could ask God to help you make it stick."

She considered his addendum. "That feels like some sort of magic spell."

He puffed his lower lip and nodded slightly. "Okay. You can leave off the prayer."

"I have your permission?"

He stared hard at her now, as if refusing to be drawn off target again.

"Okay. I forgive myself ..." Even as Eleanor started hastily, the weight of what she was about to do collapsed onto her. More deliberately, she said, "I forgive myself for judging my mother, especially regarding her faithfulness to my dad and regarding her religious beliefs. I forgive her. I forgive myself. I didn't know what I ..." She heard the echo of something she and Virgil had talked about before but shooed that away. "I didn't know what I didn't know back then. So, I forgive myself now for acting out of ignorance."

Virgil glanced toward the lake, as if to ease that weight she was hefting. "Amen."

"And, God, I'd appreciate you helping me sustain this, forgiving Connie and forgiving myself." It just came out.

That spontaneous prayer reminded her of those cries for help in the middle of the barn fire.

She snorted airily. "What do you think God says when a nonbeliever starts praying in the middle of a crisis?"

He grinned and then affected an impatient scowl. "Oh, no. Here we go again." He followed that with a deep chuckle.

She raised her eyebrows, hoping Virgil would get over his laugh and arrive at a serious answer.

He apparently got the message. "Well. I think God says, 'Good to hear from you, my dear. Help is on the way. I am right here for you.'"

"You think it was a sort of miracle that we saved so many paintings?"

"I think it was. There are other explanations, of course. But, to me, it felt like a blessing from God. Perhaps a blessing for Connie and her memory. It's impossible to know all that God is thinking at any given time. But if you believe God is loving, it's easy to accept a providential explanation about the paintings."

Eleanor was glad he was honest about his lack of sureness regarding what was in the mind of God. Maybe there was room for her to come in the door of God's house, at least to look around. Virgil left that door open for her by not attempting to close the deal right there next to the lake. No prayer of salvation. No conversion ceremony. No baptism in the lake.

Though she wasn't sure whether Lutherans did that kind of baptism. She needed to do some more research about things like that.

Before either of them turned bright red in the rays reflected off the lake, they gathered up the blanket and headed for Virgil's car. As she flopped the blanket onto the backseat, and he set the picnic basket on top of the blanket, he caught her hand.

"I know we've talked about ways you might make changes so we can pursue a relationship. But I want you to know that I'm willing to make changes too. I'm at a point in my life where I feel free to move on and find other work to do, for example."

That gentle hand gripping hers, as she leaned now on the inside of the car door, was very distracting. But Virgil was saying something important. "Are you saying you would consider leaving the church to be with me?"

He sighed and smiled lightly. "I can get a full pension and early Social Security already. I don't need to work. And it's probably time for Dove Lake Lutheran to find a younger minister with new ideas and more energy. Yes. I've been actively thinking about retiring. But I don't consider it leaving the church, just moving to a different role."

"Something more compatible with having a ... relationship

with a doubter?"

"We're all doubters, Eleanor. And we all have choices about what to do with our doubts. Willingness to learn is one of the best choices, I think." He was still holding her hand, lowering his eyes toward their fingers intertwined. "And I was thinking I would even be willing to consider a move back East, if you decided to go back to teaching there."

"A lot of options on the table."

"It seems to me that we're both free to choose a direction. Maybe we can start talking about choosing that together."

"Just talking."

"Just talking, for now."

She leaned in and kissed him on the cheek, but then she didn't pull back. Neither did he. Instead, Virgil leaned in very slightly and kissed her on the lips, slow and soft.

"Oh." She drew a long breath. "Just talking?"

"Just talking, for now."

CHAPTER THIRTY-THREE

The first week of September, Eleanor began attending a class at the Lutheran church in Heeley, Wisconsin. Pastor Randy Berkheimer taught the Sunday evening course in a cozy, little classroom. There were ten students, including Eleanor.

"I sort of felt like I was scrunching down in my seat to not look too intimidating. I'm so used to being the teacher and not the student." She was sitting with Virgil in Roger's diner on Main Street.

"When's the last time you took a class of any kind?"

She shook her head and explored the corners of the ceiling. "I can't recall. Oh, maybe my first sabbatical in 1998. I took a course at Columbia University in New York, with a very old professor whom I admired. But that was in a hundred-seat lecture hall, not a close, little classroom in the basement of the church."

"Yeah. Sorry about that basement. Their church building needs some work."

"But tell me about *your* conversation with the district supervisor."

He let go of his coffee cup and sat back. "District president, technically." He sighed. "That was easy. He questioned me for a bit, but then he might have remembered my salary and started thinking how it could be good for the church to pay a pastor with less seniority."

"I didn't know that was how it works."

"You don't need to know about it. Because I'll be retired by the end of the year."

"And the church board?"

"Well, that was much harder."

"Did you really have to tell them on the same day that you

told the district president?"

"There is some politics in churches too, you know. So I didn't want rumors to flow one direction or the other, in the days or weeks between those two conversations. Gossip is less of a problem in our church than in others, I think. But this would have been a hard secret for them to keep."

"So, what did they say?"

"One of the deacons told me I was awfully young to retire." Virgil stirred his coffee and smiled down at it. "I looked at the eighty-some-year-old gentleman and told him it was time for me to move on to other work. I'm only retiring from pastoring this church."

She smiled at the image of the old board member and the pastor young enough to be his son. "That doesn't sound like the hard part."

"No. There were tears all around. Marion Claussen started it with a very moving appreciation for my ministry here. She recalled one particular Bible study held at our house, when Joanne was alive. Marion had a sort of conversion experience there. Lots of tears from her in the board meeting, as there were at that Bible study, as I recall."

Sighing, unable to ignore the mention of Virgil's late wife, Eleanor watched his hands set down the spoon and lift his cup.

He seemed oblivious to her distracting thoughts. "Leaving will be sad, but that's just one side of the story. I've been itching to do some writing and some college teaching for a while now. This will give me a chance to pursue those dreams."

"Have you thought of taking classes yourself?"

"I have. That's one option, for sure." He set his cup down and squared up at her. "But I think we got off of your class experience too fast ... again."

"You know I don't do it consciously."

"Do what?"

"Change the subject."

"Really? You do that?"

"Mmmm."

"Like you just did, just now?"

She let go of the croissant she was about to bite and sat back for a hard laugh. "Okay. Okay. You caught me. I'll tell you about the class."

He waited for her to settle back to leaning on the table and sipping her tea. "What surprised you most about what Randy said?"

Calming her breathing, she cast another glance into the corner of the room. Two women were laughing three booths away, one chuckling, the other cackling.

"The strongest impression was his humility. He reminded me of you. I could tell he knew his stuff, that he was confident in what he was teaching. No insecurity about it."

"That's all about him, about Randy."

"Well, that's a crucial thing for me. I've been researching things online. I'm getting a grasp of the beliefs and concepts, lots of which I remember from childhood. But what matters to me now is how it's carried. The look in your eyes when we talk about your faith is vital to me. I sense no deception, no fear and no hesitation."

"Wait. Is this about Randy, or me?"

"These things are decisive for me, Virgil. I need to know if what I've been seeing from you is only about you, or if it's about the church and room there for a doubter like me."

"So, you needed to see for yourself that you can be welcomed."

"Yes. See it in someone's eyes."

Virgil lifted his gaze toward the door of the diner as the bell rang to welcome a new customer. "Yvonne." He nodded toward the arrival.

Twisting in her seat, Eleanor grinned at Yvonne, who was focusing on their table between casting her eyes toward the floor and toward the kitchen. Eleanor stood up and spun toward her.

What happened next surprised Eleanor as much as anything Yvonne had done. She shuffled right up to Eleanor and wrapped an arm around her, burying her head in the space between Eleanor's neck and shoulder.

"Oh. Yvonne. Hello. I'm ... uh ... I'm so glad to see you."

Yvonne backed away slightly. She ventured a glance at Virgil. "I'm glad to see you too. And I'm happy that you're happy."

"I'm happy? How do you know?"

"You were sad before. Very sad. The first time." She paused and looked around. "Did I see you here the first time?"

"Yes. You did. That was the first time we talked to each other."

"You were sad." She sounded much more certain about Eleanor's sadness than about the setting of that encounter.

This jostled a curiosity. "You can sense when someone is sad?"

"I know what it looks like."

"I believe you do. And it makes me feel good that you see me as happy now. It's a reminder of the good things that have happened to me this summer."

"Okay. Have a nice day." And Yvonne turned back toward the door.

Eleanor just stared, as Yvonne stepped toward the exit.

Virgil rose from his seat. "Do you wanna sit down with us, Yvonne? Have something to eat?"

His sudden movement startled Eleanor a bit. The force of his invitation surged right through her. She recovered in time to add her voice. "Yes. Yvonne. Please stay and have something with us."

Yvonne had her hand on the interior door. She turned

286

toward them and then checked the kitchen. "If you invite me to stay, it's okay. Roger says I can stay if someone invites me to be here."

Nodding at this familiar refrain, Eleanor moved toward Yvonne and reached out. "Come on. Have a seat. Tell me how you've been doing."

She and Virgil sat with Yvonne for twenty minutes, asking her polite questions and receiving monotone responses, as expected. But it seemed to Eleanor that those short replies were more abundant and that most of them were positive.

"How do you like the new worker at the house?" Eleanor had heard about the staff change the last time she visited Yvonne.

"She likes my paintings. She likes to stand and spin with me."

Eleanor grinned at Virgil who mirrored her joy. He probably understood, as she did, that this was an unqualified endorsement by Yvonne for her new caregiver.

Good for Yvonne.

After saying goodbye to Virgil, who had a meeting to prepare for at church that evening, Eleanor drove home. But first, she took Yvonne to The Dove's Nest, to claim a little time for just the two of them.

"He's a good man." Yvonne said that before climbing out of the Honda.

"Virgil?"

"Pastor."

"Oh. Yes. I agree with you. He is good."

"And true."

"Yes."

"Connie thought so."

"Right. I believe she did. Thanks for reminding me."

"I know."

"Okay. Have a good evening, Yvonne."

"Okay. You too."

When Eleanor arrived at the farm, Paul was pushing a lawnmower up the short ramp from the hill at the east edge of the yard, into the bed of his truck.

"First leaves have started falling." He nodded toward a cottonwood which was losing dull, green leaves.

"I see that. Well, I decided to wait for spring before I rebuild." She gestured with one hand toward the bare concrete that had been scraped clean in August. "No rush."

"That's good. It'll give you time to think about how you wanna set up the gallery."

"That architect, Angela, is good. I think we have a good plan. She'll send me computer drawings later this month."

"So ... you're staying around."

"I'll be here at least through the school year. And I'm planning to keep the house. Whether I live here full time or not ..." Sharing her plans with Paul was natural, but she still couldn't define what their relationship was. Perhaps that had to do with the leftovers from his relationship with Connie.

"That's good to hear. I'm sure that makes Virgil happy." He looked away as soon as he said that, perhaps worried that he had encroached on forbidden territory.

"He's a big reason I'm sticking around, of course. But lots of people have made me feel welcome around here, including you."

"That's good." He punctuated his words with a slam of the pickup gate. "Having you here makes me miss Connie a bit less, probably."

Nodding, Eleanor decided to ignore how she was still second best to her mother. "I think that's true for lots of people. And I like being the curator of her memory, at least as much as a daughter can do that."

He lifted the ramp and turned his head toward her. "I didn't mean that you're not welcome here on your own. I just miss Connie. That's all."

"I understand." She stretched what might have been a motherly smile.

As she said goodbye to Paul, the third goodbye of that evening, Eleanor noticed a warm hope that remained undiminished by letting three people that she cared about go on their way for the evening. That she had decided to settle her belongings and her heart in the farmhouse tinted those partings as pleasantly temporary.

Without planning to, on her way in the house she said a little prayer for Yvonne, always uncertain what her friend needed and always hoping she was well cared for.

When she was inside, Eleanor's phone buzzed in her purse. Jackie calling.

"How is the new school year shaping up?"

"I'm thinking about retiring."

"Oh, no. That bad."

"It's not a bad year, or a bad freshman class. I just enjoyed my summer of writing and visiting you on the farm so much, it makes it hard to get back to the grind."

"You sound like an underpaid factory worker."

"Huh. I guess I do. Spoiled child. I need to be more grateful for how nice I have things."

"Including Thomas?"

"Hmm. I'm still thinking on that."

"But you said, you believed him that he didn't have an affair with that actress."

"Not an affair, technically. But they were friendly, if not intimate."

"You're not sure it was innocent?"

"Innocent? Maybe. Mostly sure."

"Are you waiting to be totally sure before you forgive him?"

"Listen to you. Poster child for forgiveness and such. I think I liked you better as a pagan."

"Just asking."

Jackie chuckled. "So, we've had no word from Raisa on her Christmas plans. She's getting serious with this guy. So, they may be going to his parents' house."

"Okay. Well, you could *all* pile in here with me, or just you and Thomas. Whatever."

"We'll get out there, I'm sure. And we're gonna see you in a few weeks, right? October? Homecoming?"

"Yeah. While I'm there I have to meet with my renters face-to-face about long-term plans for the townhouse and meet with the realtor."

"Right. I'm not encouraging that nonsense, but I'll be glad if it brings you back here once in a while. Did you talk to Gerald about not coming back next year?"

"I did. He didn't seem heartbroken." She paused as Jackie laughed. "I think he wants to offer that visiting instructor a full-time position. And I think Dierdre is already liking department chair better than she assumed."

"Yeah. She seems like queen of the realm over there. Not a bad queen."

"Good. Good to hear."

"Well, Thomas just got home. I may go talk to him if he's in a mood for it. We'll see if forgiveness shows up here tonight."

"Okay. Blessings."

Jackie laughed. "Yes. Blessings to you too."

"Goodbye, Jackie."

"Goodbye, Eleanor."

Eleanor took off her tan jacket and walked to the coat closet next to the dining room. The coats Jackie had shipped to her filled half the closet. "Room for Virgil to move in someday." She said that aloud to herself. She wouldn't say anything like that to

Virgil for a while yet.

She paused and then stepped to the dining room table, pulling the manila folder to the edge and flipping it open. "The Barn Gallery." She couldn't incorporate the gallery under that name, of course. Others had thought of it already. But the architect's rough sketch of the new building, with those words on the artsy sign, was already established in Eleanor's imagination. It was real. The preliminary building permit and the business zoning permit from the county offered concrete affirmation of her plan—her dream.

"Well, Mom. I can't bring you back. But I can settle in right here and honor your memory and your beautiful art." She looked up at the painting hung on the dining room wall, between the windows and the living room. A man held the hand of a little girl, him hunched slightly and her skipping along, their backs as expressive as any face could be.

Eleanor grinned at the distant fields and trees in that painting, the land her mother had loved so much. And she suspected that she was coming to love it, too.

She pried herself away from those thoughts and returned to the kitchen to start the dishes. But first she glanced out the window. The setting sun was painting shadows across the concrete slab where the gallery would be. She could see it there already, in her mind's eye.

"I wish *you* could see it, Mom."

From somewhere not too distant, she felt a warm assurance that Connie was seeing her and knew all about her dream. And Eleanor thanked God for that.

EPILOGUE

She gripped the canvas in her eighty-seven-year-old hands, the frigid wind shouldering her off balance as soon as she stepped out of the barn. Cold prickles covered her forehead, one cheek and the back of one hand, where she held the side of the painting. Forcing herself to shuffle carefully on her eighty-seven-year-old feet, she bowed her head to avoid ice pellets landing on her glasses.

Crazy old woman rushing through the cold night. She chortled at the thought of it. But her laughter stopped when her left foot shot from under her and her right foot skated over the glassy pavement.

"Oh, my."

She landed with a wumph. Flat on her back.

Still clutching the painting, she lay stunned for a few seconds. She was on the pavement. She was supine on the sidewalk in the freezing cold. Oh, no. This can't be happening.

It was the very same spot.

Though not the same pavement.

This slab was elevated a few inches higher than the old sidewalk, the one on which her mother had slipped on that frozen reservoir between piles of snow. Paul had helped them replace that slab with this new cement. But the upgrade had not saved Eleanor from losing her footing in an ice storm.

She tried to roll to her side, but she was too close to the snow on that side. She huffed. "This is ridiculous."

That old slab of sidewalk, her mother's sidewalk, had been carefully removed and preserved. It now lay in the gallery—"a cheeky and winsome piece." That's what the art critic from Milwaukee had called it. "Absurd," Eleanor had called it. But

Candice had insisted. She had insisted on painting that picture of Connie lying on the sidewalk, using the actual slab of sidewalk as her canvas.

Eleanor tried to roll the other way. But what would happen to the painting? She was considering letting go of that unframed canvas. What would happen to it if she stuck it in the snow? She lay back. Flat. She would have to do a sit-up. If she could.

That made her laugh.

Now she was picturing that painting of her mother—Connie clutching a canvas and lying peacefully on that chunk of sidewalk, a churlish smile on her face, her glasses slightly askew. "Get up, Connie." That was Candice's title for the painting.

The freezing rain was starting to collect on Eleanor's glasses now. A stinging in her toes began turning toward numbness. This was a serious situation.

"Help! Help me! Help!"

A sit-up would be easier than projecting her voice from where she lay on the cold concrete.

She coached herself. "Get up, Eleanor. Get up. You don't wanna die out here. That would be tragically ironic."

The wind was wrestling the old trees on all sides of the house, each emitting deep creaks and groans in its unique voice. Then she heard another, familiar creak. The spring on the back door.

"Oh, no. Ellie. My dear. Oh, are you okay? Talk to me, honey. Are you okay?"

After skating a second and then planting both feet in the crunchy snow next to the sidewalk, Virgil appeared, leaning over her. He knelt right next to her.

"No. Don't kneel down, old man. You won't be able to get back up."

"Oh. Yes, I can. Don't you worry. I'm not as old as you are."

That started both of them laughing. Was that gallows

humor? For her, it was relief. She had fallen, just like her mother. But here was her man. He was here to give her a hand up.

"Okay. Let's set this painting aside just for a second." He planted it in the snow as if that crunchy bank were an easel frozen just for that purpose.

He pulled her hand up to his shoulder as she struggled to do that sit-up. Now they were at eye level. "You can do it, dear."

"You stand up first, Virgil. You stand first and pull me up."

He held her hand, both pulling and pushing on it to keep his balance as he craned himself back to standing. It wasn't easy, she could tell. But he was right. He could still do it.

"Now you." He held that one hand and reached for her other wrist.

She rose halfway and then slid forward, nearly toppling him backward into the snow.

"Ha. Whoa, there. Okay. Hang on. Don't pull me down." His feet were deep in the refrozen snow.

She could just see one of his house slippers poking out from the snowbank. "What are you doing out here in your slippers?"

"What are you doing out here taking a nap on the sidewalk?"

They laughed again as she finally stood. She took a deep breath and celebrated uprightness and at least momentary stability. They both turned to skate toward the back door. Eleanor hit a wet spot where the ice crunched and dissolved under her shoe.

"You turned on the sidewalk heater."

"I did. I was just coming to do that for you when I saw you flopping around out here."

"I was not flopping around." Eleanor slapped at him but stopped that when she slipped again. She clutched the backdoor handle.

Only then did Virgil return to lift the painting from the snow.

Eleanor pulled the storm door open and waited for him to get a good grip on it before pushing inside. "Ha. Oh, my. Get in here. Let me see that painting." She had a hand towel ready to receive the oil painting. "It should be okay, shouldn't it?"

"I expect so. But what about you? How are you? Did you hurt yourself when you fell?"

"You assume I fell."

"Oh. You didn't? You just lay down there for a little rest? Or was it some sort of historical reenactment, maybe?"

She cackled at the notion, laughing for several seconds before sucking in a sober breath.

"Oh, Lord. I thought I was a goner there for a second. But that would have been just too ironic."

"More than ironic. Catastrophic. I don't wanna lose you, my girl." He had stepped out of his soaked slippers by the door and was standing in the kitchen in his damp socks, holding her shoulders.

She set the painting down, propped against a cabinet.

"You came and rescued me, didn't you?"

He snickered, dots of thawing sleet speckling his glasses. "I did. I sure did. And I'll do it again if I have to. Again and again." He had her wrapped up in two arms now.

She leaned into him. "Well, let's hope *that's* not necessary."

"Oh, you know it will be. And you'll have to come and lever me up now and again. You have already, in so many ways."

"I have? Well ... maybe we can just leave that pavement heater on all winter."

He laughed.

And she knew she hadn't really changed the subject with her joke. His eyes were still locked on the same subject, the one he had been focused on since they first met.

"I love you, Virgil."
"I love you too, Eleanor."

Acknowledgements:

Thanks to Kevin Kiefer for the Starbucks story, an event he witnessed and which he told much better than Virgil does here.

Thanks to Lillian for catching some early problems with the story line. Good QA, dear. You were, of course, my inspiration for this story—me showing off to you how I could just make up a story line, as we drove through southern Wisconsin one day.

Further Reading:

See our web site and sign up for our newsletter:
https://www.jeffreymcclainjones.com

Other books by Jeff Jones:

The Love Scam
(https://www.amazon.com/dp/B07V4XF99Q)

Small Lives
(https://www.amazon.com/dp/B08HG1SHW6)

Alice's Friendship Bench
(https://www.amazon.com/dp/B0973KK3VD)

Made in the USA
Middletown, DE
11 August 2022

71162770R00177